EXIT MANAGEMENT

Naomi Booth

dead ink

For Thomas Houlton and Toby Smart

1. ELGIN MEWS

2. FREEZER

3. SAFE BOX

At minus eighteen degrees centigrade, blood begins to freeze. Tiny crystals will form in the vessels closest to the surface of the skin.

At minus nineteen degrees, blood hardens completely: water and albumin turn to ice.

At minus twenty degrees, juvenile bone tissue begins to set, cartilage splintering in fractals of frost.

At minus twenty-two degrees, even the densest blood materials start to turn: the beginnings of a human heart will still into black ice.

Part One

ELGIN MEWS

2018

Three bad things before breakfast.

One: The child in the flat next door wakes up crying again. He sleeps on the other side of the wall, and has a cough like a seal bark. Several coughs in a row, and then he can't catch his breath, and he'll start to bark-sob. No one responds when he cries like this. The rent for this apartment is astronomical— *Luxury Studio in Outer Greenwich*, the particulars had said, but now here she is, in a bedsit in Deptford sardined between this sick, sad kid and, on the other side, an older woman with alcohol-related psychosis, who screams in the night, *Where am I, where am I?* until she calls the concierge, who calls the woman's daughter in Portsmouth, who calls 999 to have her intermittently sectioned.

Two: The tiredness means she reverts to bad habits— coffee shot, three sugars, social-media surfing. Mauve nail hovering, fingertip cushioning against the silk surface of the screen. Scrolling past minor calamities (*Why Kate can wear a tiara but Meghan can't / Alison Mack went from hungry actress to brutal sex slave leader / Countdown to Brexit: what happens next?*). Then clicking through to a story about plastics. This time it's photographs of dead birds. Like a crime-scene shot: the outline of an albatross chick on wet sand, its feathers just beginning to fray away, its thin bones exposed and, where its stomach must once have been, a clutch of hard, bright objects—yellow and red bottle tops, a turquoise toothpick, a bright blue ring-pull, and other smaller objects, white, orange, brown and black, no longer recognisable. The caption on the image: *One-third of albatross chicks on the Pacific island of Medway die from plastic consumption. The parent birds bring the objects home from sea to feed their chicks.*

Three: Spiral of doom. The kid next door is really coughing now, she can hear him above the noise of the coffee machine, keening with each attempt to inhale. Looking again at the albatross chick, at the concentric, deadly objects in its tummy. Single-use objects that never go away: the piece of chewing gum she swallowed as a child; the end of coral-coloured gel-nail she'd once bitten off in a meeting and swallowed before thinking; and that night back in 2008, in the alleyway outside Roxy's in Bradford, when she'd insisted on a condom and she'd seen the empty foil packet on the floor, but no condom had re-emerged, post-coitus: so where was it? The thought of this missing prophylactic, returning to her every few months, for the last ten years. Had it been discarded, slickly, or removed backhandedly beforehand, or was it lost somewhere inside her, still there a decade on, with the childhood chewing-gum and the acrylic nail and all of the other deadly, durable objects that her body can't digest?

An email blinking on her phone.

The first good thing of the day.

This one is gonna go fast!!! Lauren you need to see it asap.

There's a fine rain across the busy high street like static interference. Three black girls in school uniform at the bus stop outside the tube station, screaming then laughing. A florist and a bougie furniture shop and a Pizza Express. A school on the corner, and in front of it a small shrine-table, with cards and teddy bears and candles. Down a side street, three Range Rovers in a row—and at the end of the street, some way off, a glimpse of the tower: Grenfell, draped in white, the sky-scraper-shroud with the green heart.

Follow the blue line on your phone, turn onto a side street: a mixture of tall white houses—bars on basement windows, obscure warning graffitied across a door—and newer blocks of flats. Trees grow from squares cut out of the pavement. When she arrives at the next intersection, she stops. Little incursions of rot in the wet petals of the cherry tree above her. She's stopped ordering cut flowers to try to cheer up her flat—that way the petals begin to go, dappled with brown. You spend thirty quid on a bouquet only to watch it turn to a vase pocked with melanoma.

A tall white guy coming towards her. A tailored silver-grey suit; a folder held over his head to guard against the drizzle. He leads with his chin, which is unusually sharp. A downturned ace of spades.

Hi, Lauren? I'm Ash. Great to meet you. Let's walk and talk. I've been brought up-to-speed on your situation by the office. You know your budget is really at the lower end of what's possible in this area. I don't discriminise. Not at all. But you do need to keep an open mind.

Where is he taking her?

Have they told you about my search requirements?

Stopping. This is what I *mean*, Lauren. Looking at her dolefully. Looking at her like a boyfriend who is telling her her flaws in the hope that she might *learn* something about herself. On your budget, you need to keep a bit of an open mind. He gestures across the road. Now this really is something special. Very well-kept block. Lovely bit of communal garden, which I don't need to tell you is unusual round here. Portobello just around the corner. What do you think?

They're looking at a geometric low-rise block. The block is set back from the street, a white stucco building put up in the '90s. The sky above it is streaked with bright pink: a sunset in torn ribbons. There are daffodils bobbing in the breeze in the shared garden.

It's not   I told your office. I'm not looking for a new-build.

Lauren, Ash says. Exaggerated sad face. You're breaking my heart here. We're both out in the rain. Why not take a quick look around? These are good flats. Purpose built, which has a lot of advantages. High fire-safety standards.

This one will go really quickly. If I were you, I'd want to get on the ladder asap.

More bad viewings.

One on a dull, warm day in May, the sky and roofs a grey-out. It's Ash who meets her again. A salesman who likes to work for it. He points her towards a tall Victorian house. Thin segment of a long, white terrace. Nice front, hey? This more your style?

Climbing a staircase behind him, a staircase that goes up and up, bending tightly. A staircase to a room with a sign that says Model; a staircase to a room for a sex-murder. On the fifth floor, a tiny, dark stretch of landing.

Now, I haven't seen this one myself yet, Lauren, but it sounds perfect for you. Unlocking the door to a small square of a room. He turns on the light switch, which fails to ignite the dead bulb hung naked from the ceiling. In one corner, a single bed. In the diagonally opposite corner, a standalone cooker, abutted by a low camping table. In the centre of the room, two deckchairs and a record player. An extremely strong smell of skunk, top-notes of semen. So many unpleasant revelations in the search for a flat so far: morbid obsessions filling walls and cabinets and display cases—collections of painted plates, of military memorabilia, of framed pictures of guide dogs, of fighting knives; a miniature shrine to Princess Diana; giant cheese plants colonising tiny spaces. Old blood smeared on walls; old blood matted into carpets. But the proximity with the masturbatory habits of strangers is the worst. The last viewing comprised one room: an unmade mattress on the floor, next to it a framed picture of J-Lo and a half-used toilet roll.

Ash striding over to a small window and opening it. You need to imagine this place with a woman's touch. I can already tell that you'd make it beautiful. I think it's got a real Parisian vibe. A slight quirk is that the bathroom's one floor down.

It's not going to work for me.

That's a real shame. Looking hurt. That wounded pose that men who are good at sales and at sexual coercion have mastered. Well, onwards and upwards. I like a challenge, Lauren.

Different agency, the very next day: plane tree leaning at an angle in front of the house, bark sloughing away, revealing underneath pristine nude tree trunk. The sky, glimpsed through new leaves, blue, scudded with fast-moving clouds. *Your thoughts and feelings drift like clouds that are moving quickly across the sky.* The new meditation app she's listening to last thing at night; soft American voice. *And if you know this, then you don't need to label yourself an anxious person, because* you *are the still sky behind those moving clouds.*

Lovely street isn't it? A white woman in a black skirt-suit. The woman smiles: lips part, teeth clench together. Miss Haigh? I'm Vicky. I'll be showing you around the property today. Immensely refined vowels. Speaking through her gritted teeth, as though her jaw is wired shut.

Following her up the steps to the house. Clamping her teeth together and parting her lips. Feels unattractive, like a grimace when she does it. The façade of the house is posh cream and the door is flanked by pillars. Follow, follow through the front door and into the hall. Under the stairs, a small door into what appears to be a cupboard.

Now, this is an extremely creative conversion, clenched-teeth woman saying.

Descend a narrow staircase into what must once have been a cellar. Put hand against the wall to steady self: plaster cool and slightly clammy to the touch like amphibious flesh. Reach the bottom and a small square room. One window, looking out onto a brick pit dug into the pavement, a slim oblong of light shining in from the street above. The pit full of old leaves and crisp packets and free newspapers. There is no furniture in the room. Just an oven against one wall and next to that a fridge and next to that a shower cubicle. One corner partitioned off into what looks like a built-in cupboard. Vicky opens the door to reveal a toilet. Smells chalky, with top-notes of mould.

Now, Vicky says. This is in your ideal area. It's a prestige address. And really, you've got everything you need right here.

Last-minute viewing, and the agent is late. Checking her phone: no new messages. Scans the street: two men in high-vis; one woman lumbering with children. Lots of scaffolding along the road, which she's been told is a good sign.

Isn't this fantastic? A voice from the front steps. Tana, an agent she's met before. I've just been looking around. When I saw this come on the books, I thought of you straight away. Wanted to get you in quick. Now smiling outwards with such force that the sinews in her neck tighten like guy ropes. You're the very first client to see this. Excited!

Tana opens the front door. Spacious entrance hall. Tiled floor and a wide staircase with a thick new carpet.

I *know*, says Tana. Squeal! Follow me.

The flat is on the first floor, at the back of the house. Stepping into a light, large room. Two large windows on the back wall and pale sunlight sheering across the cream carpet and the cream walls. Along one side of the room, a kitchen area with granite worktops: solid and white, with caramel swirls twisting through the stone.

Her phone beginning to ring in her bag.

Do you have the particulars? Tana handing them across when her phone starts up again.

Leafing through the glossy marketing pack, ignoring it. Now, says Tana. Look at this. Opening a door onto a tiny en-suite bathroom: every surface tiled. The shower's chrome-work gleaming under fierce lighting. Isn't that something?

Backing away. Moving over to the windows and looking out onto back garden: a long lawn, well-tended.

That's communal, so you'd have access to that. The gardening is covered in the service charge.

Phone ringing again; bag vibrating.

Perhaps you should get that? They're very persistent.

Buzzing stops. Then begins again. Reaching into handbag. I'll just be a second.

The voice in the phone is far away, and very close.

Lauren? Lauren, love?

Mum's voice. Her little-girl voice. Her throat is thick; voice like a child drugged; voice of a child waking from a temazepam sleep.

Mum. I can only talk for a moment, I'm just—

I know, I know you'll be dead busy at work, love, but I'm   I think your sister's   bad again. I just I can't get her out to come out of her room.

Scratchy words. Ugly, ugly noise at the end and horribly intimate: stifled choking, all the sounds of her mother's pink mouth amplified in her ear.

If she safe? Is she (whispering now, turning away from the agent) cutting again?

I don't know. I don't know, love. If I can just get her to go to the doctor. But she won't talk to me. Lauren, can you come up? Talk to her? She always listens to you.

I can't get away. Not right now. Look, Mum, I'll send you more money this month, and you can contact that woman from before, book her some more sessions?

I'll try. Yeah. But what if she won't go? Don't be cross with me then, love, will you?

Try. Just book them and tell her I've paid for them so she's got to go. Ok? Call you later, Mum, I'm in the middle of something.

Dropping phone back into bag. More money. More money this month. She budgets so carefully: the money for her rent; the money that pays off her student debts; the money she puts aside for her deposit; the money she sends home. She'll need to enter this new spend into the app, she'll need to move some funds around. Extras. There are always so many extras. Looking up, inspecting the flat, and noticing now that there is a crumb of plaster missing from the wall around the plug sock et opposite her. There's a long thread of white-plastic yarn that's come up from the carpet in one corner. The smell in here: poisonously bright; bleach and volatile paint fumes and industrial adhesives. Has the work been done too quickly? Nisha in the office bought a 'luxury' conversion last year and it had been put together maliciously; there'd been a dispute with the contractors and they'd left tiny punctures in the gas pipes and live wires under the floorboards and sewage had backed up into the shower. The whole block had to move out while the arterial system of the building was stripped away and reinstalled.

So, Tana says. Tell me what you're thinking.

I   I'm not sure. I'm not sure it feels   quite right.

Really? Tana pausing. Face blanching. Rotates her wedding ring with her right hand. I've got to level with you, Lauren.

You're not going to get better than this on your budget, and if you don't move soon, well   it's very difficult to say what's going to happen the housing market with Brexit. I'm just worried for *you*, Lauren, that's all.

Walking. Walking as far as she can until she hits a gated development or a cut-through onto a small estate that looks too dubious to wander down in the twilight. The plane trees have been pollarded down here, cut short so that the branches make leafless hands, upturned. She's not heading anywhere particular—but turning at each junction in the hope of seeing the canal. Hitting a main road, a dual carriageway without a pavement. Turning back into the streets of Little Venice and threading through again. Glossy green exterior tiles, *Drink Craft Beer*, faded Victorian adverts painted large on brickwork, Western Union, creamy Regency facades. And then she's on a bridge, and the canal must be below, but the barrier is too high for her to see down to it. Keeps on, back through the low-rises and the cherry blossom, back towards the Victorian terraces, and another high street with a fishmonger and an antiques shop and a patisserie and a tapas bar. This. This is it; this is a place to be, this street of beautiful and delicious things. Turning again, trying to loop back round. Turning onto a short street, *Elgin Mews*, a street of handsome houses painted different colours—chalky red, pale blue, light mauve. Peering into the mauve house, searching for a window into someone else's life—anyone else's clean bright life here on this street. Doesn't see, didn't see the man coming out of his front door just ahead of her, doesn't slow at all, walking straight into him—

BAM—hits his shoulder hard with her own, knocks the folder full of papers and his keys from his hands. Strange winded noise coming from him—euuuurgggghhh—and he, springing away from her. For a moment, both of them completely still outside his front door, facing one another.

Stunned by contact.

A cold current right through—adrenaline, is it, pulsing in her lips and fingertips.

Laughing, and the laugh is cold and wild. His papers licked up by the wind around them. Going for them, both of them, going for the papers, everything fluttering. Reaching, reaching up, her cold hands snatching all of this falling matter back from the sky.

Cal walks to the house along the canal path, the cool air at his cheeks, the damp air in his throat. He's been dreaming of fire again. It's his mother. Listening to reports all the time. Worrying herself about it, writing lists again—and then her worries sneak their way into his sleep and make horrible sparks in the darkness there.

Cutting back up onto the road when the canal goes underground. The keys are in his pocket. He's wearing his good work suit. Breathe, breathe deep, breathe the green, damp air. All of the flats round here are low-rise. And on József's street the houses are only on two floors. These low, safe, colourful houses. You could practically lower yourself from a window, quick army roll, barely a scratch out here.

Puts his key in the door. Metal in metal, bite of the lock: he loves this moment. He pushes the door open and the alarm starts to chime. He presses the code into the hallway pad—1 9 4 6—closes the door behind him. Nice one. Safe as houses.

József's house is fresh coffee and polished wood and verbena from the fat yellow candle that József lights to keep away mosquitoes and evil spirits in the evenings. The cleaners do a good job—two ferocious middle-aged women come in from Ilford—but he still checks on everything then runs down his list of valuables. The spare keys are in the bowl on the hallway table: check. In the kitchen, opening each of the cupboards:

Wedgewood dinnerware (48-piece set: 2 plates chipped, 1 enamel cracking)—check
Waterford tumblers in argon blue (6)—check
Waterford coupes (28, various patterns)—check
Waterford decanters (3)—check
Silver flatware, antique (12-piece place settings)—check
Frank Bowling painting (acrylic, sculptural, poured purple)—check

Retracing his steps, using a tissue to rub his finger marks from cupboard handles. He'd know, he'd surely know, instinctively and immediately, if anything were missing from József's house. Following the list anyway: an act of devotion. He checks on pictures in the living room, including the Tamás Márton oil painting over the fireplace. The biggest picture in the house. A patchwork of a sky in squares of blue, and then, below it, tesselating oranges and reds, descending into black. A sunset, maybe. Or a scorched-earth retreat.

Checks on the back garden. The sun sinking behind the house and the sky turning a wild colour—not like fire, no, like something good and sweet: like nectarine flesh. A pair of swallows fussing around a nest in the guttering. Should he get that seen to? What harm can they do? Tiny plants forcing their way up between the paving stones in purple clusters. Violets maybe? *Violets are for love,* József told him once. *And a too-soon death.* He'd stayed too long, as usual, had ended up helping József with his gardening. He won't do anything about these violets either. József likes the garden to overflow. Hates the severity and the ornamental broken shards of slate next door.

Back inside, up the stairs, checking on the paintings in the bedrooms. And that the studio is undisturbed. And finally the safe box, hidden behind a picture—another Márton—on the upstairs landing. Whatever is locked in there remains securely uncheckable. Each room is immaculate. The guests are due to arrive at 10.00 the next morning and everything is in order.

He should leave now. The job is done and if he stays any longer he'll only disturb the gleaming surfaces, leave some sort of a trace that he'll have to clean away. But he doesn't want to. Go . Not yet. The studio is where he can do least damage: the guests are not permitted in here, nor the cleaners. All of the surfaces in here already grubby: oil rags, canvases with József's thumb prints, old palettes, frames, tubes of paint, plastic containers filled with viscous yellow fluids. Smells like turps and pencil shavings. József says he doesn't really paint, but he used to do a little restoration and repair work, and he keeps his hand in. Cal, sitting down on an old stool. Picturing József working here, demitasse beside him, oil rag in his hand.

In his list of houses, none of them is like József's. The house on Herbert Crescent by St James's Park, the biggest on his list: five reception rooms, seven bedrooms, a swimming pool in the basement, a lift up to the top floor where a glass extension opens onto a terrace. An enormous, unreal gleaming space. He hates that house. Echoey and over-bright. Performing his checks, feeling like an intruder followed by a search light. Another property in Chelsea looks out onto a tree-lined lawn at the edge of the Royal Hospital. Six bedrooms and a self-contained staff flat in the basement next to a wine cellar. Their most popular property. Hates this one too: the whole place so immaculately muted (biscuit-coloured carpets, beige walls, light-grey upholstery) that he is a stain against its interior fabric. How can real people, with grubby hands and nosebleeds and sweating bodies and vomiting children live in that house? How could you shit there?

Maybe that's why they give the Curators their fancy suits? A layer of elegance that also protects the properties from direct contact with their actual bodies. An expensive version of hospital scrubs. At the interview for his job, Cal had been asked a lot of questions about his grooming habits—which he had answered evasively. At the training day, the first thing they did was measure the rookie House Curators for their suits. All of them men in their 20s and early 30s. All of them tall. Some of them so good-looking that, if you studied them for a while, their faces turned weird: Fadi, with his sharply-angled mandibles and his tiny glittering eyes; Shay with his implausible colouring: sand-coloured hair and stubble, big creamy cheeks, dark eyebrows and bright pink lips. These men, trapped together in an airless training room off the

Tottenham Court Road, made Cal think of eerily beautiful creatures caught behind glass: prismatic brightness of insect-carapaces, gruesome soft patterns of moth wings, fluttering at a window to get out.

Guesses he must be one of these weird breeds himself. He's always been told he's good-looking—but said in consternation, when girls turn him down, seeming not to understand their own reluctance. *You are* really *good-looking*, her saying. *Sorry*. And then picking up her handbag and leaving. A chronic failure to progress, that's what afflicts him, according to his brother Lewis. *You've stagnated, mate. You need to get yourself out there.* Those stages that other people seem to pass through with ease: never happened for him. Never had a steady girlfriend. School friends have mostly disappeared—into relationships or work or weed or gaming. He dropped out of university after one miserable month trying to study history in Newcastle, sitting up late at night listening to other people getting shit-faced and pulling and *living their best lives* while he: anxious, insomniac, chain smoking, not even able to keep up with the reading. He's never properly moved away from home. Never been on a plane. Never had a standard job. All of them training to be Curators for GuestHouse the same: good-looking young men who can hold a conversation with the great and the good, but are available to work antisocial hours for minimum wage on zero-hour contracts. They've all failed to progress. Fadi: kicked out of uni after a conviction for drunk driving and now has a minor methamphetamine habit. Shay: a failed music producer who lives in a squat surrounded by records he can't shift or afford to store. A beautiful group of fuck-ups and fuckheads and mummy's boys and petty criminals.

The job, the job they are required to do, is to look the part and to make things *flow*. Most of the houses on his list are occasional homes: the super-rich loaning them out to the visiting super-rich during frequent trips out of town. Guests trailing in with their children and their nannies, their PAs and their drivers and their tiny bobbing dogs, for a few days or a few weeks, and then traipsing off to other glamorous locations. Got to make sure these transitions *flow smoothly*. Greeting guests on the threshold in his good suit and introducing them to their temporary home. Handing over the leather-bound House Book, unique to each property, which details how to use the high-spec TV, the steam room, the jacuzzi. Telling them about the history of the house and the family china and the best restaurants in the area. He will offer to arrange anything they might require: a maid or a chef or a masseuse or a personal florist. He has printed leaflets for other, more discrete services (Westminster Pharmacist; Pimlico Escorts). He hands over a UK-networked phone with his number saved in the contacts (*GuestHouse Curator, Callum*). He leaves them with the keys and then, when their stay is over and the cleaning service has eradicated every sign of them, he'll steal back into the house to perform his checks. Prowling around of an evening, as the setting sun bleeds in across tiled bathroom floors and white linen, and checking inside cupboards and under beds and in hidden drawers full of jewellery. A forensic intruder. He ticks his list and then he leaves as soon as possible.

But József's house is different. József has invited him to stay. József says he likes the thought of him in the house, that he can spend the night any time he wants to. And the truth is, the reason he doesn't want to leave: he's missing József. A fucking shit ton of missing him. József has gone away for another stint of treatment. In a hospital this time. For the first year that Cal looked after the house, József was off all over the world trying different remedies. Yoga retreat in Marrakesh. Thai massage retreat in Vermont. Smoking weed for a month in Nevada. Vitamin D therapy. A week-long residency on food as pharmacology. Coming back with diarrhoea and a suitcase full of supplements. The money from GuestHouse pays for treatment costs and then József tells Cal all about his weird and wonderful trips when he returns. József makes him tea from the deadheads of flowers and informs him of the possible health benefits of eating copious amounts of raw petals. Your shit does, apparently, begin to smell of roses. Shows him the tiny puncture marks left by acupuncture and demonstrates his oxygen therapy machine, fixing the plastic mask across his face, giggling as he gulps on *energised air*.

József still looked well a year ago. But even then, it was clear that he was lonely. József always offers strange and delicious things (spirits from Italy that burn the back of the throat; pastries from the Middle East; fiery wine from the volcanic fields of Hungary) before sitting back on the sofa to tell his stories. József uses his voice differently from anyone else: he drops it, suddenly, to the softest whisper, reeling you forward in your seat. József is a storyteller. So he requires an audience. Gets extra lonely without one. And Cal loves to be that audience.

Just before he went into the hospital, on his last visit to sort the schedule, Cal had asked him about the paintings in the house, about how he had got started in the art business. József laughing, repeating the word 'business'.

Well, Callum, it was for lots of reasons. But firstly because an artist saved my life. József knows how to turn a dramatic phrase. *I arrived in London with next to nothing, sixteen years old, with only a pound note and an artist's address in my pocket. That artist was my mother's husband and I was fleeing Hungary. The year was 1963. That man saved my life and taught me everything I know about art. This picture here.* József motioning to the blaze of colour above his fireplace. *This is his work.*

Tamás Márton? Cal knows the name from his checks on the house. *He's your mother's husband? But not your father?*

Now, this is a long story, József says. *Do you have time, Callum?*

Callum does, he always does.

Now, forgive me if I repeat some things that are common knowledge about Hungary in the Second World War. You'll probably know all about the Siege of Budapest. József always begins his stories like this: *You'll likely know this about Cubism, Callum, so please forgive me…* or *Of course, as you will know, the Hungarian language is different from other European languages, coming from Ural-Altaic, like Finnish…* He never knows these things. It is one of József's many generosities, to introduce him to new things like this.

So that night, just a few weeks before he went into hospital, József had begun to tell him about his early life in Budapest: about the outbreak of the Second World War, the strange circumstances of his conception on the banks of the Danube, and the shattered city that he was born into. But suddenly, after a brilliant narration of the Siege of Budapest, József gets tired. Says he's feeling unwell; that he'll have to retire for the night. Cal, left hanging, not knowing how Tamás Márton saved József's life or how József came to be in London in the first place. These sudden slumps are more frequent now. And then Cal's dismissed. He steps out onto the cold doorstep, back along the canal towards the tube station. On the train to East Croydon, József's stories materialise again: the great rafts of ice in the Danube and the beautiful broken buildings of Budapest ghosted in the darkness of Norwood Junction. Off at Croydon, past the new office blocks and the new apartment blocks and new yoga studios, past the fried chicken shops and the off-licences and the cash-converters, over the tram lines, and then it's the steep walk up to St Cuthbert's: head down, don't look around, don't look up if you hear footsteps or voices or some sort of business or heated negotiation, keep on going, head down head down, this is how you stay out of trouble; and then, in the quiet stretch where the path borders woodland and the brambles spill over the fencing, the Carpathian Mountains are rising back around him in the blackness. Letting himself into the flat in the dark, straight to his room, past the muffled TV noises of Ma and Da in the living room, then looking up all the unfamiliar words that he can remember (*Axis Alliance* / *Arrow Cross* / *Miklós Horthy*), trying to piece József's past back together. Some nights, Cal dreams of Budapest.

A fox bark outside. Fuck, it's getting late. Avoids the canal path once it's gone dark: can't judge danger here in North London the same way as in Croydon—from a person's gait and micro-expressions and trainers. When József comes home from hospital they'll sit together in the living room again and Cal will ask him to finish the story of his arrival in London. He'll have baklava and plum brandy waiting for him. The house will be full of noise and energy and József again.

Resets the alarm and locks the door. What else will he get in for József to welcome him home? József always craves intense flavours when he's been particularly unwell. Last time, when he was just back from hospital, he asked Cal to grate a wet black truffle, dense as a blood clot, onto brioche for him. When he's been sick, József salts smoked meats so heavily that they make his lips tingle. He douses small buns in geranium oil. He rolls out tubes of marzipan and spreads them with jam. He—

Impact—impact hard through his shoulder. Body springs away from the attack. A strange, embarrassing noise of decompression—out of his own mouth, is it? Papers falling around him.

He's hit a girl. Shit, no, a woman. He's fucking hit a fucking woman. And hard, must have been hard, because his shoulder is throbbing.

Sorry. Shit, I'm so sorry. You ok?

And what will come now? She stands still, staring at him. Crying? Will she cry? Accusations? It was an accident. I was distracted. Rehearsing his defence already. And the papers: what if he loses these papers? Client information. Totally confidential. He strobes his arms, achieving nothing.

But what now? She's laughing. She's laughing and she's grabbing the papers too. She's catching up the lists of addresses and payment details and all of József's valuable belongings, she's catching them up in her hands and laughing and jumbling them back towards him.

People had told her that when she moved to London she wouldn't know who her neighbours were. That Londoners didn't speak to the people who lived next door to them. People told her that you could die in London and no one would know about it: that stacks of unopened post and the smell might be the only means of discovery. It had sounded wonderful. But it wasn't true. This morning, for instance, the child in the flat next door was cough-wailing again, and when she unlocked her front door to go to work, the mother was just there in the corridor, red-eyed, back from her nightshift. They could both hear the child. The mother put her hand over her mouth and began to shake, silently. Then Eileen, the alcoholic from the other side, coming out and shouting, *Needs to see a doctor, that bloody kid! Have you heard him? Sounds like he's bloody well got TB.* The other women spitting at her, *Mind your business*, muttering something else in Romanian, and then the woman's husband coming out too, hauling her inside their flat, and Eileen shouting, *There'll be a fight now an' all. No bloody peace here, never any bloody peace with this lot. Thank Christ they're all going to be sent BACK where they CAME from.*

Trying to chase all of this away on the way to the office with sanitiser; astringent gel dispensed in the palm, then worked all over. Wringing of clean hands. Walking down towards

Luca Borroni's office. Walking down the cool, grey corridor. Breathing deeply. Your thoughts and feelings are passing clouds. Eileen, the red-eyed-woman, the crying kid, all of the missed calls from home: temporary, fleeting, ephemera, moving quickly across the sky. There's a difficult job at hand that's going to require total concentration. This morning, she's managing the exit of one of the organisation's most unpredictable traders. Emory Parker has always been erratic in his transactions and in his behaviour. Now he's become a liability. He's an enormous white Texan, six-foot-four, and his manager is terrified of him. They're restructuring the team to eradicate him. Several meetings already with Luca to prepare him for this final encounter with Emory. She's written him a script. He only needs to follow the words on the page. She'll be there to ensure that the process goes smoothly. But he's been looking unsteady, Luca; took a couple of day for stress earlier in the week. Might need carrying in the meeting. Concentrate: needs all her powers of concentration to make sure he doesn't cock up the procedure.

Knocking on Luca's polished door. Pause. Nothing. Then knocking again and letting herself into his office.

Hi, hello, Lauren. Soft voice. He's sitting at his desk, fumbling with something in his drawer. Just coming. Just something I need to do first. Is there a slight tremor in his hands? Him taking a small brown glass bottle from his drawer and dispensing a few yellow droplets onto his tongue. Resthcue Remedy, he says, mouth still open, drops dispersing on his flabby tongue.

Walking together in silence back down the corridor towards the meeting room. Opening the door, and Emory already here. Sitting at a large conference table, enormous hands balled into fists.

Talk the talk. Adrenaline kick-in. Good morning, Emory. As you know, I'm your HR representative and I'm here to make sure that due process is followed today.

Taking her seat, motioning for Luca to sit in the chair next to her.

I knew you guys were going try to do something like this to me. Emory's voice a wail. Arms lifting theatrically. Why, Luca, why?

Emory, as we've discussed in our previous meetings, Luca is just following the procedure required as part of our reorganisation. You were given the opportunity to be accompanied by a representative today. Luca is now going to begin our meeting.

Turning towards Luca. Luca staring hard at the papers in front of him. Gone over this, already gone over this process several times: all he needs to do is read from the script. But he's frozen. He's doing something strange with his right hand, repeatedly rubbing his fingers against the papers as though he's checking the grain.

See! Emory seizing the moment. He doesn't want to do it! He knows you've got it in for me. Luca is a good guy! He knows I haven't done anything that other people aren't doing ALL THE TIME.

Nudging Luca gently with her foot under the table.

Luca widening his eyes, beginning to read from the script in a thin voice. Emory Parker, as you know, Lane&Hobart has gone through a number of organisational changes recently and your position is being made redundant. I regret to advise you that, effective immediately, your services will no longer be required by Lane&Hobart Financial Services Inc. He's reading quickly and gaining speed. To assist you in coping with this situation, we have put together a severancepackage in recognition of your years with Lane&Hobart, which includes provisions for transitionalcounsellingassistance. We have prepared a letter outlining this package which wewillgiveyou some time to consider. In the meantime, your personaleffectswillbebroughtto you, and you will need to vacate the business premises immediately, duetothesensitivenatureofyourrole. Luca looking up; darting attention like a bird. Emory silent. His lips whitening. Shaking his head repeatedly.

I—I have asked our HR executive Lauren Haigh to be here today to assist you to begin thetransitionalprocess.

No, says Emory. No, no, no. Luca! Don't let them do this. Thumping his fists down on the table, massive chest heaving upwards. The out-breath comes in hard, jerky exhalations. Chin sinking down onto chest now. Crying? Is that what's coming already? Then his head rising slowly from his sunken body. Luca, we're friends, man! he calls out.

Thank you, Luca. Lauren back in charge. That's it, that's the end of Luca's part. He can go. But Luca isn't moving.

He looks up at Emory and then he begins to reach across the table with his right hand. He's attempting the Exit Handshake. She did talk about this: she did tell him that he should try to round off the meeting in a firm but amicable manner, ideally with a handshake. But Emory is clearly in no position to accept the gesture. Emory is staring, incredulous, at the hand thrust out towards him. And Luca's hand now seeming to become progressively less convinced of its own ability to grip another's: his fingers bunching together and now his thumb disappearing in between them, so that his hand finally makes a weird, quivering claw. The three of them staring at the faltering hand, still held out over the glossy surface of the table.

That's alright, Luca, she says. I'll take it from here.

But Emory is already up on his feet. Opportunity, now, for a dramatic counter strike.

You're holding out your hand to me? Throwing his chair back, walking around the side of the table towards Luca. You're holding out your puny little hand to me, when you've just fucked me? You want me to shake that hand and say thank you very much, thank you very much Mr Borroni. Jesus Christ, it's like being fucked in the ass by Ned Flanders and then asked for a kiss.

Up on her feet. She's up on her feet now, adrenaline fully flooding in, process, process to follow. Process always to the rescue. Emory, Luca is leaving now and I'm going to give you a moment to gather yourself. Then I'll be back to talk to you about next steps.

Luca still isn't moving. Grabbing him under his right armpit. Fight, flight, freeze: he's a freezer alright. And Emory is still not done.

Luca! He's blocking their way to the door now. Luca, don't let them do this to me. I know you saw something in me. That's why you hired me. I know you saw it. I can follow your rules, I can. Please, Luca. Emory drops heavily onto his knees, raising his hands in a gesture of prayer—a surprisingly fluid genuflection for such a large man. Please, Luca. Just give me another chance.

Steering Luca out of the room, closing the door as Emory begins to sob. Directing Luca back to his office. Watching him retreat down the hallway: uncertain now of his legs, walking as though he's navigating a ship's corridor. And then she calls security.

Back at her desk, working through her emails—relentless deleting and archiving and responding. Trying. Trying to discharge the bad, nervous energy. Nothing to feel bad about. She handled things well, she kept everything under control. It was a procedurally perfect exit.

Mina, head of all things, breezing through the open-plan office, calling over with deliberate casualness. Lauren, my darling, how was it? I heard you called security?

Yeah. He made a fuss, and you know how big he is. He sobbed like a baby at the end. Nothing I couldn't handle though. He might bring an action. But we're prepared for it. It was a perfectly clean exit.

Good girl, Mina says, still walking, turning to blow her a kiss from the door.

Another viewing this evening. The same ecstatic vocabulary as always: the place is *fantastic*, *amazing location*, you're the *perfect buyer* for it, you have to see it *ASAP*. Things have gotten worse since the last viewing with Tana. Savitt&Jones, Tana's company, the largest agency in the area, emailing her: *We no longer feel confident that you're a serious buyer in a position to proceed.* The only things to come on in a week, excluding Savitt&Jones's properties, have been: a tiny bedsit stained bright yellow by nicotine, stinking of death; a basement speckled all over with black mould—the taste of toxic spores as she walked around. The agent at the end of the viewing reminding her that she was in danger of never getting on the ladder: things would only get worse; no one would sell in an uncertain market.

After the viewings, walking around, walking again towards that colourful terrace of houses, towards Elgin Mews. Inside the mauve house, a middle-aged woman, with perfect nougat highlights, backlit in the kitchen. Shift dress in pistachio-coloured silk. Pouring herself a glass of wine, releasing the tension in her neck. Two houses in darkness, and then an older couple sitting in their living room, eating olives with cocktail sticks, newspapers spread across their laps. The red house, the house in front of which she had collided with the man, was in darkness the first time she passed. But a few nights later, the man was in his kitchen with a young couple. The couple both extremely blonde. The woman in a white linen suit. The three of them speaking seriously, and then her man saying something to the other man and them shaking hands. When he opened the front door, she moved off, but not too quickly; walking with half an ear on his footsteps behind her. Perhaps he'd forgotten something. Wine, maybe? Was it a dinner party? Letting him pass her, and then turning around and walking back along the Mews. The sky burning out into indigo above the roofs of the houses.

Looking in at the windows is like looking online, only better—even more absorbing. For the whole time that she's been saving her deposit, she's been doing this. Looking at things; practising forceful domestic visualisation. Evenings spent browsing through photographs on property sites, picturing herself in a townhouse in Hampstead Heath, a luxury penthouse on the river, a converted warehouse in Southwark. Her two favourite forms of speculation: looking at houses she can't afford, and ordering expensive clothing online that she can't afford. Exquisite clothes delivered to her flat, wearing them for an evening—taking selfies, drinking wine, looking at houses while wearing them—and then, at the end of the night, folding the clothes back along the creases that had not yet hung out; placing tissue paper carefully back around soft fabric; inserting clothes back into their large plastic packages; checking the box, *Clothes are not a good fit*; in the morning, posting everything back for a refund.

The blonde couple in the red house began moving around the living room. Imagining herself into that living room: imagining it hard. She is sitting on the sofa in a powder blue pussycat blouse and buttercup pedal-pushers, her soft bare feet massaging one another. She is upstairs in a cleanly tiled bathroom, submerged in a Victorian tub, hair pinned up, body softened by oils and water. She is in the bedroom, laid on a big raft of a bed in a gold lace made-to-measure babydoll from La Perla. Or in another bedroom, at the back of the house, a nursery, with soft green walls and a cot covered in a kingfisher blue cashmere blanket, underneath which a tiny, beautiful, blur of a baby. She is standing at the side of the crib, wearing something vintage-y (Liberty print tea dress?), softly humming, and she and the baby have no needs at all: no hunger, no desire, no yearning for warmth or care or violence. Almost inert.

She had watched for a long time; she had watched until she was cold all of the way through and the blonde couple had turned out all of the lights in the house. And still the man, her man, hadn't come home.

Tonight's viewing: predictably awful. A tiny attic flat pervaded by a low hum. The agent walks around as though nothing is amiss, but a pulsing mass of wasps cluster in the main light-fitting, crawling over one another, moving perpetually into and back out of the ceiling cavity. Every so often one wasp breaks away and flies dementedly towards them, the agent turning his head and snorting.

So here she is again, wandering down Elgin Mews, staring in at the windows. The lights are on in the red house. All of the lights are on. Walking past. Walking past again. The man is in and moving around: when she sees him the second time, he's looking through the kitchen cupboards. The third time she walks down the street, he opens the front door, just as she's passing.

Hi, he says. Are you ok? I   I thought I saw you, just a minute ago.

Breaking through the fourth fucking wall. She, hyper-real. A ghost addressed at a séance. Tries to speak, but mouth falters. Then—

I, um, I'm locked out of my flat. Just waiting   just killing time until my flatmate gets home.

Oh, he says. Will you be ok?

Yes. I'll be fine. Just   so stupid of me.

You could wait   in here? If you wanted? Inside?

Inside, inside, inside.

Her face is dewy and light-seeking. Her big eyes glitter like something catching light at the bottom of a dark pool.

She is sitting on József's sofa, this strange woman he's invited in, and she is focussing all of her attention entirely on him.

Drink? Can I get you a drink?

And the way she smiles at him. As though pleasure is slowly spreading through her body. Him, going woozy. Nauseated, ever so slightly, at her proximity. His limbs might move towards her, might just reach out and touch her, and that would be totally inappropriate, an absolute fucking disaster, and how did he get into this situation, here with her in József's house anyway—

Only if you're having one. Only if you've got something open.

Well, I can open something for us. There's a drinks cabinet. That's true—the guests are due in the morning and it's all ready for them.

A sour maybe?

A sour? Right.

In the kitchen, googling *sour ingredients*. He'll have to open drawers. He'll have to use utensils. Now is the time he should tell her that this isn't his house. He definitely should tell her that right now, to avoid any possible confusion. But now is also the time that she calls through to him, I *love* your house, and the way she draws out *love*, long and smooth, and the way her sentence trails off, renders him totally fucking silent. He checks the drinks cabinet. Everything is there, ready for the guests: gin, whiskey, vodka, tequila, and there, at the back, an untouched bottle of Disaronno. There are also lemons, so he takes out four and places them on the granite worktop. He takes a napkin from a drawer and uses it to open the cupboard where the glassware lives: two squat crystal tumblers. A sharp knife, pushed testingly against the zest of the lemon, to see if he can do it. Pushed further into the skin, so that it bleeds a little bright citrus oil, and then he just does it: he cuts straight through to the granite surface, makes a drink just like József does, as if it's his kitchen. He juices the fruit into a glass and stirs it all together. He washes his hands, which are trembling slightly. Puts the emptied lemon skins into a pile to be disposed of later and wipes down the surface. There'll be time, there'll be time to sort all of this out when she leaves. You can get more lemons from the high street. And József has always said he should make himself at home. He texted just yesterday and asked Cal to come and stay with him the first night he's back from hospital. Not doing anything wrong. He's not doing anything wrong. It's just a matter of lemons.

She's curled into the corner of the sofa in the living room. She's taken her shoes off and her toenails are the colour of the inside of a shell, the same colour as her dress. He puts the drinks down. He sits right at the other end of the sofa.

So, I'm Callum, he says. People call me Cal.

Thanks so much for the drink, Cal. And for inviting me in. I'm Lauren. Sitting up straighter, crossing her legs and moving in towards him. Cheers. Reaching over with her drink.

Ta. Yeah, cheers.

So, Cal, what do you do for a living?

I   well, I'm kind of in property.

This is not really a lie. No definite lies so far. Tech-ni-cal-ly speaking. Just being scant on detail, that's all, and details are not meant for occasions like this: extraordinary occasions, where you're helping a stranger who you'll never see again. What about you? he asks.

Oh, I work in human resources.

Nice one. My mum used to do that. Making sure people are well looked after and that?

Something like that. Actually my specialism is change and exit management.

Right. Is that, like, what   getting rid of people?

She, smiling, then turning away to look around the room. Work's boring, isn't it? You like art? Tell me about this picture?

She's tilting her drink towards the Hockney in the alcove. Can't place her accent: somewhere up north maybe? A flatness when she speaks that makes her sound slightly sardonic. Is she taking the piss out of him, seeming to hang on his every word?

So, that picture is   from the early 1980s. A David Hockney.

József has told him about this picture many times: József was at Hockney's first show at the Whitechapel Gallery in 1963. It was just after his arrival in London, and József fell in love with the colour in Hockney's work. *So loud!* József always says, *Such loud, vulgar colour! Ha!* This particular picture is from much later in Hockney's career, acquired by József in the early '80s: a bright, 2D depiction of an LA swimming pool, divided into 9 squares. On the other side of the room, back by the door, an early Frank Bowling. *Bowling is another lover of colour: he came to London from Guyana and studied at the Royal College at the same time as Hockney. He poured paint directly onto the canvas to get these bright patterns. To make pictures so bright that they look like they're glowing.* All of this spilling out from him; telling her all this as though these stories are his to tell.

Right, she says. Wow. And how did you come by these beautiful pieces? Do you collect art?

No, no, not me.

Oh. Right. But whose are the pictures then?

My er, father's?

So here it is: the first hard lie. Feeling sort of easy; a curatorial lie; an artistic truth. Telling her more about the pictures. And then about a small Barbara Hepworth piece on the bureau; telling her about the studios in St Ives that József used to visit and how this work is from the '50s, at the very beginning of her period of curved abstract forms. The details come so easily—even some of the exact phrases that József uses: Hepworth was *anti-naturalism*; she works to produce *fundamental shapes*; to make the *impersonal individualised*.

Your father sounds like a fascinating man, she says. Is he still collecting art?

No, he's stopped. He's   not well right now.

Oh. Putting her glass back down carefully on the coaster and turning towards him. I'm really sorry to hear that. I hope he'll   make a quick recovery?

Doesn't speak. What can he say to this?

Her, moving closer to him on the sofa. It's not cancer is it?

No, no.

Oh. And then trying again, hopefully: A stroke?

It's multiple sclerosis, he says. Some truth in that at least.

Her moving to sit right next to him. The warmth of her arm against his. Him not moving a muscle. Hardly breathing. Her lips on his right cheek, moving slowly, softly. Then she's turning above him, moving astride him, pink dress clinging to her toffee-coloured thighs. Him, still not moving.

She takes his face in both hands. Cal. Thank you for telling me that. I feel   really close to you right now.

The flat delivery of her words. Is this sarcasm, is this all a horrible joke? But she's moving in towards him and kissing him, kissing him full on the mouth, and her mouth is soft and fresh and wet, like pulped melon. His hands moving over her now, drawing her closer, when suddenly she pulls back.

Oh Christ, she says, clambering off him and shrugging down her skirt. I can't believe I did that. You could be married? Or anything?

I'm not. Married. Or anything.

It's really late. I should be going home.

Oh, you're not   you're   'course. Sorry. Don't worry. If you need to go?

Everything falling away; his skin coolly contracting now she has withdrawn her touch. Extra lonely and embarrassed: a shrinking creature conscious of over-extension, a shamed snail withdrawing back into its shell. Can't look at her, mustn't look at her again.

I really should go. Imposing on you like this. You've been so kind. She's collecting up her handbag. That's it: she's off.

No, I haven't. Not at all.

Shall I give you my number and we can do this properly. If you'd like to?

Yeah, yeah, I would. Totally.

What about dinner next week? What about you cook for me in that gorgeous kitchen? I could do Friday night?

Yeah, definitely, let's do Friday.

Standing up, following her out, and her turning, moving towards him again, smudging her mouth, soft and warm, against the corner of his. Friday. Friday. He will see her again next Friday. His body blurring towards her, but she's already backing away, turning away again.

Can I walk you home?

Oh no. I'm really not far. Opening the front door herself. Bye, Cal.

Standing on the step a while, watching her go. Listening until her footsteps have disappeared down Elgin Mews. He'll have to go inside and clean everything. He'll have to remove every trace of them from the house, ready for the morning's guests. But, just for a moment longer, in the warm evening air: he can stand here and still feel Lauren's touch against his skin. The two of them still held together, there, in the house behind him. But he has to go home, he has to go back to Croydon; clean, check, lock up, last train through. And then the feeling is a bubble bursting into the dark night; and her touch is vaporising into Outer London.

A cobbled tributary to Liverpool Street, The Bluebird up ahead. The restaurant, dark inside, though it's the middle of the day, and artfully distressed: flowers creeping up the walls in neo-Victorian morbid print. Behind Mina's head, a display of plates, each plate depicting a tiny scene: a blue-and-white shepherd tending sheep; brown swallows, twinned in fine brush strokes and outlined in gold leaf; a gaudy bluebird, sat fatly in its nest. None of the chairs match. The surface of their lacquered table is scratched.

It's taken me weeks to get us this reservation. Mina turning the pages of her menu. I hope it's worth it. Shall we have just one *little* drink, hey? To help us through the afternoon?

Sure.

This afternoon is a disciplinary and another problem trader to dispatch.

Mina cocking her head. A waiter appearing at her side. We'll have two brambles. Not that *you* need any help, my darling. But it's been a while since we've had so many exits in one day. Tell me, how bad was the first?

The morning's exit: a potentially messy one. Another boiling hot day. The meeting had been held in a small glass-fronted room. Freddy Williams: sweating copiously. His blonde hair thickened with sweat, his ginger stubble glittering greenly, verdigrised by it.

So, the thing is, right, it was just a joke? I didn't mean to do it again. It just   happened.

Freddy's manager, Trevon, a gutless Bostonian good-cop, sitting next to Lauren, nodding empathically. I have every sympathy. I really do. You're a brilliant trader. You take all the right risks, you're bold but not reckless. We're all bummed to be losing you, buddy. And I get it, I absolutely do. They're all flirty and then they slam you with this shit. But there are certain rules that have to be followed in the workplace. So now there's a procedure we have to follow, according to Miss Haigh and her HR colleagues. It's out of my hands because of the complaints. I've done what I can, buddy. Shaking his head sadly, turning to her to make this all go away.

Mr Williams. Freddy, this is the second time we've met to discuss   this issue. In the previous meeting, you were told to treat our discussion as a final warning. And we're now in a position where we need to terminate your contract of employment on the grounds of gross misconduct. You have on three separate occasions emailed a photograph of your genitals to a female colleague—

But that's what I'm saying! It wasn't *my* dick. And she's not really a colleague. She's   admin, isn't she? If you look at the pictures, you can see that they're all different penises! They're not mine. They're joke penises! One of them's circumcised. I can show you I'm not circumcised, I can prove it right now!

Please   sit back down, Mr Williams, I don't need to see proof of anything. At this point it really doesn't matter whose   penis you posted.

It was just—

I shouldn't have to tell you again that sending obscene materials at work, of whoever's genitals, constitutes gross misconduct. Your admin colleague would be well within her rights to bring a case against you for harassment. We are terminating your contract with immediate effect. Recite the script from memory now; her holy catechism: To assist you in coping with this situation, we have put together a severance package in recognition of your years with Lane&Hobart Financial Services Inc, which includes provisions for transitional counselling assistance. We have prepared a letter outlining this package which we will give you some time to consider. In the meantime, your personal effects will be brought to you, and you will need to vacate the business premises immediately, due to the sensitive nature of your role.

Freddy Williams' gasps, horrible strangled little noises, hardly, hardly audible through her unfaltering performance.

It wasn't the easiest of exits. Running her finger down the menu. Snail porridge. Salmon with liquorice gel. But she'll have whatever Mina orders for her. He got upset, said it was all a joke, said it wasn't his   penis. But he knows he doesn't have a leg to stand on. He went out whimpering in the end, and thanking me for my help. I've promised him a reference.

Waiter arriving with their drinks. Are they ready to order? We'll have two cucumber gazpacho and two duck with blood pudding. Mina snapping her menu shut, holding it out towards the waiter, looking in the opposite direction until he has left. You need the red meat, darling. Winking at her. I'm doing the milk round again at the end of the month. Do you think I'll find anyone as talented as you? Of course I won't! Ha! I'm going to focus on finding reward specialists this time. We need some good cops too. Do you remember our milk round, darling? I knew straight away that you were something extraordinary.

Love at first sight, when Lauren first saw Mina. Five years ago, finishing her degree in business at Bristol. Wanting to reach the City, wanting to get away from the grime of Bristol and start afresh. Dev, her boyfriend, had made some money from online poker. Whenever Dev won, he treated her to extravagant gifts: easy come, easy go. Dining in restaurants on the waterfront; parties on boats where cocaine was poured out in fat smooth lines, sweet as icing sugar. Dev chose to live in something very similar to a squat at the edge of St Paul's with four of his friends. Technically, they were called *guardians* of the property they inhabited: they were part of a scheme to keep vacant properties protected. Dev all evangelical about it: paying minimal rent to live on the top floor of a derelict warehouse right at the edge of the city centre. Calling it their penthouse. Stud walls they'd put up to make separate sleeping areas but the rest of the space one large communal living room strewn with decks and records and burnt-out blunts and semi-conscious strangers. The makeshift toilet and shower cubicle—unspeakably bad. After a night out with

Dev, at a restaurant or a new club, this is where they would end up: back at the warehouse on a mattress on the floor. No curtains in Dev's sleeping segment and so she would lie awake in the starlight, listening to the late-night movements of the other men, studying the industrial stains that had bled out onto the concrete floor. Praying that she wouldn't need to use the toilet until dawn.

Bristol was not what she had hoped for. The warehouse produced a feeling like sea-sickness: waking in the night, not knowing where she was, she'd be back in another industrial room, a derelict mill at the edge of Huddersfield, where she'd woken once, years ago, not knowing where she was. The smell of damp, the speakers and sound equipment around her, the old industrial marks on the concrete floor. It was barely light. Out. She'd been out with one of her father's friends, out on the mad mile in Batley. She was seventeen and no one could hurt her now: not if she wanted it more than they did. But where was she? One man was sleeping on the floor, another was pressed hard against her on an old sofa. She knew neither of them. Neither was the man she had gone out with. Her mouth burning, sickly sweet orange: Southern Comfort. She would never again drink Southern Comfort. Getting up from the sofa. Vomit sting at the back of her throat. Vomiting twice in quick succession. The men waking. Making no eye contact with her or each other. *Come on*, one of them says, and they all trail out of the derelict mill to the canal side. *There's a bus route up there*, he says, pointing up the valley, and he hands her a tenner. The other one already a way down the canal path, and this one chasing after him now shouting, *Oi, dickhead, wait up.* And so she, walking along a steep valley road as the sun rose, her throat raw, her thighs trembling, the light unbearably delicate. And blood, she finds blood when she gets home; but only a little.

One morning, Dev sleeping soundly, she's woken by a crying gull. The concrete around her; the marks on the floor; the smell of chalky damp. Rising, silently, writing Dev a note. Outlining her future plans and asking him not to contact her again. Collecting up the things he'd bought for her (silk nightdress, bottle of perfume, a diamond pendant), and then creeping out past all of the separate sleeping compartments. Just before 5am. Walking back to her digs through the empty city streets. Shivering, cold and alive, in the bright blue morning as gulls wheel and caw above.

Later that day. Later that day she first saw Mina. Showering back at her flat, putting on the good clothes, the fierce makeup. Loud music, heavy beat. Psyched up, totally psyched up for the grad fair. Mina gleaming at the Lane&Hobart stall. Ferociously clean. No smile. No smile for Lauren, but baring her tiny symmetrical teeth: a greeting and a warning off. Navy wool suit. Cream silk vest. Gold and diamond collar around her throat. Arms crossed in front. Hair all peroxide. Untouchable. Mina. So clean. Like she would never be grubby, no matter what you did to her.

Tell me something interesting about yourself, pretty girl. I've met with too many boring boys today. Mina speaking with sing-song polish; and with the taunting intimacy of someone who despises most human beings.

Empty in that moment: nothing to say. And then all of the adrenaline, the surge that makes something from nothing. Her voice saying: *I'm good at ending things.*

You are? Mina looking amused.

Yes. I'm future focussed.

Two rounds of interviews, and then she's through, through to the Graduate Trainee Scheme in Human Resources at Lane&Hobart Financial Services Inc. Mina taking her under her wing: teaching her about equal opportunities monitoring and about due process in redundancy. And teaching her where to go out in London and the importance of hand sanitiser after all journeys and how to gauge a man's net-worth from his shoes and that you must absolutely never match your shoes to your handbag unless you wanted to be mistaken for a Russian prostitute when you went to Mahiki. Mina, born in Tallinn, educated at Stanford, living in London since her 20s. Passing on her knowledge of the world, including her tried-and-tested pre-date routine: a visit to a spa for a massage, a high-protein snack, and masturbation in the bath an hour before going out. *You should never be dependent on a man for warmth, sustenance or pleasure, my darling. You must never go out hungry. A woman needs to learn to take care of herself.*

Mina's paying for lunch in The Bluebird, and Mina wants intel.

Anyway, darling, less about work. Tell me about this new boy and his house. Mina sitting back in her chair and sipping her drink. She likes to intersperse her thinking about HR strategy with other kinds of strategic planning. It keeps her fresh.

Well. The house is   bohemian, I guess you'd say. It's near the canal. Little Venice. It's full of pictures. Paintings. Absolutely everywhere.

That's a smart investment.

It doesn't seem like it's an investment, exactly. It's sort of haphazard. A passion project, I suppose.

Room for improvement, hey? Work for you to do there. And the boy, what about this boy?

Little bubbles clustering on the stem of her straw; stirring, watching them disperse. Lime, pinioned at the bottom of the glass. Fraying its pulpy flesh. The boy. Callum. This is what she won't tell Mina: about his uncertain, hungry manner. His obvious desire to touch her. When Cal speaks, he does so out of one side of his mouth and then he screws his features up as though he already regrets what he's saying and when his face rests again, he glances at you with those eyes—completely lost. Completely needful. That she finds his hunger for her such a pull that she lost control, for just a moment. She hadn't been prepared. She had gone out hungry. It was a chance encounter, after all. That she'd practically jumped him. That feeling: that death-spiral of desire that had launched her towards him. The feeling she still can't entirely subdue, can't domesticate like Mina seems able to do so proficiently. She knows what she's supposed to do: never put out on the first night; gather information; ensure that she can manoeuvre, that the relationship will help to move her up in the world. *Your erotic capital, my darling*, Mina is fond of saying, *is the most valuable thing you have. Don't squander it.* But every so often, still, it happens: a chance encounter that catches her off guard, a desire so strong that she can't pull back. On the back seat of a Vauxhall with an Uber driver, bright blue eyes, sleeves of tattoos, who kept telling her that he'd even turned off the app for her; that doorman last month outside a bar in Kensington Gardens, an enormous ex-squaddie who'd sat her on top of a dumpster and kissed her inner thighs with total concentration. Leaning back, closing her eyes, she was a stone thrown in a deep well then, an object with high velocity, rising and then falling into unknowable darkness. And they were falling together, her and these hard-but-tender men, these broken, beautiful men with precarious jobs and shattered cheekbones and scant prospects, they were hurtling into that darkness together. But only for a moment. She'd remember herself almost immediately afterwards. Her velocity was upwards. A momentary lapse, that's all these encounters were. No numbers ever exchanged. *You're a hard bitch, aren't you? Well fuck you very much.*

But Callum is legit. There's scope here. Plenty of it. Mina will approve.

Callum? So, he's in property, he says. He's   going through a difficult time at the moment. Knowing that Mina admires someone who can put on a good show in trying circumstances: His father's very ill. Dying, I think.

Ah. And what's the plan now, darling? Next steps?

Dinner. At his. Though he's being a bit   evasive.

Huh. Don't let him wriggle off the hook. It's got to be at his. It's a good sign that you've been to the house already, but that doesn't mean anything: the wife could be away, or the girlfriend not living there. Remember Reshana. You need to sweep the place.

Reshana: a warning for them all. Reshana was a recruit to the grad scheme at the same time as her: Bajan, Oxford-educated, serious but not *too* serious, deadly good-looking— *Reshana's got the full package, she's the Real Deal, that girl's going to go far*: Mina on repeat. A few months in, Reshana had started dating a French trader from another firm who blew hot and cold. But he always had excuses that checked out. Stayed just the right side of plausibility. And then he disappeared for several months, totally ghosted her, finally returning with effusive apologies and compliments and an exquisite silk dress. He'd been on an extended business trip to Shanghai, he said. Things had gotten too much with work and he'd just needed a break. When she finally spent the night at his flat, she performed the sweep while he was showering, checking every space she could for clues of a wife: his walk-in wardrobe held six silk gowns in different colours—pristine, hanging in their cellophane, ready to be gifted. Reshana's trader was a warning to all of them: they must perform the sweep as early on as possible.

And Callum's shoes?

Nice. Maybe not quite what you'd expect with his suit. But still, nice.

This is a lie; Cal's shoes were clearly from the high street. But Mina's rules aren't fool-proof, right?

Very good, Mina says.

There is one   snag. There's something   I haven't been entirely honest about. I haven't told him where I live. He thinks   well it's complicated. But he thinks I live close-by to him, in Little Venice. It's part of how we met and now I don't know how to back-track.

Hmm. Mina leaning back and sipping her drink. This is a problem that will give her some enjoyment. Well, of course, you wouldn't want him to know you live in Deptford. He never needs to know about your place. This could be good for you, Lauren. It will force you to keep your guard up. Just say you want to go out for dinner. See if he can afford you. Keep your domestic arrangements private. He doesn't need to know about your little flat or the details of your council tax or your epilation schedule.

The waiter arrives. Mina leaning back, looking away, allowing the man to present her with her food.

Now. Leaning forward. Lifting cutlery, slicing cleanly through the blood pudding. Who is it we're getting rid of this afternoon?

The thing is, the thing is, it's impossible to work out how bad the situation really is. It feels pretty bad. For instance, he can't sit down in József's living room. Every time he tries, he feels like he needs to piss, and he has to get up and move around. But also: he feels this way a lot of the time. Things bother him, they bother him way more than they should. And these aren't necessarily terrible things, objectively speaking: for instance, he still thinks a lot about last summer, when his brother brought his girlfriend over, and he asked how her cat was. Just trying to make conversation. He knew how much she loved that cat. She'd shown him a whole load of pictures the first time they'd met. So. Many. Pictures. What he didn't know was that the cat had gone missing. He asked about the cat and then she'd run out of the living room crying, and Lewis had called him a bellend, and told him he'd found the frigging cat in the car park, totally pulverised after falling from the twelfth-floor balcony of their new flat, but he hadn't told her that, *So thanks a lot for bringing it up, bellend*. Now, objectively, he'd done nothing wrong, but he still felt fucking shite about it, like he'd let his brother down. Can't look Cheryl in the eye even now or trust himself to speak to her. He hoards his own failures and mistakes. He knows that he does this. Thinks about them, lists them, recounts all of his inadequacies to himself late at night. Another example—

even this, even the one supposedly good thing he has: his relationship with József, his access to Elgin Mews—even before this   problem   with Lauren, he found himself anxious about it. Sometimes. Because: isn't it weird? Doesn't it make him weird to be hanging on the every word of an elderly client, to be so attached to him and his house? To think that they're friends? Fuck's sake. Fuck's sake. But József has told him, József has told him repeatedly that it's ok for him to stay here, that he wants him to use the house. That they truly are friends. *Please! Stay whenever you like, dear boy. My home is your home.* And here's the real problem: if you feel bad about everything, how can you work out if something is *really* bad?

Going through to the kitchen. Talk to Marc to settle these nerves. But the fact that Marc's here, prepping a meal for him: further proof that things aren't right. Marc is one of the private chefs he books for clients. He realised, the morning after his night with Lauren, that József's house was booked out on the following Saturday, the very next morning after their proposed date. He'd also realised that he should meet Lauren on neutral ground, somewhere that meant he didn't need to carry on lying. He'd tried his best to rearrange, to put Lauren off the idea of dinner at 'his', to take her out for a meal instead. But she'd been totally insistent. She'd even hinted that he might have something to hide. *Cal, you're not trying to keep me away from your beautiful house are you?? I want another look at those paintings. XX*

He was forced onto the defensive: he had to have her over for dinner, to show that he had nothing to hide. Which meant keeping up the lie. Is there a philosophical term for this? Other than fuck fuck fucking doomed? Marc has been a total legend. Offered to do the evening on the cheap and said that he could clear the kitchen completely, so that there'd be no sign of the meal in the morning. Marc is used to working in other people's houses and leaving no trace. Just like him. But he's also rolling up his thin cigarettes on the kitchen worktops and tiny threads of tobacco are dropping onto the floor. Will he catch all of them in his clean up? And he smokes his rollies on the back doorstep, flicking the stubs out into the garden. Cal will have to search those out later, in the dark, to make sure the garden is immaculate.

What's the matter, bro? You want a roll-up? A little snifter? Shaking his head.

You look well edgey, mate. You must really like this girl? Don't let it show so much. They don't like it, you know. Laughing. Punching him on the shoulder.

Return to the living room to pace. In his suit, because what else does he wear in this house? But even that feels wrong now, part of the deceit. He needs a plan, that's what he needs. They'll have the meal here together, and then he'll explain. He'll say: Funny story this, Lauren, but this house, this house we've just had dinner in together, it isn't really my house. I don't own it. It's just that I'm allowed to use it, for this one evening. I live with my parents in Croydon. Fucking sexy right?

What would József think about this predicament? He stares at the picture above the fireplace, the Tamás Márton, the blaze of fire: József's most prized painting. *That man saved my life. He taught me everything I know about art.* The story of this painting that József had left unfinished. The basics, Cal knows: József's mother, Klara, had been a young Jewish poet living in Budapest when war broke out in 1944. She had married the artist and critic Tamás Márton that same year, and they had fled from the city when things became too dangerous. They had hidden in the countryside, and escaped the worst of things in Budapest. They returned to the city when the Soviets arrived. But something terrible had happened to Klara out there. *She was still alive, though! To still being alive!* József had raised his glass, just before dismissing Cal. *I'm sorry, dear boy, I'm too tired. Would you mind if we stopped there?*

To still being alive. József would laugh at this situation. *It's nothing!* he'd say. *Are you still alive? Yes? Then there is hope!* József will be back soon, fit as a fiddle, to tell the rest of his story, to make everything feel hopeful, reversible, retrievable.

There's a hard knock at the door. Cal's blood runs cold.

They sit at the kitchen table eating venison wellington and drinking pinot noir and she has this brilliant look on her face, as though she is so excited she might burst if she doesn't try to hold it in, which she does by pursing her lips and dimpling up her cheeks. Lauren asks Marc about everything:

what region the wine is from, what all the different cheeses are, even where the tablecloth is from. Marc is only too happy to step in and talk to her. He's started doing this little fake roll on his *r*s, as though he's French or something. Marc has lived his whole life in Brixton. Lauren listens hard to everything he's saying, and when Marc winks at Cal as he leaves the table for a rollie, Cal feels like he might be sick. Pours himself more wine, though he's already pretty fuzzed. Thinks of József, in the hospital right now in his burgundy pyjamas eating God knows what, while they sit here at his kitchen table, picking over cubes of salted cheese and butter-tablet fudge. He almost says it then, he almost blurts it out: *Listen, Lauren, funny story this...* but when he glances over at her, she's licking the salt from her fingertips, shyly. She catches his eye and looks down.

Sorry, she says. It's just so delicious. Her lips are stained slightly from the wine and her cheeks are dark red too. And now she's reaching across to him, she really is, she's leaning across to kiss him, and his hands are in her soft hair and they are standing up simultaneously, they're moving together, he's stumbling backwards, but they're still kissing, they're moving together towards the front room, and they're kissing and kissing, lying together on the sofa, their legs all caught up, he can feel her soft wet mouth and her soft warm skin, he can taste the salt on her lips and the edges of her hair fluttering into his mouth, and there are noises from the kitchen—Marc clearing things away—and she moves his hand between her soft warm thighs, and he hears the front door closing, and they are alone here now, and he's sinking, sinking, sinking—

Tacky skin. Skin of cheek bonded to something cool and sticky. Eyelids fluttering. Pulling away. Attempting to locate himself; for moments he is lost, brain flickering ineffectively like a dodgy GPS signal. He's in the living room, in József's living room, the Tamás Márton picture in front of him, his cheek stuck to the chesterfield sofa. No memory of falling asleep here. But, dawning on him, with the dreadful force of a repressed inevitability, the knowledge that it is the morning after the night before: it is Saturday morning and the guests from Dubai will be arriving imminently. On the floor: Lauren's shimmering green dress, shrugged off and discarded like an empty snake skin. Lauren. Fucking hell. Where is she? Checking his phone. 06.57. He still has time, just, to tidy up before they arrive. The guests are due at nine.

Lauren? Him calling out to the empty kitchen. Could she be upstairs? He can hear no movement. Lauren? Calling out on the upstairs landing. The door to József's bedroom open a fraction. The master suite. He pushes the door and sights Lauren in the middle of József's bed under the freshly laundered Egyptian cotton. Stirring, she: a soft, happy moan from under the sheets.

Shit. You've got to get out of that bed.

Lauren lifting her head. Morning. Then letting her head fall back to the pillow. You fell asleep downstairs and I didn't want to disturb you. Why don't you get in? Pulling back the duvet. She's wearing violet lace underwear. The smell of her warm body rising up like hot milky tea. Her body, her bare, brown, curved body, ghosting backwards, a laminate of hot virtual encounters: photos, videos, porn sites. Has he ever seen a body like this before? irl? Hasn't it always been just glimpses? A tiny triangle of nipple escaping the edge of a push up bra; fingers looped over the edge of elastic, pulling knickers to one side, and a triangle of pubis, mouse-brown or black or shockingly naked. Of the last girl—a Christmas pull, neither of their hearts in it—all he'd seen was her buttocks and the soft, minky fuzz of the hair between them.

Him standing still: trying to set the image of her body in his mind in perpetuity. Excited and fucking horrified. Lauren. Fuck. I'm really sorry but we've got to get out of the house. Quickly.

Oh. Is it work stuff? Pulling the duvet back around her.

Yeah, yeah, work stuff. I'll get your dress.

Coming back into the bedroom with her clothes and she's in the en-suite; he can hear her in the shower. All those tiny droplets of water against the glass screen, all over the tiles, all over the marble floor, all around the sink, that will now need to be eradicated. The bedcovers look ok but there are creases in the sheet where Lauren has been lying. And a soft musky smell rising from the heat of the bed: the traces of her perfume. There are some spare sheets in one of the guest bedrooms but he's never made a bed this big before. If he strips the bed now, could Lauren help him? No, that's a stupid fucking idea: he'd seem like a total psychopath, ejecting her from the bed and then asking her to remake it.

I knew you'd have beautiful towels, she's saying. Hydro-cotton, right?

Right, he says, sorrowfully.

Takes him forty minutes to get her out of the house. Fobs her off without breakfast or coffee but promises to take her out soon to make amends. As soon as she's gone, he strips to his pants and begins to clean the house. Uses his sock to towel down the shower cubicle. Locates spare bedding and does his best to achieve a straight edge. Picks Marc's damp cigarette butts out of the soil in the back garden. At 08.55, puts his suit back on. At 09.12, Mr and Mrs Al-Futtaim and their maid arrive by chauffer-driven car. Cal standing on the threshold and extending his hand. Smiling so hard that his teeth sand against one another. Welcoming them into the house, running through the book with them. A layer of sweat on his back, his shirt sticking to his skin.

Leaving, he glances back at the house. A memory of Lauren last night—of the way she and then the house, circled close around him—shivering back through him. A woman's figure at the front room window. Mrs Al-Futtaim, adjusting the curtains. The house is theirs now. But Lauren and Cal's bodies are all over it too. They've left the kind of traces that only crime scene luminol could show in a beautiful, ghastly gleaming blue.

The same old man. The same old man working away on the platform edge at Dewsbury train station for years. For as long as she can remember. Doubled over by the stairs with a small metal scraping device, some sort of stripping knife, working away at the edges of a piece of chewing gum that has been ground in. The chewing gum is now so grey that it's difficult to distinguish from the ground. These flattened, ossified discs everywhere, all across the platform. A boy approaches the stairs and spits his gum out onto the ground. The old man lifts his head for a moment, ignores the boy, talks tenderly to a passing pigeon.

It's hot even here, even in West Yorkshire. Air the temperature of blood. It was a mistake to walk. Along the top road, at the edge of the park, there is still no breeze. From up here, you can see down through the estate and all the way across to the opposite side of the valley. In the bottom of the valley is the rugby ground. Behind it, the river glitters intermittently. Then the valley rises up again: brown and then bright green in patches and then darkening again, all the way up to the moors, to Emley Moor mast. She knows the smell of the toilets of the rugby club house in the valley bottom and the soapy taste of the bitter there. She knows that beside that glittering river, gangs of kids will be clustered, drinking diamond white in the heat and sucking on nitrous. The other side of the valley is landfill; it might be green in places, but underneath the new turf it is a vast compaction of discarded, degrading *stuff*—microbial anerobic heat, liquefaction, acid-formation, void-pockets of methane, volatile metal concentrates, leachate running off and downwards into poisonous substrate. It fucking stinks when the wind blows. But there is no wind today, no let-up in the heat.

The road down into the estate is a steep incline. At the top of the hill, boxy red brick semis, pebble-dashed at first-floor level. Nan's old house. Front porch a mess. That would never have happened when Nan was here. Emptied. Emptied of her. Don't look, don't look at it. Just walk past. Keep on to the house that Lauren grew up in, which is lived in now by a family with four boys: net curtains, plant pots out front. Next to it there's a vacant—a house sealed up, perforated metal covers on the door and windows. The semi-circle of grass that once seemed huge: *No ball games*, red plastic bin for dog faeces, yellow plastic bin for hypodermic needles. Down the hill, the estate's architecture changes: on the right, rows of maisonettes, built perpendicular to the main street so that they sit along the hillside like terraces, looking across to the valley. On the left, the posher red brick semis: closes and cul-de-sacs. Three lads standing on a corner. Too young to know her, probably. The last time she came home, a boy she'd known from school had spotted her at the edge of the estate. Mike Hepworth jogging up alongside her, jibbering in a way that told her he'd been up all night. Telling her that his dad had been in a bad way, but that they were through the worst of it now: *dark times*. Telling her about his job at the abattoir across in Birstall and how it was reliable money, how they all had a laugh anyway. And people eat meat, don't they, so why should they get all funny about people working in abattoirs? Some girls did, some girls got funny when he said he worked at the abattoir. But they had a laugh. And you get used to the smell. All this before the bus stop, as though she cared about his father and his job and his pulling prospects. Then he had asked her to come to the Social for a drink that night; loads of people would be out, payday before Christmas. Her telling him, politely but firmly, that she couldn't. That she lived in London now and was only back over Christmas for a couple of nights.

Oh, yeah, Mike saying, in an understanding tone. *You always were a stuck-up bitch, weren't you?* And then singing softly, *Lauren Haigh is a slag, Lauren Haigh is a slag,* just like they used to at school. And by the time the bus pulled up he was shouting it at her.

Passes the boys. They do not whistle, they do not cat call, they do not insult her when she fails to respond. Walks on without incident. But this   nothing   isn't it slightly disconcerting? Did they not see her at all? At the bottom of the hill: Lucinda's portacabin. This is where she first learned it: how to knit frustration into ambition in the dark art of the beauty ritual. She'd been an amateur at first, no real discipline. Kerry and her practising together. Kerry was in her class at school and lived with her mum in a care home and said that all she had to do was sit on the old feller's laps, nothing else, and they'd give her a fiver a time and then they had money for supplies. Kerry did her eyelashes on Saturdays: a thin line of glue along her closed upper eyelid and then Kerry's fudgey fingers pressing against her skin. Skewiff, clumps of rubberised glue always balled along the lower lashes. They needed to get their act together. They learned to steam each other's faces, gleefully attacked each other's noses with tiny metal devices to perform extractions; fake-tanned one another using enormous application mittens, diagnosing emergent cellulite; dyed each other's lashes with black hair colour, eyes streaming with peroxide; straightened one another's hair, bearing singe marks on the upper curve of their ears and the napes of their necks. Finally, the professionals were required. Lucinda did hair and beauty and Lee, her boyfriend, always revolving in a barber's chair, did short-term loans if you couldn't pay up front. Lauren took a part-time job at the solicitors' in town. All of her money spent at Lucinda's: every fortnight, her tan topped up, her nails replaced, her eyelashes extended and every last strand of hair torn from her pudendum. That pain, channelled: with each burning rip, focussing on the possible outcome of the next night out, the next exam, the next interview. The pain proving her determination to herself: she would get what she wanted; she would get out of here.

In front of the flats now, and people are out in the gardens. A girl in a bikini in a large rubber ring on the parched grass and one laid on a towel next to her. Two toddlers in a paddling pool. Topless lads and a dog searching for shade and some old-timers drinking cans on deckchairs. They're playing music from someone's phone—a tinny version of 'Blurred Lines'. No one calls out to her. No one even sees her. And it's good not to be noticed. It's good. Much better. But also: lonely, a strange feeling of lonely. Just a tiny bit. Not much. Still better. Still much better than being known here. Than being stuck here.

She has a key, but she rings the bell to the flat once to give a warning. Unlocking the door. Hallway dark. The smell is sour. Her mother, stumbling in from the lounge.

Lauren, love!

Scratchy little-girl voice setting her on edge already. Her mother hugs her close. Then pushes her away, to look at her properly.

You look well, Lauren. You do. You look right well.

Then she rubs her hand across her face. Self-consciously? She's not been up long by the look of it: last night's mascara in clumps; Lycra top and trackies; very little jewellery. Samantha, Sammy, Sam-love: looking so small in the hallway with her matted mane of black hair and her black-smudge eyes. All through Lauren's childhood, her mum had looked like this: like a neglected child. And when she was up, she was up: living room picnics at teatime with chewy Fruit Salads and Irn-Bru and Cyndi Lauper, all three of them dancing: Sammy, Lauren and little Amy. Sammy like a fond big sister, plaiting their hair, letting them share her lipsticks.

But when she was down, she was down: comatose in the bathtub, unrousable, 999; men knocking-on for her at all hours, *Sammy, Sam-love, coming out with us for a bit?* Her hardly able to walk, but going with them, always going: *I'll be back soon, Lauren, promise. Look after your sister. There's a fiver under the microwave.* Always leaving, always being walked out on her Bambi-stumble-legs. Them, these men, walking her out to God knew where: Lauren's father first, then his friends after he'd fucked off, and later, when things were really bad, even the Church of the Latter Day Saints getting in on the action—an earnest pair of young men in suits knocking-on for her, drunk-walking her to Bible class in town. Her wild with laughing, *They're going to teach me something, Lauren love! They're praying for me!*

But always pulling through in the end. Never down for long. And always the hope, or delusion, that things were about to get better. Lauren sends her money each month, but there's always extras besides: *I just need it to tide myself over, love, until they get the benefits sorted, until I get the housing application in, until I can see the doctor for a prescription, until your sister is better, until until until…*

What time is it, love? You early? I was going to get dressed up, make something for us to eat.

Her mother never cooks.

It's two o'clock, Mum. Exactly when I said I'd arrive.

Oh. Must have lost track. I'll put the kettle on any road. Calling up the stairs: Amy, Amy, she's here! Our Lauren's here!

Watching her mother navigate the kitchen: the teabags are in a cupboard alongside glass bottles of coral-coloured fish paste and cans of energy drinks. Lauren goes for the milk: the fridge is full of avocados and mould. She doesn't look well, Sammy doesn't look well. She's thinner than at Christmas. She's wearing thick tracksuit bottoms and it's 30 degrees outside.

Now then. I got biscuits in. Posh ones. Where did I put them? Going through the kitchen cupboards again. Her hands shaking.

Were you out last night, Mum?

No, no. I hardly go out now, you know. I don't like leaving your sister for too long. Your Aunty Michaela came round for a few drinks and we watched a film together. She coughs. Few too many ciggies. I'm regretting that this morning. Going to do that hypnotherapy soon. Doctor says I can get on the waiting list. These'll do for now, will they? Tearing at a packet and then shaking out large, chocolate-chip biscuits onto a plate. We'll get a Chinese tonight. My treat. Teabags into three mugs, drenching them in boiling water. Let's go and be snuggly, love.

The living room is where the sour smell is coming from. Her mum has slept on the sofa. There are cans of Red Bull on the floor and empty plastic bottles: mixers. At Christmas, Lauren found a ghost apple under the sofa in here: an old core, which had accumulated layers of soft, wispy mould, growing back into the shape of a full white fruit. It had disintegrated when she touched it, spores catching on her fingers like spiderweb.

You need some air in here, Mum. Opening the living room curtains, opening a window. Watching Sammy carefully as she drinks her tea. She's tanned too much and now it's starting to show. Something still so young about her. Not just her voice: it's the way she sits; the way she hunches over her tea. But dark brown age spots across her forehead and cheeks too. Her eyelash extensions have been on far too long: you can see where the glue meets the natural lash, a good half centimetre in front of her mother's eyes, and the lashes are clumped together. Her mum rubs her hand around the back of the neck and up into her hair.

I'm not at my best, I know, love. I just   I don't know what to do about… Voice dropping, nodding her head in the direction of the staircase.

These cookies are bad. Lauren dunks one. Wet biscuit dissolving in her mouth. It tastes of refined sugar, of cheap bad carbs that kill you prematurely; of her Nan.

What's been happening, then? Is it just more of the same?

Her mother gripping her mug now, looking around the room, soliciting the dado rail and Artex ceiling for support. Oh, Lauren, love, don't be like that. Please, I can't take you being so hard. Part of it is this flat. You know I've always hated this flat. The bloke next door is serious, you know. Dealing. I get all sorts coming to the door now. It's no good for your sister. She's terrified of everything. She hardly goes out you now. Says she doesn't want to leave me alone, not with everything next door. But I've told her over and over: I've always been able to look after myself. She doesn't need to worry about me. I think it's her who's scared. I think she might be getting   what do they call it? Fear of going out? Ag-or-a-phobia.

What happened with the counsellor?

A hundred pounds she'd sent to her to make an appointment for Amy. And where had that gone?

Love, that's what I'm saying. She hardly goes out. I couldn't get her to go. I think she's still   processing all of that stuff. You know. With Liam. Blaming herself. Still thinking about it.

It's five years on? How can she still be thinking about it, five years on?

Amy, who everyone wants to take care of. Amy with her cartoon-girl eyes, her lower lids that flinch upwards and flutter uncontrollably if she notices you looking at her. Amy who is small and high-voiced like their mother. Amy who has been the focus of intermittent concern ever since the Terrible Thing, as in, *How's your Amy after that terrible thing*? And letters from the college offering counselling, and their mother going on and on about it, saying that it's hard to get over a *terrible thing* like that, and she'll need to stay living at home with her. Throwing around acronyms from Google searches: PTSD and CBT and EFT.

The Terrible Thing happened five years ago. The Terrible Thing happened on the night of Amy's eighteenth birthday.

Lauren and her mum watched the Terrible Thing on CCTV at Dewsbury Police Station with Liam's dad and an officer from the British Transport Police. They watched it without sound: the chaos of the teenage bodies, their silent mouths wide open, Liam's dad vomiting in the corridor after.

On the night of the Terrible Thing, Amy was out with Ruby and Liam, down where the old train line used to be— the long, grassy indentation that runs round one side of town in a semi-circle. Sitting at the edge of the old train tunnel, drinking, daring one another to run into the darkness. They drank and drank until they were jittery with sugar. They decided to go through to Leeds, to a club Ruby knew, where the bouncer was a friend and might let them in. They ran up to town, to the real station, for the last train through.

In the footage, Liam looks drunk, badly drunk. When they hit the platform, he grabs Amy's head and kisses her wildly. *Fuck off*, Ruby's silent big mouth shouts on the CCTV as Lauren watches. *You two can't leave me out*. She pushes Liam. He wanders off towards the end of the platform. He sits down there, on the platform edge, swings his legs, sings out silently into the dark blue star-skittered sky. He throws a bottle across the tracks and it bounces, intact, onto the opposite line. *You're drunk!* Ruby shouts and takes Amy's hand. *Liam. Is. Really. Drunk.* Off-camera, the train is approaching. Amy is floppy and she leans into Ruby, into her clean, shiny, going-out hair. *Get up, dickhead!* Ruby shouts. *Train's here.* But Liam isn't getting up. Liam is being sick down his front.

Liam isn't moving. And the train is pulling in towards him. And Ruby is silently shouting *GET UP GET UP GET UP*. And he isn't moving. And Amy is screaming. And the train is screeching. And Liam is keeling backwards onto platform, his legs still bent downwards, disappearing under the train. And he is making no sound.

Liam had both legs amputated just above the knee. He'd been very lucky, everyone said. He could have keeled forward instead of back when he passed out and then he'd have been done for.

They'd all of them encouraged Amy to tell the story of that night, over and over. But she'd stopped wanting to talk about it ages ago. Mum still fixated on it though: talking to her friends about it, about what Amy needs next, about the course of her trauma, about how depressed Amy is. And what good has it done them all, dwelling on it like this? Wrapping Amy in cotton wool?

Lauren ejects the memory. That's what you do. Push the exit button. Move on. Fuck's sake.

Even Liam's doing alright now, she says to her mother. He's got prosthetics and is re-doing his A Levels last I heard. It's just Amy who isn't moving on. We've made her worse, going on about it. Encouraging her to stay at home.

Lauren. Don't be   don't say that, love. Don't be cross with me. There's something   going on with her. I don't know. You know   she keeps talking about your dad. Hasn't mentioned him for years. I don't know what…

Her mother putting one hand over her face. Making no sound, but then rubbing her forehead hard.

This carpet. This manky, matted thing under their feet. Probably fitted in the 1970s. God only knows what it has accumulated over the decades. In the old house at the top of the estate, when Lauren was a child, she once dropped a book under her bed. Reached underneath her mattress, feeling around for it, and the carpet felt strange: cool and soft and feathery. Dangling herself over the edge, angling her nightlight to get a better look: under the bed, around the clothes and old toys shoved under there, the carpet silvery white and shimmering. The whole surface alive with movement. Carpet moths. A massive secret colony of carpet moths living under her childhood bed. This is the thing about her mother: she's soft and she's lax and she never sorts things out. She's a child. Still. And she'll just let things rot and fester and grow all around them; like the mould in this flat, spreading in the dark fridge and under the furniture.

I'll talk to her, Lauren says. I'll sort this out.

Knocking twice in quick succession on Amy's door. No answer. Pushing the door open a fraction; it drags against the traction of the carpet. Amy is on her bed, curled up on her side, with her back to Lauren. Introverted pose. Who ever really knew what was going on with Amy? She'd been like this for years. Flat voice. Unsmiling face. Curled in on herself in this awful room. The room is teeming with grubby stuff. On her bed, an orange and red cloth with a dense print, probably from one of the sari stalls on the market. The walls and wardrobe doors completely covered by collage: pictures and postcards and photographs and birthday cards and programmes and cinema stubs; there are even receipts and Blu-Tacked bus tickets. A series of photographs of Amy and Liam as really small children, yellow spoil marks creeping across them. The room is damp behind this layer of paper: a carol sheet pinned up from a school Christmas play is curling away from the wall at its corners. Mould and incense. Isn't incense a known carcinogen? The room is a poisonous paper cocoon. Visually repellent. Totally fucking morbid.

Amy, she says.

Amy doesn't move.

Amy. Lauren sits down on the single bed, reaches out to touch her shoulder.

Jumping, Amy jumping, then squirming over to face Lauren. She's wearing huge earphones, which she takes off now.

Oh. It's you. Hi, you. Sitting up now, leaning over to rest her chin on Lauren's shoulder, nestling her face into her neck. How long have you been here?

Not long.

Amy looks thinner than Mum. Lips bright red. Eyes gritty black. Hair plaited messily to one side. Arms bare and latticed over with thin scars, old and new.

Doesn't anyone is this house make an effort, anymore?

We don't all want to look so   glossy.

Well, I'm going to make you look a bit glossier. And then we're going to go out for a Chinese tonight.

I don't want to, Lauren. I just—

Shhh. No arguments. Lie down.

Amy pouting, but then wriggling down the bed so her head is in Lauren's lap. She's brought her a bag of goodies; she always does when she comes home. Every time she buys an expensive lipstick or an exfoliant, she's given little sachets and pots of other expensive things to try. She collects these things for Amy. Now then. She tears a white plastic packet with her teeth, squeezes droplets of oil onto her fingertips. You're dehydrated. On your forehead. This is neroli. Fingertips making circles across Amy's face, skin moving over the surface of her bones. Amy's eyes are closed, but even now her lower lids are doing that strange, upwards flutter; convulsively flinching. You'll get dried out and desiccated, like Mum, if you're not careful.

I'm not careful.

Well you fucking should be. Primer. A pea of clear serum on her index fingertip. Smeared onto Amy's forehead, bridge of nose, cheek bones, chin. Now we're ready to start makeup.

You do all this, before you even *start*? How can you spend that much time in front of a mirror?

That's right, Amy. Cooing directly into Amy's ear. Because you're busy spending your time in far more productive and important ways.

Beginning with the base: a thick liquid beige dispensed onto the side of her hand. Then a small brush, mixing the colour into the yellow oil that has slightly separated from it. Covering Amy's face, quick, deft brushstrokes down either side of her nose. You need to start protecting yourself, Amy. Bobbi Brown. Biscuit. SPF 15.

I like the feel of the wind on my face. Amy, speaking in someone else's voice.

Keep your eyes closed.

A smudge of bronzer over her cheekbones.

I wish you did. I wish you did like the wind on your face. Instead of being here cooped up with Mum the whole time, so that she can obsess about you. How many ways has Amy been damaged? Let me count the ways…

Amy's lips beginning to tremble. Her throat swallowing, repeatedly.

Don't you dare cry. I'm about to make you look extremely beautiful.

One of Amy's eyes palpitating madly now. Mushroom shadow across the whole eye socket. Two coats of mascara whilst her eyes stay closed. Pencil round the edge of her lips, the bow at the top, the triangular point at the bottom. Strobes of iridescent highlighter over her brow bones and the tops of her cheeks and her collar bones.

You're finished.

Amy opening her eyes. Her pupils dilating, then retracting.

Get up, have a look.

Opening the wardrobe door and then the two of them standing in front of the mirror inside it. Tipping Amy's chin upwards. Look at us.

We look   unreal.

Their echoing features, their nacreous skin.

Amy, we're going out tonight. You need to get out, you know. You need to start looking after yourself properly.

Because hasn't she tried? Hasn't she tried for long enough to look after Amy? To protect her? At cost. At great fucking personal cost. Enough, enough already. Years of trying to keep her safe, and now look: she can't take care of herself at the most basic level. Years of dreading Saturday night: that bus trip across to Leeds, both of them with their overnight bags on their laps, sitting tight until the tower blocks zone into sight. The field that they walk across first, between the main road and the tower blocks, in which a solitary Shire horse is tethered with a heavy chain, the chain fastened to a ring that is concreted into the ground. The horse has a beard and turns in slow, sad circles. The betting shop, the motorway junction, the Jewish cemetery. As they get closer, the tower blocks shut out the light: enormous monoliths twenty-storeys high, looming above them in euphemistic pastel shades—soft pink, duck-egg blue, duckling yellow. They make their way up, up into the sky, in the lift that smells sharply of urine and skunk—when it's working—ammonia paint-strippering the back of your throat. Disembarking on their father's floor. *What if I jump, what if I just went mad and jumped?*

Amy saying. *Go on then*, Lauren says. *You mad bint. Let me help you.* And they tussle at the edge, Amy screaming and laughing. Every Saturday night the same: Amy in front of the TV, their dad playing cards with his mates in the kitchen, Lauren spiking her coke with their vodka and watching the sun set over the M1 out of the big living room window. In the summer, the sky the brightest auburn-pink, a colour that she loved, a colour like gold melting in fire. Until she doesn't love it anymore: until those friends, those friends of her dad's, take her on trips to casinos and curry houses, to nightclubs and B&Bs on the south side of the city, and she learns to recognise that the colour of the sunset above the M1 is the same colour as blood in your urine. *Yeah, alright, give it a rest, I'll go with him, yeah yeah, I'll go, I'll go Dad, alright. Amy's staying at home with you, right? Just keep Amy at home with you, yeah? She's too young to go out, I'll go, I'll fucking go with him, fucking alright.*

Eating sweet and gelatinous orange chunks of meat at the Chinese restaurant in town. They've managed to get Amy out of the house, but she's quiet and eats mechanically. Their mum over-excited, asking people in the restaurant to take pictures of the three of them with her phone. That woman who keeps staring, a woman over in the back corner. And now she's up and coming over to the table. Shel, it's Shel from the supermarket. Years since Lauren's seen her, but still the same striped highlights, the same gold studs, the same pink nails.

Samantha Haigh, look at you out with your girls. Don't you look a picture. Your Lauren's the spit of you when you were her age.

Mum smiling, clutching herself: made up.

Heard you were down in Lahn-dan, Lauren. How you getting on?

Yeah, ok, thanks.

Got a good job and that? Yeah? You're best off out of it. It's Poles as well as Pakis now. Nowt left in the town centre for us.

Her mum laughs. All nerves, all placatory. Glancing at Amy. Voice fluttering. Don't be like that about it, Shel.

Shel and those other middle-aged white women Lauren used to work with on Saturdays at the supermarket, those solicitous, salt-of-the-earth women—*How are you, Mr Patel? Family keeping well? Those boys of yours staying out of trouble?*— and then the moment after—*Did you smell him? Wanted to put a tissue over my face. Bloody hell.*

Grubby, grubby thinking. So much grubby thinking. In the City, you can't talk like this. Everyone using the officially-sanctioned language of equality and diversity. Clean language. Legally-acceptable language. There's an equality framework. The City is the proof that if you work hard enough, you can get away from all of this   grubbiness. A clean meritocracy: her and Reshana on the grad scheme, traders from all over the world making their money in London. Your worth in the work that you do, the revenue you bring in: in you fulfilling your defined function. No one talking about bodies stinking, no one blaming their failures on other people. Isn't the City proof of progress? Proof that things can be clean and fair?   Just as long as you don't think about who cleans the toilets: just as long as you don't think about the demographics of who cleans the toilets. Third-party, outsourced, not your responsibility. And don't think about how sometimes there's something   almost grubby, in the conversations in the shared kitchen: *Congrats Helen! Where will you have the baby? My brother works in obstetrics, you know, and all of these women keep arriving from Nigeria. Terrible complications, real nightmare stuff. And then he clocks that they're all registered to the same address in Tower Hamlets. Healthcare tourism, isn't it? That's what people see, and they think it's the EU, you know?* Don't think about it, don't think about it. You've worked so hard: and if you work this hard, you deserve to leave all this   behind you. And isn't she an equalities champion? Equal opportunities, equal opportunities as sanctioned by law. But don't think about what happens inside police cells. And don't think about Paul in payroll: *Alright, Lauren. How was your weekend? Shitty story about those girls in Rochdale. Did you see it? They think they're fair game, that's the problem. Anyway, when are you letting me take you out?* Paul from payroll who wants to school you in the racial dynamics of sexual exploitation and take you out for dinner and a fuck.

And then you're back up here, and here is Pam, bold as brass with her grubby thinking and her grubby language. And isn't it all still here: that supermarket fucking stink? And isn't it even worse now? No progress, no progress at all with all the: *They've taken all the work. They're raping our girls. I just want Brexit done so they'll all go back*. And that manager from Bury—who sidled up behind the customer care desk at the supermarket and put his dirty little white hands up the girls' overalls, while the older women looked away or were suddenly busy: *You been on the fish counter, Lindsey? Oof, I can smell it on you, love. Ha ha ha*—him still running the show. And the two elderly white women who did the cleaning, two sisters who lived together on an old farm at the edge of Roberttown, who stank so strongly you knew when they'd come in through the doors. And they cleaned slowly and methodically, their backs stooped with decades of work, their arms strong, and the smell of sweat and lanolin coming off them in waves. They reeked like old wax jackets, they moved like creaking crones. And no one spoke to them and they didn't use the staff room. You'd swerve across an aisle to avoid saying hello to them. And after their morning shift the sisters went into town, and cleaned gratis: charity shops, church halls, youth clubs, you'd see them everywhere with their old vacuums, cleaning up all the town's filth for free. But no one acknowledging them, no, no one talking to them, no one wondering if they even had hot water, just hating on Mr Patel, who stinks, doesn't he bloody stink. The whole grubby lot of it still going in that overlit asbestos shack of a supermarket down the road.

A silent teenager coming to clear their plates; a boy with a bowed head, soft chevron of black hair on his upper lip. Not looking, studiously not looking at them as he starts to scrape away the leftover food.

Oh, whatever, Cath, you can go all PC, but you know it's true. Why do you think your Lauren's so bloody far away, eh? She's always been a smart one. Doesn't get that from you, does she? Ha! Take care of yourself, Lauren love.

When Shel walks away, Amy starts to cry.

Making her bed up on the sofa in the living room. Sitting on top of the duvet. It's still too hot to try to sleep. This room is almost as bad as Amy's: stuff everywhere—photos of the two of them as kids, photos of their mother as a grinning teenager hanging off her dad's neck, papers, pill packets, dead or dying plants thick with dust, discarded baby wipes, cosmetics cases, empty avocado skins. She can hear her mum watching TV above her, watching the news on the tiny set she has in her bedroom. There are fires near Manchester, great fires across the moor tops that people can see from the city. Army called in. Never been such fires before. Never been such heat in the north. When she tries to google anything, there it is: a news stream of fire.

Being back here, it always makes this happen. All these problems, which are nothing to do with her, which she can do nothing about, rushing right up to her. Brexit, wildfire, grubby backwards thinking. Anxious, anxious feeling. Right inside her. Twinge. A twinge deep in her pelvis. That fucking condom. Some little shred of it still there? Breaking down.

Toxic shock. The shock, the shock when the bleeding had started. So bright. Endometrial tissue   breaking down spluttering out—Fuck's sake. Exit this. Needs to exit this. Needs to get back to her own life, her own clean life which is not here, which is not these thoughts, which is not in these grubby things. Earplugs in. Corpse pose and listen to the meditation app. Passing clouds, these thoughts are passing clouds. Breathe and breathe and breathe. Until calm again. She'll be out of here tomorrow. These things will recede again. She is moving away and up, up into a world where all of this grubbiness is distant. Changes into the silk nightdress she has brought with her. Angles her phone above her in the semi-dark. Camera flashes with light: face, lifted up towards the screen; hair falling backwards; body, arching up towards the screen in soft plum silk. Attaching the photo, sending it to Callum: *When are you taking me out? It's been too long. Look at me languishing! xx*

Inadequate light in the cramped upstairs bathroom, but this will have to do. Locks the door and takes out her bottles. Lines them up on the sink. Turquoise bottle first, the cleansing lotion that smells of eucalyptus. Work it across your face, circling across eye sockets, cheekbones, to the edges of your jaw: mini-facial massage, for circulation and tissue plumpness. A muslin cloth soaked in water, spread across your face—as hot as you can bear it. Work the cloth across your face and neck, index finger into corners of nostrils, eyebrows, right into the roots of your eyelashes. Pat face with a clean towel until it feels tight and dry. Spray with astringent toner, until skin slightly stings. Three golden globs onto your fingers, work the serum across your face. A syringe of power-extract, patted into places of high vulnerability: the edges of your eyes, up to your temples, around your lip line. A small white tube of lip protector. A scoop of pink night cream. Mist of vaporised grape water. And, finally, two elixir supplement pills: firm, youthful skin from the inside out. Even when you sleep, you're working on yourself: you're protected.

Protect yourself. Always protect yourself. You need to take care of yourself, Lauren, love. Nan. Her nan talking. Five-foot-two. Dewsbury through and through. Immaculately turned out, fierce as a terrier. Raging-loud cardigans from M&S, chicken chasseur in the microwave, and *I've had more sex than you've had hot dinners, my love.* Never seemed old, but never seemed young. Must have been forty-five when Lauren was born, working night shifts at the Fox's biscuit factory in Batley— managing the line, hairnet secured, blue rubber gloves, her clothes beneath the little white coat always smelling of the Chanel No.5 she bought herself at Christmas and of crunch creams. The bumper bags of broken biscuits—Party Rings, Jam'n'Cream, Viennese, sugar dust at the bottom—always on the kitchen side. Her house just up from theirs, the front porch immaculate, bleach and a hard brush of the step every Sunday. Her nan who worked through the nights and came and took care of her and Amy during the days, put food on for them, let them watch cartoons while she stood in the doorway smoking and shouting to the neighbours. When did she sleep? Never. Hard lines round her mouth, hard lines on her forehead. But bright, always bright and fierce, lipstick on, shoulder-pads, hair spritzed to solid. And when Mum had her bad patches, they'd go and sleep together at Nan's, Amy and her sharing a single bed in the cold, clean spare room: *You're in charge now, Lauren, you understand, while I'm out at work? You and your sister are not to leave this house under any circumstances and you don't let anyone in, not even your mother, do you understand?* And food was laid out for them each evening, and clothes were washed, and there was brushing of teeth, and Nan would let them look at her glossies: *Hello!* and *Take a Break* and *TV Times*. And when it was time for them to go back home, she hadn't wanted to. Hadn't wanted to go. That last time, she'd cried, in fact. Tried to push her face into her nan's neck: Chanel No.5, biscuit sugar. *Don't you dare*, Nan'd said, *don't you dare, Lauren Haigh. Not you. Your mum has always been soft, that's been her problem. Always been like it, right from the off. Following anyone around, anyone who'd give her any attention. Doing anything they ask of her. She's no backbone. She even used to sit like him, your Grandad Ray. Her father.* Who was known in the family as Granddad Bastard, though Lauren had never met him: he'd died in his early 40s, a weak heart, too much booze, a disastrous fall in an icy alleyway on Christmas Eve, her nan never knowing the details—whether it was a fight, a mugging, a drunken stumble—but he'd fallen badly and hit his head, bitten his tongue, and there he stayed on the icy cobbles behind The Albion, paralytic, choking on his own blood, discovered late one Christmas Day morning by Jeannie Murgatoryd who slopped out the bar. *They were soft, both of them, your mother and your grandad. But not you. You're like me. Hardworking. Hard as nails. You're going to have to take care of yourself, Lauren love, do you hear me?* Pushed off, sitting up like a big girl, wiping sleeve across face. *You're going to have to take care of yourself, just like I always did. There's no one else. There's no one who can take care of you, and don't believe anyone who says they can. But you've got yourself, Lauren love, that's what you've got. Hard as nails.* Going back there. Walking her sister home. Their mother tearful and over-affectionate. *I've missed you, I've missed you my babies*, her sour breath, her tacky lips on their cheeks and necks. Never staying there again, never back to Nan's cold clean house again. Nan, dead that next year from emphysema. You've got to take care of yourself. There's no one else who can take care of you.

Moving back towards the stairs, standing for a moment outside Amy's room. There is no sound. Pushing the door. Amy has fallen asleep with her makeup on, curled on her side, her big headphones wrapped around her head again. Why doesn't she take any care of herself? Because she's never learned. She's never had to, because they've cocooned her. Because their mum has kept her here like this. Because Sammy has kept her in this grubby little nest. All of this stuff. All of this stuff all over the room. All of this detritus from the past. It's not just morbid. It's some kind of fire hazard. Quietly, meticulously, beginning to remove the debris from the walls. One-by-one, the photos and the postcards and the gig tickets. Drawing out the pins from the blown, damp plaster. They have barely held. Nails scratch at old Blu-Tac while Amy sleeps.

When she has finished, she pushes three tall stacks of curled paper under the bed. Bare, bare room now and the textured wallpaper an uneven nicotine colour. Walls perforated all over with tiny holes and tears. Clean slate though. Past erased. All that mouldering stuff cleared. Clean slate for Amy. That's what she needs. This is the sort of room you want to leave. She leaves it.

This dude, this Tony Steadman, has kept him waiting for over an hour. Cal sits on the leather sofa in the beige front room, back straight, folder in front of him, checking his watch every thirty seconds. The client could arrive at any moment, so this is how he has to be: locked in ready-to-greetness. Every so often, DLR train juddering past, ornaments on the glass exhibition stand jittering. He's handing over a flat in Canary Wharf. When this *Tony Steadman* finally arrives he's an hour and a half late. No apology. Stinking of aftershave and booze. He gives the flat the once over. A woman waits in the hallway, mute, while he inspects the place. Short white babydoll dress, very high heels and a lot of makeup. Holding an expensive overnight bag. It's relatively rare to get Londoners staying in the GuestHouse properties; when they do, it's often for illicit stuff rather than business—people who don't want to be seen at a hotel. This could be an affair, or a more clandestine transaction. Is the woman regretting the whole thing? Is she ok? Is this business for her, or something else? Tony Steadman still moving around the flat, opening the kitchen cupboards, looking out of the windows, making dissatisfied grunts. Cal catches the woman's eye, smiles at her, trying to say by widening his eyes, *What a fucking tool? Are you ok?* The woman shifts her pose so that she's leaning against the wall and away from Cal.

Nah, Tony says when he's finished pacing around. This is *way* too small for us.

Cal goes over the flat's advantages and then lists other properties they have in the area; this is what you're meant to do if a client is dissatisfied.

Tony looking at him like he's ridiculous. A laugh in his voice. I'm going to have to get a hotel, mate. Glancing across at the woman. Penthouse suite. Tell you what, I'll pay the first night, like, and you sort it out with the boss, right? Folding a twenty into Cal's top pocket, winking at him, walking back out, the woman following. Where had the twenty come from? Cal hadn't seen it in the man's hand. He hadn't taken it out of his wallet. It's this magic trick they have, these wealthy, bullish men, of tipping you with a wave of the hand. Who teaches them how to do it? Twenty is ok though. He can take Lauren for a drink somewhere with twenty. He needs to invite her somewhere really nice so they can talk properly; so he can explain about the house and József. He'll have to. He'll have to because József's coming home tomorrow. He turns off all of the uplighters in the flat. DLR train shuddering past again. In the dark, in this stranger's flat, he looks out at Canary Wharf and the water in the river: one solid glossy reflective surface, black lacquered and unreal.

By the time he gets back to Croydon it's almost midnight. Lets himself in quietly. His parents are still up: his ma's voice in the kitchen. They haven't heard him come in. He moves towards his room slowly. Loitering with intent. Wants to hear what she's saying, to check on her tone. She's been bad again, lately. It always starts with the repetition of the same conversation, the same worry, over and over. Then she'll stop sleeping. Then he'll find her nocturnal lists around the house. Last week, he found two. The first, a list of essential objects:

Wedding rings
Photo albums
Keys
Passports
Insurance docs
Bank book

The second was more opaque. A to-do list? A series of questions or research notes?

ACM cladding or High-pressure laminate?
Check on fire breaks
Fire Marshalls—frequency??
A-F rating for flammability
Building regs—does Housing Association have sign-off?

Whatever it is, it's fire related. This is where all her anxieties are focussed again. She's been listening to the reports on Grenfell. And stories about other places too: a recent fire in East London, which spread in minutes along wood-clad balconies. A public meeting that she had on on the radio, people shouting: *It's a death-trap, the whole estate is a death-trap! No one should go back inside until you take that cladding away.*

St Cuthbert's House, where his parents have lived for thirty years, is on six storeys. The block is owned by the Housing Association, a mix of private and social housing. They're on the third floor. Whenever Ma starts going on about it, Da says that they're the lucky ones: and he's in the trade, he knows how things work. *You can't ever eliminate all risk, but the fire risk is   tolerable   here*, he says. *Tolerable?* Ma coming back at it, *Tolerable? What sort of a word is that? That's not your word. That's official speak isn't it?* Da saying, *Simmer down, Gaynor love, you're getting yourself worked up over nothing.* If the cladding were to be replaced, it could cost them tens of thousands. They own their flat. They might have to sell it to afford the repairs. There are sufficient fire-breaks, he says. Why is she so worried, still? Why can't she ever appreciate her bloody good luck? *And what about the top floor?* she says. *Is the risk 'tolerable' if you live up there too?* The top floor is emergency housing, and full of families: a young girl, Esin, younger than him at least, who lives up there with her baby boy. Ma goes up there sometimes, finding things in her drawers from when him and Lewis were little, faded bibs and fuzzy felts, and taking them up there so that she can play with the baby. *And what about Lewis's block? HPL that is. Twelfth floor they're on.*

Yeah, these lists of hers are to do with fire, no question. He knows how his mum's mind works. He knows it because it's how his mind works too. He's learned these anxious tics from her. The middle-of-the-night, heart-palpitating lists of doom. Used to be that he would wake in a sweat, the taste of black smoke on his tongue, blood pounding, ready to run, ready to jump, ready to do anything to escape. He was young then. Just a boy. Nine years old. 9/11. That long September of watching fire: the images stored somewhere deep, replayed in his dreams for years after. *You boys should be out playing,* his da saying, *while the nights are still light, playing cricket or biking or running around Coombe Wood. You don't know how lucky you are.* But instead, him and Lewis were watching on the TV, over and over, like everyone else, the flash of light, billowing smoke clouds, the towers burning downwards, until, crash, boom, all fall down. And that footage, poor quality, from far away, but picking it up all the same, the TV-news zooming in on those small figures. Jumping from the upper floors. So high. So high it made the figures tiny and unreal. Jumping matchstick men. Except that they were real. Except that bad things were real, even when far away and small. How could you do it? How could you bring yourself to jump from so high? Only if the fire was so bad, so hot and choking black, that you would escape it any way at all. And that was what his thinking turned to all that month, and the next, and all the first year at the new high school: what would you do, what would you do, if the fire came and you were trapped? What would you do to outrun it? His mother drilling him: *What do you do, Cal? You're in the science block and a fire starts. What floor is Ibram's flat? And you smell smoke while you're staying there. What do you do? We'd use sheets, Mum. We'd soak sheets.*

We'd use wet towels. Over our heads. Crouch down low. That's right. Good boy, Cal. For a long while, every place he went, checking quickly: which way would the fire burn through, where were his nearest exits, how would he get out?

There are other things she worries about too: carbon monoxide poisoning; dioxins and particulate matter and heart disease; new viruses; Lewis developing sepsis and Cheryl not recognising the symptoms; Da still on the roofs, getting older and less sharp, but still up on the roofs in all weathers; the men who sometimes loiter in the block's shared areas; Esin up on the top floor and the other girls who have to walk through the estate; him out at all hours. But fire is the most persistent, the most constant of her worries. She's fretting in the kitchen now; he can hear it. She's got that querulous edge to her voice. But she's not talking about cladding. She's not talking about fire, not now at any rate. Nah, she's on about the cars at the edge of the estate, the pimped-up cars that sometimes pull up and then tear off, racing one another.

It only takes a child to step out, she's saying, or one of them to lose control. And that's it. They'd be dead. Do you think they're in gangs? How do they afford those cars anyway? They look so young. It's drugs, isn't it, Trev?

Da clattering about, putting the washing up away. Look, they're probably still living at home, spending every penny they've got on spoilers. They're no more gangsters than our Cal is.

Well what about our Cal? You never want to talk about him, but he's out all hours, wearing that suit. He's definitely smoking again.

So what, Gayn, you think Cal is in a gang now, just because he works odd hours and smokes the odd spliff?

Well, I don't believe this *house curator* stuff. No one's heard of it. What does he know about property? I think someone's taking him for a ride. It's not right, Trev. You know how he is. He'd be easy prey. What if he's   carrying things for them? You know, dodgy packages.

He is frozen in the hallway: suspended animation, like the cat he sometimes catches mid-shit behind József's roses. He should move; he shouldn't stay here eavesdropping, waiting for the terrible things they're going to say about him.

He doesn't move.

Look. Da talking again. Voice of reason. Cal's not a gangster! He hasn't got the nouse for it, love. Cal's problem is that he's always been a bit on the useless side. He smokes his smokes, he plays his video games, he sleeps, he eats, he does this little job, hoovering the carpets of the rich and famous, whatever it is. Pretty boy, isn't he? He's anxious, you know that. He gets it from you. He's too anxious for anything criminal. Snowflakes, that's what they call them, isn't it? This lot? Too frightened to go out into the world and make anything of themselves. Look, love, he barely managed a month up in Newcastle, he's not going to be doing anything dangerous. We've spoiled him, that's what it is, Gaynor, my love. I know you don't like to hear it, but if it had been up to me they'd both have been out the house at eighteen, like we were. Making their own way in the world, standing on their own two feet.

He's barely here as it is. He's a good boy, a sensitive boy, our Cal. That's not a fault. But you think I've made him   useless? Like me. Like me. That's what you mean, isn't it? His mother starting to cry. I knew we should never have brought them up near London. What did I say?

You said, let's go back home, where there's no jobs and lots of heroin.

Where there's fresh air and a landscape that gives you ambitions! His ma sniff-cry-laughing now.

Gaynor, love, Lewis is doing fine. He'll propose to that daft girl soon. Nothing to worry about on that front. And we just need to put our foot down with Cal. But there's no use thinking about it when you're like this. You know how you get. You're looking for things to worry about tonight. He just needs to—

Gurgling. Grey, soapy water circling down the plug hole. His parents moving towards the door. He darts to his room. What was it his da might have said at the end? He just needs to   be more self-reliant; stand on his own two feet; move out. That would have been it: move out. That was what his father was always trying to get at, when they had their little chats in the pub at the bottom of the estate. Sitting him down with a pint of something dark and flat, telling him again the story of his father, Cal's grandfather, Harry Thomas, and how he'd had to fend for himself from the very start. At fourteen, his mother dead, Harry had left home and pitched a tent at the edge of Ruabon Moors, back in North Wales. He'd got a job at the limeworks and he'd lived on the moor for two whole years before he got himself a place in the village. Worked hard all his life and eventually bought his own council house. That was self-reliance. That was how men used to look after themselves and their families. Slap on the back; a clout towards independence. But there are no limeworks here, Cal always wants to say, and next to no jobs without a degree. Zero hours and no job security whatever you did. What was he meant to do to become self-reliant? Pitch a tent at the edge of the M25 and walk to a digital start-up in Soho each morning? Sleep on a delivery bike, waiting for a takeaway order to come through?

He searches out the little bit of weed he has in a tin in a drawer and rolls a tiny spliff, which almost falls apart as he lights it. Can't even roll a proper fucking joint. Useless fuck. Opens his window as wide as it will go. A car alarm. The orange of the night sky. The orange of the street lights. The heat in the city is making tarmac split, making roads crumble, making train tracks melt. Needs to do something, something mindless but absorbing, something to stop the thoughts, something to stop this bad feeling spreading. *Useless. Like me.* He starts up two chats on different apps with girls he'll never meet. Opening his tablet: Apps/ *Gone Home*. It's a first-person game: you walk through a house, your family house in Portland, Oregon, that you've come back to. But no one's here. Your family are missing and you're looking for clues. You pull a book from a shelf, open a drawer, look through boxes down in the cellar. You sift through photographs and the clothes in a packed suitcase and your father's desk. You wander through the house, picking things up and turning them over; a bit like your daytime, your daytime wandering through houses in which you don't belong. You suck on your weak spliff and sink back onto the bed. And then your phone flashes: Lauren. Lauren. Lauren.

Alarm. His head is blank, grey matter: concrete, shot through and cracking. Groaning. Why alarm, why so early? Then remembers: today is the day. József is getting out. József is coming home! Due to meet him at the hospital in central London at midday and then they'll go back home together. He's got no handovers; he's free to stay the night. Again. Best not to bring it up, best not to think about it. He's going to sort out things for József, get him settled back in so he can recover, and then he's going to sort out the other thing. Yeah, he is. He's going to do it all properly. Are you still alive? Then there is hope! Now József is coming home, he's going to tell Lauren the truth. And they can start again, properly, without any of the misunderstanding. Whistling, as he gets dressed, whistling in a way that is almost cheerful. That tune his mother taught him to use when he was young if he needed to piss and there was nowhere to go.

Arrives at the hospital early. József is on the tenth floor. This hospital: not what you picture when you think of a hospital, not at all. Not what he pictures anyway. When his grandma was dying, they visited every weekend at the hospital in Wrexham. Doubly-incontinent by that point, she barely knew who they were, and the ward always stank of cabbage and pepper and diarrhoea. But this hospital, József's hospital, smells of roses. For real. Must be something they use to polish the floors. Asking for directions at the reception desk, down the gleaming walkway, knocking on József's door.

His voice: punchy and energetic! Enter!

But when Cal does Enter! József is not looking punchy and energetic. He's fully dressed, sitting up on his bed with his legs stretched out in front of him. His suit slightly too big for him now and something about the way his body is posed that's wrong. Head tilted forward to the right. Looking like he's got a slow puncture.

Callum, Callum, József saying and lifting his tan, trembling hands towards him. Leaning in and József clasping his face, kisses him on both cheeks. Sit down, my dear. I'm afraid I'm still waiting for the consultant to discharge me. It seems to be taking a long time for him to do his rounds.

S'okay. There's no hurry. A large window at the side of the bed, overlooking the river. The sky is bright blue and wildly three-dimensional: clouds suspended just above them in fat, slow-drifting plumes. You can practically see the whole city from here: the brown river, the old buildings of Westminster, the newer buildings jutting into the sky—slim, circular, gleaming. And the building work everywhere: clusters of cranes, bright flashing lights, naked lift shafts rising from the ground before anything else.

It's not a bad view, József saying. But I won't be sorry to leave it. One gets so very bored. They repeat the menu after a week. And look at this. József pointing to a large, faded print of a painting of Waterloo Bridge hanging on the wall opposite. How could you do that to Monet? Shrink him and make him colourless? It's intolerable.

When József stops talking, his body and face slacken almost immediately. It's uncanny, this slackness, this version of József's body which seems liable to stop at any moment. Cal wants to animate him again, to make him move, and speak—anything to make him himself again. But he can't think of anything to say.

József speaks again after a while. How is the house?

The house is fine. It's good. I had the gardener come over last week. Your thistles are coming out.

Ah, thank you. I've been worried about them in this heat. And have we had many guests?

Yes, it's been steady. The office are pleased with it. Someone in every weekend. One couple stayed for a week.

The Saudis? Or that family from Dubai?

The Saudis, I think.

And what about you, dear Cal? Have you stayed there?

Yeah. Yeah. I did one night.

Good boy! This is what I asked you to do. Why do you look so… Breaking off. Making a sucking sound. Then speaking again, but it's not quite right—a lisp there on certain words: So morose about it? I need to ask you…

József taking Cal's hand, but turning his head slowly to the side, away from him. Is he exhausted already from the talking? Or looking at the river? Now his head is falling forwards again.

József? What's going on? Do I need to call someone?

József doesn't speak. Makes the sucking sound again; he is dribbling, long lines of clear, viscous spittle between his chin and the pillow. József lets go of Cal's hand and shoos at him: a dismissive movement.

Alright. Alright. I'll go and get a coffee then, shall I?

When he returns, the consultant is sitting in the chair at the side of József's bed. He is wearing a blue striped shirt and a dicky bow and his clothes look immaculate.

Ah, Callum, how *are* you?

In this hospital, people greet you as though you are fond friends.

I'm ok, ta, he says.

Pleased to be getting the old man home, eh?

Cal doesn't like this tone at all. It's unnerving. Similar cheerful chatting last time, so now he knows that Dr Rasheed delivers horrific news as though he's issuing an invite to something wonderful: *There might start to be some incontinence at this stage*! he had said when they were discharged before. Something to really look forward to!

Yeah, he says. It'll be good to have him settled back at home.

But you're worried? Perfectly understandable, young man. Commendable in fact. I'm just going over everything with József, so we all know what to expect. As you're both aware, this can be a degenerative condition. Still smiling; making *degenerative* sound like something rare and wonderful. So far, it hasn't been a consistent pattern. That's one of the *curious* things about this condition. One can be much improved, just as József has been, for very long stretches of time. But we believe József now has what we call *secondary progressive MS*. That means the symptoms may not significantly improve this time and, given József's age, we're thinking of management of symptoms and pain now. We're going to do everything that we know has some positive benefit. József has been given a programme of exercises to keep his muscle strength up. He'll need some support in adhering to that. We'll carry on with the anticonvulsants, some SSRIs to help mood and some good, strong painkillers. And sleeping tablets, but only to be used sparingly. Now, this is potentially a very potent mix of drugs, so we need to be sure that you're methodical about taking them. Ticking his pen at József, who actually seems to be enjoying this, smiling into his chest.

This can be a challenging time. There's a heightened risk of infection. And swallowing may become a   significant difficulty. So we're only discharging József on the assurance that there'll be someone around at all times to support him. Otherwise, we'd be recommending a different kind of clinical setting for   this stage.

Dr Rasheed is looking at him. József is looking at him too. A smile: an apology smile and tiny shrug of the shoulders.

What? Me?

Yes, Callum! József is under the impression that you'll be—

Yeah. Sorry, Dr Rasheed. I just got confused. The nurse will still come in, like before, if we need him, yeah? But yeah, of course, I'll be there. Can we go now?

Fumbling for his keys on the threshold. It's difficult, because he's holding József's arm and carrying his case. He puts the case down, but doesn't want to let go of József's arm. He'd seemed ok again, when they left the hospital, but when it came to getting up from the tube, he just couldn't. He had attempted and then had looked up at Cal, pleadingly. Cal had half-dragged, half-pushed him off the train and the momentum seemed to get him going again.

Now József is shaking him off. Stop fussing, Callum! You don't need to carry me over the threshold like a blushing bride. Ha!

Cal inserts the key. Bite of metal. Pushes open the door, which brushes over the mat. Types in the code, turning to fetch the case and József, but József pushing past him, straight into the living room, collapsing onto the sofa.

It smells too clean in here! It's like the hospital!

But Cal can tell that he's happy. I'm putting the kettle on.

The kitchen is immaculate. He asked the cleaners to do a deep clean and it smells of grapefruit, like it always does when they've finished. At home, when his ma cleans, the smell is unpleasant: chemical, somehow worse than the dirt that's being removed. Smell of old scouring pads and bleach and traces of sour milk and urine. But József's house smells of verbena and rosemary and mint, of all of the good things. Kettle gleaming. Oven top gleaming. Cupboard handles gleaming. Fucking hell, it's only a clean kitchen! Stupid with happiness, stupid with happiness that József is home.

Coffee? Tea? Calling through to him.

Ah, tea, I think. Jasmine.

Opens the kitchen cupboards: beautiful packets and packages and embossed tins. Knows exactly where the jasmine is. Reordered it a week ago after a guest had depleted the stock. Placing a tightly-budded flower into a china cup and pouring the scalding water on top. Waiting for it to begin opening. Then carrying it through on a tray, with a plate of brittle cantuccini biscuits from the local deli that he knows József likes.

It's still warm, but József has drawn a blanket across his legs and is half lying on the couch, hand over his eyes. Cal puts the tray down on the table in front of him. József doesn't seem to see it. Should he start a conversation? Ask József a question, so that he can tell him a story and stop thinking about the hospital, if that's what it is he's thinking about?

Callum, we need to talk about a few things.

Ok, he says, sitting in the big armchair. Yeah, sure, let's talk.

I'm sorry about springing that on you, at the hospital. I wanted to talk it through with you before Rasheed came along. I intended to, but then I became   tired. It seemed to slip my mind.

That's ok. I don't mind. You want me to stay here sometimes? After tonight?

I know you have other commitments. I know you might not be able to be here every day. But I have a   proposal for you. Turning his head now and looking at Cal. You like it here, don't you, Callum? You've been making yourself at home while I've been away?

Yeah, it's alright, your house. Not too shabby. Grinning. József smiling too. Where is this going? Has he heard about Lauren, somehow?

Good. Good boy. I'm pleased. This is my proposal. Or, that's too grand. My idea. You heard Dr Rasheed. I need someone here, some of the time at least. You won't have to do all that much. The nurse will come when things get bad. But I need someone to check on me. Embarrassing as that is. We don't know how long   it might take, but we must not be sentimental about this, Callum. Or at least, we must make plans despite being sentimental. You have always been a sweet, sweet boy to me. Listen to me carefully, Callum. I would like to leave this house to you, this house and my paintings—shhh. Don't try to speak. You haven't heard my proposal, my idea, yet. You have to do something for me. Something that will give me piece of mind. I need someone to keep an eye on me. And if things get bad, really bad, I may need someone to help me. I want to   stay here, at home, Callum. At the end. I don't want to go to another hospital. Do you understand? And if I deteriorate, and I can't   help myself, you might need to   help me. Do you understand what I'm saying?

Face feeling strange: flushing. Tick of blood in his lips and his ears. It's the look that József is giving him. It is the most determined look. Is József asking him to nurse him? Or something more? He looks grave, so very grave.

What did I say, Callum? Now is not the time to be sentimental. Do you understand what I am asking?

Can't think. Can't think properly. Always going to pot when something important is happening. About to cry, maybe? God, what's going on? What is József asking?

Do you agree? You understand, Callum, what you are agreeing to? To help me, at the end, if I can't   help myself?

Anything. He'll do anything for József. He'll do whatever it is that József is asking from him. Cal nods.

József slowly closing his eyes. Good, sweet boy, he says.

The bar is crush-full of people. Brightly-lit, laughing, drinking people—confident people who can make jokes and tell anecdotes and can hold a proper conversation. Lauren sent the address of the bar: this is where he's supposed to go. Forces a way in, asks for a beer. The barman asks which beer? He's going to get it wrong: whatever he asks for, it will be wrong. He's wearing his suit, and that's wrong. No one else in the bar is wearing a suit. It's 32 degrees. He can't even dress right. And why is he still pretending to be the kind of man who needs to wear a suit? Today his main professional tasks have been: picking up a repeat prescription; weeding the back garden; helping József into the bath; reading to him, while he floated happily, until the water cooled; helping József out of the bath, towelling him down, pretending not to see his body, but secretly noticing how it is changing—bending differently, joints giving way unpredictably, little spasms in his calves and his thighs.

A Red Stripe? he says.

We don't do Red Stripe, pal, the man says. We've got a selection of craft beers and a number of guest Belgian lambics at the moment.

Right. Deploying something he's learned from József: What do you recommend then? This, József says, is a way to discover new things, and to make people feel their expertise is appreciated.

Doesn't seem do the trick here. The guy doesn't crack a smile.

The Mort Subite's got a kick to it. Want to try it?

Nah, mate, I'll take it. I'm sure it's good. Thanks.

Finds a seat at a corner table. Feeling even worse about the suit, which has mostly hung in the wardrobe in his temporary room, across the hall from József, for the last fortnight. The men in here wear garish colours. A young white guy at the bar is in a bright green cap, which he wears popped up off the top of his head. Another guy by the door in a bright pink t-shirt. One man wearing red braces over a yellow t-shirt. Why did he choose to wear a navy suit like he's been to a fucking funeral? And will Lauren get suspicious: him wearing the same thing all three times they've met? About to pour his beer into a glass. Checking around. Is it the right thing to do? Maybe the guy gave him the glass because he looks like the kind of guy who would need it; like when you're given you a fork instead of chopsticks at a Chinese restaurant. Fucking clueless. Some people are drinking from bottles. Others have beer in glasses. Lauren will know which is right. And if he gets it wrong, maybe she'll be able to tell that he's got everything wrong. She'll be able to tell that he's never been to a bar like this before. She'll know he doesn't belong round here. But good. Lauren knowing must be good. In the long run. He needs to tell her the truth, put things on an honest footing. He needs to tell her about József. Tonight. Tonight is the night.

It's been a good day with József. One of the best. After his bath, both of them happy and relaxed, they'd sat together for a while in the living room, playing records. József wasn't tired, didn't seem tired at all: in fact, he had so much energy that his hands were twitching a little. Cal then trying to engage him in something, so that he didn't get distracted or frustrated, like he sometimes does when he has these bursts.

A gambit for him: *You know, you never finished your story about Tamás Márton. You never told me about your arrival in London.*

I didn't? József saying: mock horror. *And you've been waiting all this time for an old man's life story?* Laughing and leaning his head back against the sofa.

Well, where did we get to? Let's see, let's see. My mother, Klara, had fled Budapest with Tamás. Yes? It was a good life that they were leaving behind. Tamás was just becoming well-known. My mother was writing poetry. They had an apartment and they loved the city. My mother knew everyone: writers, artists, civil servants, princesses from Hungary's ancient families, social democrats. Everyone! But things began to change once the war started. Not immediately. These things happen gradually, you know, Callum. For a while, it always seems that nothing is really going to happen. There's a lull, you see, whenever things are changing behind the scenes. Hungary had joined together with the Axis powers, with Germany and Italy. She joined forces with the Nazis, but then Horthy betrayed the Nazis by negotiating with the enemy—but that is another story! Where was I? So, there were rumours about these Nazis, about what they were doing, but no one knew for sure. And then it started. Jews in Hungary began to disappear from official positions. There were stories that their property was being taken, that men were being conscripted and forced to work in the mines. Late one night—this would have been in 1944, in the springtime— Tamás received a telephone call from a friend in the civil service, telling him to get Klara out of the city immediately. Straight away. That very night or the next day at the latest. Tamás rang around, desperately searching for somewhere to go. Some wealthy friends who were leaving for the West told him about a remote villa, hidden in woodland, far out of the city. Tamás and Klara locked up their apartment, they carried only essentials on their backs—flour, lard, candles, wine, money, jewellery—and they tracked out along the Danube together before dawn.

The village they fled to was a mixture of peasant huts and lavish châteaux. Many of the wealthiest Budapest families had already fled, leaving these holiday homes behind. All of these empty villas, buried in the woods, were now full of escapees and refugees. When Tamás and my mother found their house, it was already inhabited: an elderly Jewish man and his family were living in the cellar. They stayed here, in this clandestine community, in this new village of itinerants, while the Germans occupied Hungary, deposed her Prime Minister, arrested her civil servants and dissidents, deported her Jews to Poland, tortured and killed her Roma. There were Hungarian Nazis too, you see, and a new fascist leader, Ferenc Szálasi. His Arrow Cross squads were searching along the Danube for Jews and gypsies, tracking them like animals. The village remained blessedly out of sight for a while, too small to be of interest or miraculously forgotten. They lived on hope and lard and plum brandy: the Soviets were advancing, the Soviets would set them free! Liberation was on its way! They played card games in the evenings by candlelight, and they shared the Russian words that they knew, so that they would be able to greet their liberators. Ha! But, there were fearful tales too, of course, about the brutality of the soldiers from the East. For years, people had been frightened of communism—people had said it was theft by the state, that the Russian people lived in abject poverty, that they were subjected to routine violence and state executions. So what were they to think now? They lived in hope and fear of the Russian soldiers arriving.

Shall I go on, Callum?

Yeah, yeah. If you're not too tired?

Well, they survived the winter and early in the new year, two soldiers approached the village on horseback through the snow. Fine horsemen, magnificent bearings. Those who had a little Russian shouted out a welcome to them. The soldiers grinned, magnanimous. They shook hands with the men and they kissed the women. They laughed at the fatness of one of the peasants, calling him a bourgeois and demanding that he hand over his coat. A young woman in the village who had lived in Prague acted as translator. They asked to look around each villa. When they came to Tamás and Klara's adopted home, they whistled, like appreciative guests. The old man, Schwarz, rushed forward to one of the soldiers, overcome. The man held him back by both arms, and then laughed, kissing him gently on his cheeks, from right to left.

The soldiers left later that evening and the villagers talked of their fine manners and great horsemanship. Some began to make plans to return to the city after the inevitable Soviet victory. The next evening the soldiers returned with more men on horseback. They had brought a sled with bells on it. People cheered again. But the soldiers had submachine guns slung around their necks and they moved in small bands, three or four of them, to each villa. The same two soldiers returned to Tamás and Klara's house, with two new men. The soldier greeted the old man again, kissed him on both cheeks, and then nuzzled a machine gun between his shoulder blades. This soldier picked through all of the family's belongings, taking all of the valuables. He stripped the men of their watches and the women of their rings. The Russians took all the flour and wine from the kitchen and then they said their farewells like old friends, clapping Tamás and the old man on the back.

The Soviets passed through the village frequently after that. They would appear in a kitchen without warning and sweep away all of the supplies. They were advancing on Budapest now and the final siege was about to begin. The village had become an important strategic position. A large Soviet corps rolled in, on horseback and in tanks. They requisitioned every house. Tamás and Klara slept in the kitchen along with the Schwarz family.

There were broken vehicles everywhere. The ground around the village was churned like a battlefield. The Russians butchered machinery and animals in the gardens. The village's women were forced to work in the kitchens, peeling potatoes and stewing meat all day long. The men were ordered to work: they chopped down every telegraph post, every gate post, trees from the edge of the forest, to make new posts for the Russians to string electrical wire. Then they were ordered to hack holes in the roads with pickaxes, for mines to be planted in case the Russians needed to retreat. And every man was offered poppy seed for the procurement of girls. The villagers covered their daughters' faces with soot or dressed them like old women. People were telling stories: that the Soviets grabbed women and dragged them into the woods. The stories from the city were worse. One night, Tamás came back from tree-felling to discover Klara sobbing in the kitchen, her right hand trembling uncontrollably. She was being comforted by Maria, the old man's daughter, and the way Maria looked up at Tamás when he came in—afraid and hateful—made him know immediately what had happened.

That was Tamás's introduction to communism. These men had marched for years. Some of them were in the same soiled uniforms they'd worn at Stalingrad. It was so much, it was so frequent, the violence, these attacks on women, that the National Committee suspended the ban on abortions immediately after the war. There were thousands of abandoned babies. Babies born in the aftermath of the liberation were declared orphans and would be taken care of by the state. So that was how my mother became pregnant with me. I know nothing of my biological father. He could have been Russian or Uzbek or Kirghizian or Mongolian or Ukrainian or Siberian. I know only that he was a Soviet soldier. And that my mother didn't abandon me. No! She loved me! Truly, dear boy! She always said that I was the proof that she was still alive. She would say: József, you are the proof of my hope, and she would kiss me, my mother, over and over, until I became furious!

József laughing and raising his glass now: *To still being alive!*

But what happened to you after that? Cal asking, not having the heart to tell József that he's already told him this part of the story, that this is where he broke off the last time, before he went into hospital.

Oh, well. Let me go back. The Siege of Budapest lasted for two long months. The Soviets bombarded the city, destroying the last of the Nazi forces. Tamás and my mother could hear the canons from the village, they could see explosives flashing in the sky. The nights were long, shot through with the sounds of ice cracking on the Danube as well as the sounds of war. The village listened as Buda was being destroyed. They dared not think of their work, their furniture, their pictures, their favourite tearooms and restaurants, the ancient buildings, or their friends and their families cowering in cellars in the city. They thought only of their flour supply, the lard they had buried to hide it from the Soviets, and how much longer they could last.

One freezing February morning, children ran from house to house: Buda is free! Hungary is free! The Germans were defeated. And people in the village began to make plans to return to the city. Klara and Tamás packed their few remaining goods (watches and money gone, a little soap and coffee left) and walked the 20 kilometres back along the Danube to the city. The smell when they got there was unbearable: brick dust thick in the air, and rotting matter too. Remember, Klara is pregnant with me now. My poor mother. Half of the buildings had been destroyed, everything had been looted. The city was in tatters. And bodies, bodies in tatters too. Bodies collected in small piles at the ends of streets, awaiting burial in the mass graves. Can you imagine? Tamás and Klara's building was still standing, but their apartment had been ransacked: the pictures had been taken by the Nazis; the furniture had been smashed up and burned by the Soviets, who had also stripped out the wiring; bandits had sifted through what remained, taking cutlery and china, ripping pages out of books to burn in the hearth. All of Tamás's work was gone.

Klara set about making their flat habitable again with frenzied energy. She went out each day, salvaging things from piles of rubble around the city. People dug through the rubble, every day, sifting for valuables. They had no money. Inflation meant that buying food was almost impossible and they lived on black bread, bartered with things that Klara found. People dug in the dead of night in the gardens of empty Jewish properties, in the gardens of those who had disappeared, in the graveyards—anywhere they could think of—hoping to find buried gold or even just flour. Klara's parents, wealthy factory owners in Upper Hungary, had disappeared. No one knew where. Their factory had been requisitioned by the Nazis and now it was controlled by the Soviets. All empty property had been seized. Everyone had someone who was gone, someone they were waiting for. Where were her parents? Had they been taken to a concentration camp? Had they starved in a cellar? No one could tell her. Sometimes, in those years after the war, a gaunt, filthy figure stumbled back into the city, returned from a concentration camp or released from a Soviet work camp. But most of the missing were never returned.

By the time Klara was heavily pregnant, Tamás could hardly bear to be in this tattered city. He could not paint. I had grown big between them. He pleaded with her to give the baby up as an orphan, he pleaded with her to leave the country with him. But she refused on both counts. She was writing again, feverish writing. There were new opportunities, you see—journals, publishing houses—springing up now that censorship was easing. There was a brief   interregnum, that lull again, while things changed, while the Soviet censorship machinery warmed up. But my mother thought that this was how things would always be. New things were flourishing out of the ruins! New things growing like weeds, springing up from the demolition sites! Communism was hope for her.

But this was no good for Tamás. He had begun to hate his old acquaintances who had stayed in the city and survived. They had all been so complacent, him too; they had allowed Hungary to stall its way out of democracy before the war, they had sat down to dinner before 1944 with friends they knew supported national socialism, talking about it all in a civilised way, as though who they supported and their politics was merely academic, an engaging dinner party topic of conversation. He had a friend who had told him outright that he supported national socialism just a few weeks before he and Klara had fled; he had shared brandy and cigars with the man. And now, just as they had let the Hungarian Nazis and Arrow Cross take over, another terror was settling in. There were uniforms everywhere in the streets. People were disappearing from their apartments. People were being marched away in the street. And no one seemed to think this was too bad; it was so much quieter than how things had happened with the Nazis. The city preferred not to speak of it. But Tamás recognised it: he walked along Andrássy Road, past the infamous number 60, the old flaying house where the Arrow Cross had been quartered. People had been taken into this house and never returned; people were tortured and destroyed in the dark cellars, just yards away from the pavement where others still walked. And now, on the balcony, there were young men again, standing about in new uniforms, laughing, smoking, stretching themselves up to their full heights, showing their gums when they grinned.

Tamás couldn't stand it and, when I was born, he couldn't stand to think of us staying in the city. His own parents had escaped during the war to France and then on to London. He wanted to leave too, and to take me and Klara with him. He knew things would get worse. But Klara refused to go. Budapest was being given a new start! All of the destruction would be worth it if they could build a new, socialist Hungary! Most Hungarians had already stopped speaking of this supposed 'Time of Liberation': you see, their language betrayed what they could not say explicitly. There was no liberation! They just talked now about 'Before the Siege' and 'After the Siege'. But my mother, my dear mother doggedly hung on to hope. Sartre had just been translated into Hungarian! She was committed as a writer to the freedom of a classless society! She said that Tamás had become a backward-looking reactionary: that he was clinging on to a way of life that was dead. That he wanted to return to a 'free' Budapest that had never, in fact, been free.

Shall I go on, Callum? Really? You aren't bored yet, my dear?

No! Go on, if you're ok to?

Well, Tamás left Hungary in 1948, when I was almost two years old, without Klara. As soon as I could walk, my mother took me on circuits of the city, and told me the history of its bourgeois ruins: This was the Royal Palace, she'd say, and she let me climb the wall to stare through the railings. This tasteless eyesore was where the Regent Horthy resided and ruled! We'd walk up Castle Hill to the Bastion Parade, which had been the grandest part of the Inner City: whole walls were missing, great rooms suspended high up in the sky. This is where the dignitaries used to promenade, each day at noon, the duchesses and the princesses and the diplomats, my mother told me. There's no problem with them not paying their taxes now. Ha! They have nothing left to pay with.

In the springtime, my mother would tell me about the trees that used to line our street and blossom in front of our window. Once there had been almond trees and plantains and great horse chestnuts. The trees had been blasted or chopped down for firewood in the siege, but once upon a time the city had been green and pink and white—not just the colour of dust.

Of course, Tamás was right. Things got worse. No one had any money. So many buildings were destroyed that everyone was lived in co-tenancies: we shared our old apartment with a young couple. My mother had her gold tooth extracted to buy us meat and potatoes one winter. The Soviets were restrained in those first few years after the war. But then the Hungarian communists who had been in training in Moscow returned and took control.

My mother realised these things too late. But when she realised, when the people realised, the most remarkable thing happened: people took to the streets. There was a revolution! This was 1956. It started with the students, but then it grew, until it seemed like everyone was fighting together. People in the streets hit out at tanks and guns with their bare fists! Imagine, Callum! The government fell and new workers' councils took control. It was the biggest uprising, the biggest threat to Soviet control since the war. The soldiers, you see, the rank and file at least, had turned against the Soviets too. It seemed as though *we might win! It truly did! But the Soviets sent in their forces. They occupied Budapest. The fighting in the poorest districts, in Csepel on the Danube, that was the fiercest. But they defeated us, eventually. After the new government was installed, life became very dangerous for my mother, and for me too. We went into hiding. We slept in backrooms and cellars around the city, and in Pécs in the Mecsek Mountains. We were never anywhere for more than a few weeks at a time. Years, Callum, we lived like this! But still she would not try to leave the country. This is my home, she would say, Hungarian is the language I must write in! My mother, who was so well read, you know—who had grown up with Goethe and Shakespeare and Dante as well as Arany and Vörösmarty and Jókai. She could have written in any language she chose! But no. Only Hungarian would do. Hungary is alone in the world, she said, and our language needs me. Not English; not French; not even Italian! She waited until I had an escape route. Tamás arranged it, somehow, sending tickets and currency and false passports for us both, stamped with the Koussuth coat of arms. But of course she didn't come with me. She took me to the Arlberg Express, and told me to be brave, and kissed my face over and over and turned to go: and I didn't beg, or make a scene. I didn't refuse to leave without her. I just left. I am ashamed to say, I left with some enthusiasm. I was off into the world! Into this new world of the West, this world of shops full of new books and new watches and anything you wanted to eat and bright abundance beyond belief! First to Switzerland, then through Italy to France, and finally on to London. Remember, I was just a boy then, excited by such shiny things.*

Once I was gone, my mother came out into the open and she denounced the Soviets and new government. Communism, she said, was the most beautiful idea that we had and the best chance for all of us. But communism had never existed! Especially not in Russia! She wrote this in poems, she posted it onto walls, she shouted it from street corners. Many of our friends had committed suicide in the years after the war: an actress my mother had been friendly with poisoned herself; a doctor, a famous neurologist she knew, injected himself fatally with morphine. More people committed suicide during the liberation than during the war. But my mother chose a most unusual and spectacular method. She refused her chance to leave the country and then she made herself intolerable to the regime. Tamás always said: Your mother committed suicide by words.

József breaks. Takes a drink. He's starting to flag, but he's not finished yet.

When I arrived in London, Tamás took me in. He didn't ask what had happened to my mother. He must have known, in his heart, that she would never leave. He gave me tea and a room and said I could come and go as I pleased. I spent the days with him in his tiny studio in Vauxhall, watching him paint, helping with supplies and equipment and assisting in any small way I could: cleaning brushes, making coffee, meeting with sitters. He would talk at length while he painted, telling me about the village that he and my mother stayed in, and the Siege of Budapest, telling me everything that I've just told you, and far more besides. Railing against the communists in Hungary and the artists and writers who had stayed and supported them! The artists and writers who were less brave than my mother, the ones who had become propogandists. People's faith in each other had been destroyed, he used to say: Fascism, communism and now the commodity, they have destroyed any hope that we can deal with each other fairly. But art, Tamás always said, true art, exists to keep us from falling into total despair. In painting, he used to say, the artist's loss, everything good that's been taken away or destroyed, it bursts into something new!

József motions towards the painting above the fireplace, the huge abstract picture in luminous colour. *This is a painting by Tamás Márton, my mother's husband, the artist who saved my life. It was the first painting that I ever bought.*

And what happened, Cal asks, *to Tamás?*

Ah! Well, as you know, he became a renowned artist. From the '70s, at least, his work became well known. There were exhibitions in Paris and Venice and Toronto. He rarely went to such things, you know, but I did, and I represented his work. I even gave speeches for him on occasion! But he grew more and more restless. More disappointed. He moved to America in the '80s. America was his beacon of hope then. They are serious about art! he'd say. They are serious about the imagination! But they disappointed him too. I am a stranger in the world, he said to me on the telephone, towards the end. Wherever I go now, I am a stranger. That is the path that I have chosen. By then, dear boy, he was almost a recluse. He could barely see, and yet he was still painting. Every day! Beautiful, blue blurred landscapes. I tried to help him. I visited and helped him in his studio again. I offered to stay. I would have stayed there, I would have stayed with him, of course. But he hated my fussing. He died in the winter of 1989. Alone in New York. And he had never once returned to Hungary. József lifting his head and looking directly at Cal now. *He didn't have anyone to help him. At the end. Such a revered artist, and he was alone.* József closes his eyes. *I'll stop now, if I may, dear boy.*

All of this. Everything that József has lived through. And here he is, pissing about getting nervous in a bar and telling pitiful lies. He has to tell Lauren. He is going to tell Lauren. There's got to be a way to make things right. You're alive? Then there's hope. Right? Pouring his beer into his glass. Looking up, and there she is, approaching through the busy bar. In a pale-blue silk shirt, open a long way down. In a tight skirt and extremely high heels. Standing up while she's still several feet away. Feeling immediately foolish but he can't help it. It's involuntary. His body just starts up towards her, and now he's standing there, waiting for her.

Her grinning. Goofy and gorgeous. Hi.

Hi, he says. Both standing at the table. Then her, leaning over, kissing him on the cheek. The smell of clean hair, soft skin, something warm and sweet in the nook of her neck. She puts her bag down and sits.

Sudden death? Turning the bottle of beer on the table towards her. I've never heard of that. But then I don't know anything about beers. I expect you're an expert. It was real ale for a while, wasn't it? And now it's all craft beer?

Nah. I'm not an expert in anything. Can I buy you a drink though?

Thanks. The Malbec here is good, I think. A carafe, maybe? Push the boat out?

A carafe. Of Malbec. Coming up.

They don't do a carafe of Malbec. It's by the bottle. So he puts the forty-five quid onto his card. No overheads at József's, but not much of an income since he cut back his hours at GuestHouse. The problem is that it's easy to do, if you ride out the initial low-level nausea: this spending money like you're someone who has money to spend. Wearing someone else's suit. Simulating the life that someone else might lead. It's easy to do in the way that ice-skating is easy when you first get some speed up at the RocknRoller and you're into a glide and you're accelerating and you're staying up, you're actually staying up, but you know, you know that something bad is coming—collision, humiliation, face-smashed-on-ice—because what you don't know how to do is actually stop. That is: all of this is only easy because stopping is harder and requires some actual fucking expertise. Fuck's sake. He's an amateur. He's such a useless amateur. Sort it out.

Carrying the bottle and two glasses. And here she is, believing in him. Looking at him like that. And him, letting her look and letting her crunch the screw-cap open and pour the wine. Her shifting her chair so that she's sitting even closer to him, her leg right up against his.

Cheers, she says, lifting her glass to her lips. She doesn't take her eyes off him. Busy day at work? she asks.

Yeah, sort of busy, he says. You?

Always.

You been away? he asks. Last week was it? Sorry it's taken a while for us to meet.

Yeah. I just went back to see family. Briefly.

Nice one. Everything ok?

It will be. My sister's just   going through some stuff.

That sounds   supportive of you. Going up to see her, I mean.

Yeah. Well, you can be too supportive. It's too much. Sometimes people need to learn to grow on their own, without support. Sometimes the support can stop them from developing.

Yeah, maybe, he's saying. That's what my da's always saying. Stand on your own two feet or you'll lose your leg muscles. But what if your leg muscles are, I don't know, in spasm? Then you can't stand on your own two feet unsupported, can you? Staring down at his hands. *De-gen-er-a-tive.* Ah man. Sorry, that's such a bleak and stupid thing to say. Sorry. I'm sure it's nothing like that with your sister.

Lauren's hand on his thigh, moving upwards ever so slightly. Are you ok, Callum? Is it   your father? You seem a bit   on edge?

Now is the moment. Now is the time to try to decelerate: to tell her that József is not his father. That his real father is perfectly well, fighting fit in fact, probably right now playing darts in his local, the barking Alsatian tethered on the flat roof, challenging anyone unfortunate enough to cross his path to a friendly arm-wrestle.

I'm ok. He   well, I've actually been taking care of him today. He came home from hospital.

Lauren's hand staying there on his thigh, sure and warm. It must be very hard caring for someone   who's so unwell. You're under a lot of pressure. It's important that you take time to care for yourself. You need support too.

Still not saying anything. Still letting her believe that it's his father who's sick. Fucking useless cowardly idiot. And it's not even true that it's hard. Well, it can be   challenging caring for József. But in some ways this is the happiest he has ever been. He gets to make József comfortable, and he's better at it than anyone else. József needs him. József wants him to be there. He's actually being *useful*.

Lauren is talking about the sort of support you could be entitled to as a carer. Him, nodding along. Then she is talking about the sort of counselling services she has access to through work. Then she is saying, let's leave all this family stuff behind us for tonight, shall we? Maybe we both need a break?

Do you have any other   places? she's asking. Shy. But probing. Besides Elgin Mews, I mean? Somewhere we might be able to go? So you can have a break from your father and relax?

Other places?

Yeah man. Their flat in Croydon. His ma at the kitchen counter, making shepherd's pie on a Friday night, ready with the trays and the bottle of sherry and the TV guide for when his da gets home from the pub.

All of the empty homes on his list, the shadows moving slowly across their immaculate upholstery and perfectly posed artefacts as the sun sets. The others do sometimes access these houses for shifty purposes. But he won't do it. If he took her to Chelsea, to the white and gold house, they'd only inhabit one tiny corner of the vast theatre, like furtive animals who've found a way in behind the scenes. It would only make the lie bigger and deeper.

Yes, other places. Do you? Have any? Lauren trailing her fingers along the back of his hand.

I   Nothing I could get access to right now. Downing the last of his beer. It's going to his head already. Sensations surging outwards: the pulse in his temples, the pulse in his fingertips, his blood quickening itself outwards, towards her.

That's a shame. Her singsong careless voice. I was looking forward to tonight.

Her touch on the back of his hand. She's retracted her fingers, but he can still feel the trace of them there. Fourth dimension. This is it. Fadi once explained it to him during a cigarette break on a training day. He'd scored earlier that morning. *The fourth dimension, Cal, yeah, it's this streaming continuity of all actions through time, so that your body is still connected, back through time, right, in a blurred snake of movement, to everything that your body has ever done and to everything that your body has ever touched.* Cal had laughed when Fadi told him: *Mate, I fucking hope not. Who wants to be stuck to their past?* But he can feel it now, he can feel every different way her body has touched his, every moment that they've been together, he can still feel her skin against his, her body, nude and warm, arched back against him on the sofa in József's living room. Fucking hell. Fucking hell.

Maybe we could go back to your place? he says. If that's…?

No. Answering quickly. We can't. My flatmate
doesn't like guests.

Right. Yeah. Of course. No worries. I didn't think… He doesn't think. He's looking at her lips, which are dark and mat. And the skin of her throat, which is supple, glistening slightly in the heat. Can I   Can I just   kiss   you? Hopeless, fucking hopeless, already reaching out towards her with both hands.

They are on Elgin Mews. They are walking together down the Mews. He is drunk. he is really, really wasted. Here you are again, you fucking idiot. How could he have let this happen? *Maybe you can come in for a nightcap?* he'd said as they left the bar. *Maybe he'll be asleep and we won't even disturb him?*

You have to keep your own life going, Lauren had said. *I'm sure that's what your father wants.*

And he'd nodded as though this was true and very sensible. So now here they are outside József's house, and he can see that József is not in bed, not at all. The lights are off upstairs, but the living room is glowing.

Oh dear, Lauren says. Do we have a problem? Making that prospect sound delicious. What are we going to do? Asking, cool and low. Daddy's at home and we've got nowhere to go.

I...

József is probably on the sofa, under his cashmere rug. If he's not in bed, perhaps he got tired and fell asleep there. Worst case scenario: he stayed downstairs too long, lost the energy to get back up, and is stuck there, awake but unable to move. Fuck.

I should go in. See if he needs any help.

Of course, she says. But don't forget that you need time to yourself too. It's your house and you deserve some time off in it.

It's not. Quiet voice, shaky. It's not, and I...

Shhhh. Lauren putting her finger across his mouth, pressing it hard. You're drunk, Cal. Tired and emotional, right? She takes his hands in hers. She laces her fingers through his, tightly. Standing close to him. Her breath on his lips. So when will I see you again? When can I visit?

I just need to, he says, I just want to   make things right. I'll sort it and then   yeah, come over.

I'd like that. I'd like that   a lot.

You'll be alright? Getting home?

Yeah, I'll be alright. Message me a date, ok?

Putting his key in the door. Listening to her footsteps moving further off. Is she still there? He turns to look down the street, flutters his fingers towards her. But there is just darkness and then the bite of his key in the lock.

Waiting at the end of the street. Traffic noise behind her, warm petrol sky. Cal turns her way, looks down the Mews, shivers his fingers in a strange little wave. But he can't locate her. Can he? She doesn't move. When Cal has been swallowed by the house, she waits a moment. Then she's walking back down the Mews. She keeps to the other side of the road, and when she gets to the red house, she slows right down. Living room all lit up. Callum super visible. Bending over the sofa. Grappling with something. Up and down, up and down. A thin, elderly man, brought up to standing. But the man can't stand: he's bent over like a mangled coat hanger. Cal trying to keep the man up, holding him in his arms right in front of the window. Then they move away into the hall. The room is an empty light box. Alone, alone in the dark. She stays there watching until she is sure they will not return.

They are listening to madcap music. This is one part of József's grand plan for how they will spend their evenings. They will educate one another. Last week it was films: they ate baklava and drank sweet spirits, and József introduced him to *Blue*. Now, *Blue* is not what you'd usually think of as a film. It consists of a single shot of the colour blue, which fills the screen, while the filmmaker talks about his life and dreamy music plays in the background. József had told him to close his eyes and see if he could still see the blue as the sounds washed over him. And afterwards, he told him about Derek Jarman, the director, and about his illness and his final years, about his love of his garden in Dungeness: a weird, post-apocalyptic landscape that he filled with colour. When Cal knelt at his side at the end of the evening to offer his help up the stairs, József had said, *I think I'll be fine on my own. Dear boy.* Stroking Cal's head and kissing the top of it. *Dear boy.* Those words had held Cal safe in his sleep in the room across the hall.

The following night Cal introduced József to *True Grit*. He'd googled like mad, so he could tell him everything about the Coen brothers, and the music, and the actors. But József had fallen asleep halfway through.

Now they've moved on to music. József prefaces tonight's record with a brief introduction: Bella Bartók, József tells him, as you'll know, my dear, was one of the 20th century's greatest composers. And one of Hungary's most famous musicians. In his early work you can hear it, you can hear that old Hungary: the folk music, the Gypsy music, all of the things that the Nazis tried to eradicate. From these old things, out of the ruins of that music, Bartók makes something new. Something so discordant and strange, something that had never been heard before.

Cal and József are listening to an early concerto: strange, dissonant, shivery music, occasionally swelling into something more strident. The sky outside is the flesh of a blood orange. And the clouds in it are red, underlit; as though just beyond sight, below the rooftops opposite, the world is all on fire. József leans his head back against the sofa; his eyes are closed. Listening to music seems to be better than reading to him just now; when they listen to music, he is able to drift between alertness, rest and sleep, without worrying too much about it. Now, for instance, József might be asleep, though he was talking animatedly just a few moments ago. Something flickers in his left cheek. A small muscle spasm, moving the corner of József's mouth up and down. He must be asleep, or this would bother him. He would slap at his own muscle, as he sometimes does now, as though dashing a fly.

When the concerto has finished, Cal tidies up their dinner things. They ate on trays tonight, at his suggestion. József seeing it as some kind of adventure. He's been extending his cooking repertoire. Tonight, József shouted through instructions as he fried trout fillets with dill and made a beetroot salad. Then Angel Delight for dessert: József's guilty pleasure. Cal rinses the plates and stacks them in the drainer.

He polishes up the silverware, drops the knives and forks back into the drawer. Finds himself a can of Red Stripe (his guilty pleasure), pours it into a tumbler. And then he pads back into the living room, restarts the record, leans back in the armchair, closes his eyes and concentrates.

József's voice finding him in the dark. We need to talk about last night, Callum. Different. Sounding different from earlier. Something shifted. This happens now. He'll nap and wake in a completely different mood.

Cal alert now, eyes open.

József is sitting upright, with his blanket pulled up around him.

I'm sorry, Cal saying. I shouldn't have gone out for so long. It was my fault, and I—

No! It was not your fault. Resolute voice. The same voice that he used last night when Cal had gotten in. József had given firm, well-constructed directions from the off. His tone of voice saying: I have been thinking this situation over and have long decided on the best way to proceed. How long had he been there, thinking that situation through? When Cal came in, he knew instantly that something was wrong. It was the smell. Nothing overpowering, but something subtly different. Something sharp and earthy. Straight into the living room, and he had found József laid on his side on the sofa. An excruciated pose. *Callum,* József had said, flat and decisive, *my legs have given out and I've had an accident. The worst kind of accident. You need to carry me to the bathroom and put me in the large shower.*

He had frozen, just for a moment, trying to work out what had happened.

Now, Callum! Lift me up immediately, please.

So Cal carried him up the stairs and followed his instructions. Placed him fully clothed in the shower tray. Then stripped him and directed warm water onto him and his clothes, until the water ran clear. Scooped József back out, towelled him, talcumed him, put him in clean pyjamas, lifted him into his bed. And then József had wept.

This is what I meant, József had said, drying his face with the flat of the palm. *If my body is giving up, then it's time. It's time, Callum.*

Not answering. Pretending not to hear him. Taking the soiled clothes down to the washer and putting the load on. Making tea and rose biscuits, taking them up for József to have in bed. Then finding him already asleep.

What happened last night was not your fault. It was no one's fault. But you can't be here all the time. We might need to look into alternatives. For night care. Until—

I can! The thought of a stranger, even of Jacob—the private nurse who sometimes comes in the daytime; strong, serious, gentle Jacob who practised paediatric medicine in Accra before coming to London—even the thought of him dressing József in his pyjamas, holding him and lifting him at his most vulnerable, into his bed, is painful. I can be here! I won't go out for as long again. I don't need to go out at all.

Listen to yourself, Callum. You can't stay here every night, tending an old, incontinent man. Things are going get worse now. It would be sensible for us to suppose this.

That's not true. We don't know how things are going to play out.

A local doctor had visited the day after József's discharge. She hadn't had Dr Rasheed's cheerful manner and József hadn't warmed to her. She'd murmured something on the way out, something about the value of *specialist care for these final stages*. Final stages. But what did she know? She'd seen József when he was exhausted and trembly, not when he was talking about Bartók and practically dancing.

We don't know anything for sure. They're always getting things wrong. This could be just another intermittent stage. And then, when you're better again, they might find new—

Stop it. Stop it, please, Cal. This doesn't help.

But things change all the time.

They do. But I am an old man and we need to make plans for   the worst. Last night, you see, I spent an hour lying in my own excrement. I had some time to think about this. Ha!

And that's why I won't go out. Not for long. We can get everything delivered. I never need to go far.

József laughing now. Sweet boy! And what about this young woman you were meeting? The one who makes you walk around in a delirious, love-struck haze? Do you think she'll be delivered?

Lauren. It is painful to think of not seeing her. Hurts the surface of his body; a total throb.

I   Maybe she could come and meet you. We could   have her over? Maybe?

You think this bright young thing wants to come and visit with a frail old man?

You're not frail. You were just   tired.

My good, sweet boy. Not everyone has your gift for caring. You mustn't expect it of her.

Already imagining it. József can tell her about Bartók and Jarman and Budapest too. She loved hearing the stories about József's paintings, about Hockney and Bowling and Hepworth and Márton: József can tell her so much more.

I could invite her, Cal says. If that's ok? I could cook dinner for us all next week?

Well. Perhaps. I can't trust myself, you know that. I don't know what will happen, or how I'll feel next week. But if you're here, and she knows not to expect too much, then perhaps. And, of course, I am curious to see the beautiful girl who has so captivated my dear, dear Callum.

What will he do, though? What will he do about the   misunderstanding between him and Lauren? He'll be honest from now on; got to be.

There's something, Cal says. There's a   problem. A misunderstanding between us.

Between us? József holds his hand against his chest.

No, no. Not us. Between me and Lauren. I   I   she's confused about   who my father is.

Is there some mystery you haven't told me? Your parents are from Wales, yes? I suppose, on a deeper level, everyone's confused about their parentage. I, for instance, effectively have two fathers. A Soviet I never met, and Tamás, who—

Nah, it's not like that. I   Oh man. I told her   she got the wrong end of the stick. She thinks that you're my father.

József pulls a strange face. Like something bitter and unexpected is in his mouth. You said that? You said that I was your father?

It just   it just sort of came out. I didn't know how to explain us living here…

József shaking his head. It is a terrible thing to do, to disown or deny your own father. Some things are difficult to explain, I see that. I would be proud to be your father, Callum. But I am not. You must tell her the truth.

I know. I will. I will. We'll sort everything out. I'm alive, right? So there's hope?

There is a breeze, the faintest of breezes, prickling the skin of her arms. Shiver, the ghost of a shiver as she approaches on the Mews. So wonderful, this current of air, after another day of city heat, after a tube train filled with sweating bodies, the shared air hot and damp and dense. Sanitise. Need to sanitise. Antibacterial hand gel dispensed and worked across her hands on the way. And here now. Arriving. Breathe in. No.12. Callum's house all lit up, all four of its large front windows filled with light. Anticipation of all sorts of good things fluttering inside her: Red wine. Bloody meat. Silk against her skin. Heritage wallpaper. Designer glassware. Ivory lace. A baby, a silent, eyes-closed baby, tucked into sleep in the upstairs room.

The door opens. It is not Callum. It is the old man. The coat hanger of a man. Smiling, moving back into the hall.

Come in, come in, please. I'm József.

The long hallway studded with pictures. Verbena, meat cooking, expensive cologne. He takes her jacket, leads her through to the living room.

It is such a pleasure to meet you, he says. I have heard so much about you. And, of course, you are even more beautiful than Callum led me to believe!

The man is smaller and more delicate than Callum. Dark-skinned and slightly stooped. Colossal white eyebrows. She can't see any immediate resemblance between them.

Pleased to meet you. Lean in, kiss him lightly on both cheeks. She does not wish to touch this elderly man. Where is Cal? József is moving around the house with such ease. Such propriety. And his familiarity with her, his easy compliments—about her beauty and now about the wine she has brought—set her on edge. Overbearing. He's in charge of all of this, setting the course of the evening, when it should be Cal. Where the fuck is Cal? Slight panic. Little stab of adrenaline. Is he even here?

József leaves the room to bring her wine, returns with something chilled; the colour of pear flesh.

I thought we would start with this. Callum says you enjoy wine? I have something very special for dessert. He'll be through in a moment. He has been cooking for most of the afternoon, you know. We're in for a real treat.

While he speaks, she's checking for signs of weakness. He doesn't look sick at all. He's energetic, in fact: so much so that he seems unable to sit still. He's up now, for instance, fiddling with the record player. His skin, though, is a little sallow: the colour of an old bruise. Looks like he would be tender to the touch.

How have you   been feeling? Delicately put, but not gentle. I know things have been   difficult. With your   health issues.

Stiffening. The old man stiffening just a little.

Sip of wine: a sharp, cold, pleasant sensation.

How sweet of you to ask. Sing-song words, a tight smile. He speaks loudly, as though for an audience, so that Callum must now be able to hear his voice above the sound of spattering oil in the kitchen—if that is where Callum is. Thank you for your concern, Lauren. I'm feeling quite well this evening. And Callum has been taking wonderful care of me.

Is there anyone else? Helping? Other   family members?

Ah! Callum and I manage quite well. Don't we, dear boy?

There he is. There he is in the doorway. Like a shy teenager. Face half in shadow; furtive—something furtive and profoundly introverted about his stance. He doesn't move towards her, he doesn't greet her. Just stands there as though he's not allowed to come and sit with the grown-ups.

Come in, then, dear, József says. Don't dawdle in the hallway.

Sitting beside her on the sofa now, smudging his mouth against her cheek. As though József is introducing them: the both of them awkward with one another. Why, why this way round? And why is she letting this bother her so much? Don't lose your nerve: I am deserving of good things. I am deserving of being in this house.

Squeeze Cal's leg. This wine is delicious. And the food smells amazing.

Oh, József organised everything.

József? Other well-to-do families address each other by first names. Mina always refers to her mother as Signe, for instance. But something's off. Shifting; some dynamic shifting strangely here.

And now I'm going to leave the two of you to have a little chat. József springs up quite suddenly, not quite controlling the movement: white wine over the edge of his glass.

She whispers into Callum's ear: He's spilled his wine.

It doesn't matter, he says. I'll clear it in a bit.

What did he mean, *little chat*? Unnerved, a flutter in her stomach that's turning to panic. Breathe. Breathe and master it. Turn towards him little-by-little: magenta satin dress; glossed hair; cheekbones brushed with bronze; nude, glistening lips. The effect is gratifying: Callum's eyes move hungrily across her.

I need to talk to you about something.

Fucking right. Her instincts are always fucking right: something is amiss. A number of scenarios occur simultaneously: Callum's father is about to die, RN; Callum is already married; Callum is embroiled in some sort of complicated situation or serious accusation; Callum's father and/or him are involved in something illegal—the art is money laundering. Prepares herself, silently, for what will come next; prepares to respond quickly to whatever shocking or unpleasant news she is about to receive.

Ok. You can tell me anything, Cal.

It's about   József.

Your father?

Well, that's just it. Him rubbing the flat of his palm hard against one eye and then the other. He's not my father. I don't know why I said it in the first place. I'm sorry. I'm such a fucking idiot. He's not really my father. But once I'd said it   I don't know, it sort of felt true. I mean, I wanted it to be true. It's pathetic, I know.

Perfectly still. She remains perfectly still. Erect and alert as a hare, ready to make any of the sudden cerebral movements that might be required of her.

So, not your biological father?

No. Yes, not my biological father...

So your   step-father? That's no big—

No, no, that's not it. I didn't grow up with him. I grew up in Croydon. I live in Croydon. My dad is called Trevor. He's a roofer. My mum works at the council. Part-time. On reception. She's called Gaynor.

Something falls away. Sense of safety gone. Alone in this house with two men: and what does she really know about either of them? Cal looks more afraid than her; but that's no guarantee of anything. She's seen the frightened wildness that can set in before a trader loses it; the confession, the confession that can seem like an intimacy just before a man goes for you.

Cal's starting to attack his own hands, which are quivering. Picking at his cuticles.

Cal, just tell me what it is you have to say. Feeling for her phone, covertly clutching her bag and getting ready to spring away.

He looks up then, looks right at her with his sorrowful eyes. I started working for this property company, looking after people's houses, a couple of years ago now, and that's how I got to know him. József. This is his house. And he became   I don't know. We became close. That must be why I said it. I don't know why I said it. It was a lie, but it didn't feel like a lie. Not right away.

So   let me get this right. You work   for him?

It's not like that, exactly. I'm sort of   living here now. And. Him leaning in, whispering now. He says wants me to have the house. When he   He doesn't have anyone else. No family. I don't know if I—

Pushes her finger across his lips. If he's quiet then she can think. Her mind works quickly. She just needs to make sure she has all the information.

So, he is sick? József? That is true? And this isn't your house, but you do live here?

Him nodding.

And he wants to leave this house to you?

Nodding.

Are you   together? I mean, sleeping together? Watching his face carefully.

Fuck. No. Bewildered, seems to be. It's not anything like that   I mean, I do   I do   I care for him. He's been kinder to me than anyone else. But, like I say, it's more like he's   I don't know. Family. Like family.

Naïve. This is so naïve as to be delusional. Or stupid. Surely József is Cal's sugar daddy? Or wants to be, if he's not already? Sick doesn't mean he's not thirsty. Is he even sick?

I'm not explaining things right. He's only ever asked me for one thing. He's never asked—

What thing?

From the look on Cal's face, she's getting to the heart of it now.

Closes his mouth.

Nothing, nothing. I'm making it sound all wrong. But if we have dinner, you'll see. He's so great. He knows so much about the world, and he's travelled and met all of these famous artists. You'll see, you'll see what he's like.

They sit: triumvirate. A low chandelier above them. The rest of the kitchen in shadow. The meal is good. She picks out the toasted almonds and lets them sit on her tongue, prickling with sea salt. She sucks up the samphire and hollandaise. She drinks more of the wine. Cal speaks every so often, complimenting József on aspects of the meal. József is curt with him. Beginning to sound angry, even. He's getting tired, she can see that, and he doesn't even attempt to disguise it. Fuck them both. Fuck Cal's pathetic fabrications, fuck József's superiority, making her feel as though she doesn't belong here, as though he's giving her a gift just by letting her inside his beautiful house to eat his beautiful food. Eat up every mouthful, because she fucking deserves it. József designed the menu, so she compliments him. Asks him repeated questions with ferocious politeness. Questions he is less and less able to reply to.

Cal says you've travelled a lot, József? It's an unusual name, Márton. Where are you from? I mean, your family?

He raises his head, stares for a moment, and then scowls. Lets his head sink.

Are you feeling tired? Callum asks. I could do you a tray?

József shaking his head. But he is struggling with his cutlery. He can't get any purchase with his knife on his samphire and his left hand keeps tightening up involuntarily into a fist.

Callum stopping eating and watching him now.

What beautiful pictures you have, József, she says, flaking the flesh of the fish on her plate, placing it precisely into her mouth. Cal says you used to be a collector and dealer. That must have been *fascinating*.

He doesn't even try to raise his head this time. A noise uttered into his chest.

Twirling black linguine deftly with her fork; depositing it neatly into her mouth.

And you love cooking as well as art? Cal says you put together everything for tonight? How wonderful of you.

József clatters his knife and fork down against his plate. His left hand now wound-up like a snail shell. With his right hand he grabs at the food on his plate, taking some samphire between three fingers and pushing it towards his mouth. It is in approximately the right place, but he has to use force to make it slide from the edge of his cheek fully into his mouth. His fingers and his lips are slicked over with yellow hollandaise.

Oh. Oh dear, she says.

Callum standing up. You're tired! Why didn't you tell me you were so tired? I'll take you up. I'll feed you upstairs. Him moving around the table, pulling József's chair out.

Iaaaa. József shouting. Iaa don't want to...

He gets tired so quickly. It comes from nowhere sometimes. But he should have told me. You should have told me!

Callum hoisting József up under his armpits. Him hanging from Callum's arms. And then he groans. A dark patch begins to bloom in the groin of József's khaki-coloured trousers. The patch seeps slowly downwards. There is a muffled spattering sound as urine hits the parquet floor.

Oh, she says again. She folds her napkin up neatly on the table.

You should have told me! Callum shouts. Hauling József's body upwards. Half dragging him now, up and out of the kitchen.

Can't eat anymore. Not with the puddle of József's urine glistening on the floor. Proper big gulp of wine and pours herself more. She moves back into the living room with her glass. Muffled noises from upstairs: Callum trying to insist on something, József protesting. Moving over to the window, to the small, curled green object that is displayed just in front of it. The shape is vaguely unpleasant. Barbara Hepworth, Callum told her when she was first here, an artist born in her neck of the woods, in Wakefield. The small sculpture

151

is a whorl: the horrible, tightening intimacy of a shell; the curling, waxy mechanism of the human ear. The human body insistently close.

I'll just clean up in here. Callum calling through from the kitchen. I won't be long. His voice is bright and false. She's not going to offer to help to clean up the piss of the man he pretended was his father. The man who barely spoke to her at dinner. She's not going to clean up piss at the end of a long day with a man who has lied to her for two months.

Cal emerging now with a bottle of cherry brandy, two small glasses and a glossy tart.

Frangipane. New cherries, him saying. Sitting down, then putting his face into his hands. No sound, but his back heaving up and down.

Everything's fucked, isn't it? I wanted to make things alright. But you didn't get to really meet him, not how he usually is. And now József's totally distraught. I've fucked it up, haven't I?

Running her hand up and down his spine. Working the tiny knuckle bones in his neck. Look, Cal, József's obviously sick. Really sick. Are you looking after him completely on your own?

Cal's back still heaving.

Yeah. I mean, there's visiting doctors and a nurse, Jacob, who comes sometimes too. It's not too much. Not usually. I just hate   seeing him like this. And now   now he's saying it's going to get worse. He's asked me to   oh fuck. Fucking hell. He keeps asking me if I'll   act for him.

Still hasn't looked up at her. Still bent over, head in hands. She can't get a read on him. Is he going to be sick?

Act for him? I'm not sure I   What do you mean?

Silence for a bit. And then:

He's asked me to   Shit. I think   he's asked me to   take care of him. And then, if things   when things   go downhill. If he can't do it himself   He doesn't want to be completely dependent, you know? I think he wants me to   Fuck. I'm supposed to know, when things get too bad. If he can't say, I'm supposed to make the decision. And   help him…

He looks up now. Eyes brimful and frightened.

Help him? How? Do you mean   do you mean   to end   things?

A faint pulse, or a spasm, in his cheek. He's trying hard not to cry.

I guess. I guess. I don't know. I think that's what he means.

And you've   agreed?

I mean, I've stayed here. I haven't refused. But now he's started saying it'll be time soon. And it's not time. I know it's not. In the morning he'll be fine again. It's still intermittent.

Things falling into place now. Of course. Of course. He knows it, József knows that it's time for him to go. That's what it is: that's why Callum's in this house. That's why they're both here. That's the reason for this strange set-up and this weird energy. This is part of József's exit strategy. The condescension, the belligerence: all of that is just stalling because József knows it's inevitable. Because he knows that he'll have to depend on them. That he needs their help now that he's close to the end. He needs to make a show of his superiority, a final flourish. She recognises them now: all the signs of a grandiose man on his way out.

How? How would you   do it?

I don't   know   I can't   His pills, I suppose. He says he could take the sleeping pills and the painkillers together, if he needed to. They're strong and they'd do it. And if he couldn't, I suppose that's how I'd   But that's what I'm saying: we don't need to think about it. It'll be ages, yet. Cal's upper lip starting to go.

She cups her hand around the back of his head. Pulls his head towards her chest. Kisses his ear—this idiot, lying boy, this soft lad who can't do the one thing that József has asked of him, who doesn't realise that this is why he's in this house at all—and then whispers into his hair: It's going to be alright.

Yeah, I know, I know. Tomorrow morning he'll be fine again. You saw how he was when you first arrived. That's József. It's just that he gets   tired easily. Tomorrow morning he'll be alright again.

Well, maybe things will be clearer tomorrow, she says. How about I come back tomorrow evening? We can talk things over. I can help you   decide what to do next.

Yeah. Yeah. Ok. Then you'll see. He'll be totally A-ok. You'll get it then.

Pour me some of this brandy, then, she says. One for the road.

They've barely spoken all day. When he went in first thing, József declined to be dressed and turned his head away. Didn't want breakfast or lunch. Never mind, just get on with the things that need doing. He's already washed everything that József was wearing last night. Cleaned the kitchen up properly, disinfected the parquet. Picked up the dry cleaning. Been to the shops so that they're stocked for the next few days with olives and blue cheese and sardines. He makes up a tray for József—marmalade toast and pomegranate juice. He must be starving by now.

Knocking on the door again. It's after 4pm, got to get him to eat something. No reply. Push, push the door open. Steal in.

József is curled up on his side, so it's difficult to tell if he's sleeping. Stepping closer to the bed. Whispering: József?

József's head turns slightly on the pillow. He reaches out with a trembling, naked hand, and Cal rushes to his side, putting the tray on the floor. József might be trying to smile; it's difficult to tell sometimes.

I'm sorry, Callum. His words slow and slightly slurred.

It's a bad day, that's all it is, just a bad day.

I'm sorry that last night   didn't go as we planned. But you told her, yes? You explained the situation? Things are alright between you and   Lauren?

I told her. Things are   ok. I think she wants   to help us.

Callum, I don't want anyone else to help us. Please listen to me. What I said last night is true.

Cal shaking his head.

I'm an old, sick man. I've lived long enough, dear boy. It's a privilege to have grown old. Oh, I know how lucky I am to have grown old! I've had this illness for more than a decade, and still I've been happy. Still I've lived how I wanted to live. But I feel   different. Something in my throat. And things out in the world   turning full circle. The past repeating: here, and in America, and back in Hungary. All the way back round. That fascist way of thinking again. The nationalists. Vicious. Such petty, vicious thinking. I don't have the energy left for it. There's something I need to tell you, dear Cal. While I   can. There's a safe box in the hall, hidden behind Tamás's painting there. You know it?

Nodding; the safe he checks after guests, the safe he checks to make sure it hasn't been tampered with.

József's speech is effortful, but he's taking his time, trying to make every word as loud and clear as possible: Inside that safe is a box, containing the ashes of the great artist Tamás Márton. It is my wish that my own ashes to be kept with Tamás's, that we be kept together. You will make sure that we remain together, yes? I don't care where, but together, yes? Tamás Márton is the man to whom I owe the utmost filiality.

Cal squeezing József's fingers together, trying to gather them into reciprocity. There's no response.

Do you understand? József says, I have no   record of where my mother's body   of what they did with   her.

Nodding. I understand. But you don't need to be thinking of any of this. Not yet. It's just a bad day. Tomorrow things will look different.

József retracts his hand, and they both watch it slowly unspooling on top of the covers.

It was supposed to be a straightforward exit. They'd followed procedure to the letter. Everything fine in the preliminary meetings. A usually mild-mannered man, Stefan Meier. Had given the impression that he might be secretly quite relieved if he was to leave the company. He's a little older than most of the traders, a little more cautious. He'd been in the same position for five years. Mid-range suits and mid-range shoes. Nothing flashy, nothing reckless. Small talk about holidays and his children's school costs and his family back in Frankfurt.

At the first meeting: Lauren and the manager setting things out. Him listening carefully.

We've called this meeting as the first step in preparing you for the possibility that your role might be made redundant.

Yes, thank you.

Explaining the process that would follow, him thanking her repeatedly and fervently, so much so that she'd asked at the end: You do understand, Stefan, that your role is at risk?

Yes, yes. I do understand. Thank you, Ms Haigh, for setting things out so clearly. Thank you.

Handshake for her and his manager, and then he'd left the room.

This afternoon, the second meeting: seeming slightly more jittery, but still compliant enough. He'd been offered the opportunity for someone to accompany him to the meeting, but he'd attended alone. Lauren explaining clearly that his role was being made redundant, that he would be given three months of gardening leave with full pay with immediate effect. Because of the business-sensitive nature of his role, they'd need to accompany him back to his desk to collect any personal belongings and then he'd be required to leave the building.

Thank you. Yes. Can I   I just   I feel a little   I think I need a moment?

Lauren explaining that counselling was available through the transitional assistance package, immediately if necessary, and that he was welcome to use the phone in the room to make a call. Then stepping out into the hallway with his manager, Joanne.

Sometimes it takes a moment for it to really sink in, she says.

Maybe. The team manager, their much lauded and only female team leader, an American-Japanese graduate of Yale who'd spent twenty years in Zurich and whose instincts were usually exceptionally good. I'm slightly concerned about him. He's been acting   a little out of the ordinary. We may need to—

BAM

A loud, dull bang. What the fuck. What the fuck? An attack? A distant attack—somewhere in Canary Wharf? Or lower down, one of the lower floors of this tower?

Dropping to the ground. She's dropped to the ground and Joanne is holding on to the wall. Both of them staring around, whites of the eyes now.

Another bang. Inside the meeting room.

Joanne stepping towards the door. Lauren up on her feet and barring her way.

No. Go back to your office. I'll take care of this.

An emergency point down the corridor. Using the phone there to call security. Waiting back outside the door; waiting until things have been quiet for more than a minute, and then opening the door just a fraction. Stefan there, with one of the chairs held almost above his head; seeing her, freezing, the chair wobbling above him. Then slamming it down onto the centre of the glass boardroom table. A dull thud on contact. Several deep cracks at the middle of the table. No shatter.

I'm sorry. I don't know   what I was thinking. Him slumping back against the wall.

Her afternoon only getting worse. Phone flashing again and again inside her handbag. Her mother calling repeatedly. So much admin to sort out for Stefan Meier now. Booking him into a clinic for the next two days, various phone calls to authorise that payment—and then she had to contact Meier's wife. And as she manages all this, the thought of Callum and József cycling in her mind too. The messiness of it, of József's piss on the floor, and Callum hauling him out of the room, and then Callum's dry heaving on the sofa. Tonight, after she's dealt with all this, she is going to have sort that out too. Her mother can wait.

*   *   *

Leaving the office, fishing her phone out of her handbag: thirteen missed calls and one voicemail. In the first, her mother's voice rushing straight in, high-pitched, glitching in weird places: Lauren, love, I think she's properly lost it this time. Your sister. She's saying such things. Lauren. She says that you destroyed all her stuff, all of her keepsakes, when you came up. She says you're a psycho, Lauren. Years ago now, she's talking about. She's never   she's never said a word against you before. I can't understand her. She says that you must've known, that you must've known what he was like   what your Dad was like. Ring me back. I don't know what to do. She's locked herself in the loo, and you're not answering your phone. I don't know what to do. I don't know what to do. Please, love, call me back.

Almost at the tube. Sense of panic rising, breathing coming shallow in her chest. But what can she do now, if her sister doesn't see how much she's already done to try to take care of her? How much she did to protect her? Veers out of the commuting flow, searches on her phone. Sends some links to her mother: an NHS info page and a number. What else can she do? Everything they try only makes things worse. Dropping the phone back into her handbag. Back into the flow. Escalator inexorably down.

*　　*　　*

Elgin Mews. Walking slowly along in front of the calm and tasteful facades of Elgin Mews. Antibacterial gel from her handbag, rubbing, rubbing over her hands. Walking slowly until she is collected and calm. Deep breath. Knock knock. Cal opens the door of the red house. Face washed out, eyes tender and pinkish and ugly.

I'm not even sure you should come in. That's the first thing he says to her. Sorry. He's in a bad way. He's not even got out of bed today.

What now? Now he's not even going to let her in?

You need a break, she says. Look at you. If József is in bed, we can have a quiet chat downstairs. He won't even know I'm here. We need to sort this situation out. Stepping into the house, Cal moving backwards.

They sit in the living room. Him incapable of basic hosting. Has to go through to the kitchen to get a bottle of wine herself. Inspecting the wine rack: a pinot. She fucking needs this. Pours them both a glass. Breathe. Breathes to steady herself, because her voice will otherwise be angry. Stop gripping the wine glass so hard.

Tell me what's happened, she says. Tell me about how things have been today.

Of course he won't ask about her. Of course he won't ask her about her day. If things have been difficult for her, if she's ok. Of course no one will ever ask her if she's fucking ok.

He thinks it's time, Cal saying weakly. He says it's close to the time. But it's not. This is just what happens. Things get worse and then they get better again. It's happened loads of times. He's just having a bad day.

The pinot is vinegar bright and stinging the back of her throat. Cal: slumped there. Pathetic in his denial. Totally unable to act.

Ok, her saying. Am I right in thinking that József   wants to choose when it should happen? He wants to orchestrate it himself, right? And you agreed. So maybe he doesn't want a long, lingering, drawn out   thing.

Yeah, right. But I don't think he's in a state to decide. I should wait another week, and then go back to the consultant to ask for a treatment review. There'll be other things we can try. Different medications. It's not   it's not the final stages. Not yet.

He's already downed his drink. He pours himself another glass. And then he starts going on about what a great time they had just last week, watching films together, talking about Budapest. And then he's telling her about some artist, some Tamás Márton, whose pictures apparently hang around the house. Down in her bag, her phone flashing again. She's the one who'll have to do it. Of course. She's always the one who always has to sort it all out, in the end, the one who works out what needs to be done and actually does it.

Helping Callum up to the bedroom. Two bottles of wine and nothing to eat. Stay the night, he's saying, collapsing onto the bed. Stay with me. I know you won't believe me. I know it's too soon and all that. But I love you. I think I do. It's fucked up, I know. But I do. You're the fourth fucking dimension.

He falls asleep quickly, mouth gasping open, top lip arching upwards like a child's. Lying down next to him. Waiting until his breathing is settled, until he is deeply, safely asleep. And then she rises. Everything so luxurious in this house that her movements are silence. Feet muffled in the thick, gold-coloured pile. Moving so quietly that it's as though she's progressing through a dream. Is she floating? Crossing the hall and pushing open the door to the master bedroom. József, an old, tiny thing, curled on his side in the massive bed. Sitting down beside him. The curtains open; there is moonlight. Looking at his head on the pillow. He's so small; a sea creature prised from its shell; helpless, naked, bereft. He opens his eyes, but he does not look at her.

A scene from long ago: Amy playing in the back garden of the old house, the house at the top of the estate. Small still—no older than five or six. Something has happened and Amy is frightened. What is it? A dog; it is a dog barking close by, along the ginnel that runs behind their garden, behind the bright orange wooden fencing. The dog has started up, suddenly, just the other side of the wood, loud and hungry, and has made Amy start to cry. Her face streaming with tears and mucus. Where is their mother? Not around. Out with their dad and his mates, getting fucked up? Lauren left in charge, as usual, and now Amy is acting up. It's just a dog, why is she so scared of a dog behind a fence? Lauren moving close to Amy, right in front of her. Look, there's nothing to be scared of. Her sister still crying. And then: bam. Slapping her hard across the face. Amy frozen, her little red mouth open, her cheek welling up already. Shock. Standing still and staring around her, as though afraid that the ground under her feet might give way if she moves in any direction. The way Amy had looked up at her, her little gelatinous eyes taking it all in for the first time: Lauren in front of her, standing resolute and unrepentant; the broken washing wheel with its tangle of blue plastic strings in the garden behind them; their pebble-dashed box of a house, filled with their cheap plastic toys and their mother's cheap jewellery and their pink synthetic highly flammable clothes. Lauren was showing her something horrible but true: she was teaching her that she needed to take care of herself. That you can't trust anyone, not even those you love. Especially not those you love. Amy should have learned. But she didn't. Later that day, she'd climbed onto Lauren's lap and wanted to cuddle. Love you, love you, Law, she'd said. And she'd asked to sleep in bed with her that night. She should have been firmer with Amy back then and then after everything with Liam: she's been too soft with her, and now Amy can't look after herself at all. She hadn't ever learned the lesson that she'd tried to teach her.

But József: József knows what needs to be done. He knows how to take care of himself and he's made a plan. If she'd pissed herself like that, she'd want out too. She'd want to bribe strangers to deal with it; no family around you, no one you knew. Self-sufficient. Like Nan, like her nan. She knew how to look after herself. How to get a job done. Her nan, working and working, and telling none of them about the emphysema. Who was with her, she'd asked Aunty Bess, years later. Was anyone with her when she   went? *I was there,* Bess said, *the day before. But that was how she would've wanted it, your nan. Like cats, you know. They take themselves off on their own, when they know it's their time.* Clear eyed, Bessie was. No weeping.

There are pills on the bedside table next to a glass of water. Checking the label on the brown bottle: Methylmorphine. Do not exceed recommended dose. Depressing the safety lid, shaking the pills into her hand. They have a brittle, bright pink coating, like children's sweets. With her other hand, taking hold of József's face, turning his head towards her and forcing her fingers deep into his cheeks. Pushing his jaw apart. He does not look at her, but he does not resist. Beginning to drop the pills between his lips. And him beginning to swallow. Pushing them down, one after the other, fingers scuffing against his rough, thin lips, and he is swallowing; he is joining in. His Adam's apple, in the semi-dark, bobbing up and down, and up and down. Gagging, briefly, near silent. She lifts the glass; he sips the water. Her rubbing his windpipe, easing it all back down. Him, soft as a kitten. Keeping on until all the pills have disappeared into his small, dark body. His face wet and still. And then she is floating back to Callum's bed.

Part Two

FREEZER

2019

Winter. Waking into early darkness. Believing it is morning is an act of faith. A hard frost glinting in the street lights on the pavements of Little Venice. No birdsong. Frost barely thawing through the sunless days. Nails flaking in the cold. Skin dulled. Every London creature looking hunted and sun-starved. A thin mist over the canal, over the Thames, all around the office for weeks: a mist that makes people appear and disappear like figments. A mist that makes everything a dangerous surprise: the snaking river, South Quay Bridge, Canary Wharf tower, each of them emerging suddenly in front of you.

February: the worst month of all. A trader in one of her teams committing suicide. News of a stillbirth: a woman in the admin pool for whom Mina had just organised a baby shower, the baby coming early, the baby coming cold. *What will they do with the gifts*, Mina saying, *what will they do with them? Should we offer to take them away?* As though this was their responsibility. As though it was their fault they'd bought lovely gifts that would now be—what? Landfill? Grave goods? Awful, awful, but it wasn't their fault. You have to push through, you have to push through. It is almost spring. Things will change soon.

But Cal is still as bad as ever. He's back at work, though God knows how. She can ask him to do the smallest thing, like fix her a drink or a sandwich, and he will leave to do it, be gone for ages, and then wander back in, having forgotten entirely what he is about. Sometimes she'll go to look for him and find him standing in front of one of József's paintings, just staring. Or he's loitering on the top landing, pawing at the wall. Or she'll hear him in József's studio, murmuring: hoping he's on the phone; knowing he isn't.

In those first few weeks after József's death—late summer, the house filled with golden light, the tree next door dropping pears over the wall (*our wall, our house,* she always reminds him, she always reminds herself), which she picked up, alone in the garden at night, the moon bright in the sky above her, taking the soft, cold fruit and binning it before it could moulder—Cal was a child again. His pale, credulous face, pulpy from crying. Everything she said to him needing to be repeated, as though the news of József's death had rendered him hard of hearing. Impact causing tinnitus? She had taken care of Every. Little. Thing. The call to the doctor on that very first morning. The death certificate, the private ambulance. No one seemed surprised. No difficult questions posed. No post-mortem required, unless they would like to consent to one for medical research purposes? No, they would not like to consent. Which was fine, which we absolutely understand. Did people not ask questions of you if you lived in a house like this? Did they only ever offer sympathy? The mortuary, where a matronly woman took her hand and told her that the lights were always kept on, that she wasn't to worry because there was always someone on duty here with them. *Them.* And then she had almost faltered: the care for these cold, lonely bodies. Christ. What had she done? What had she done?

When she got back to the house, she had started on the paperwork immediately. Ferociously. Things were in good order. Józscf had planned well for all of this, and for Cal. True to his word. She spoke with the solicitor, who had detailed instructions. She organised the cremation, quickly. There'd been an obituary in *The Times—József Márton: Hungarian art dealer who championed Modern British Art.* And then the solicitor had arranged the memorial: more than a hundred people and Cal knew none of them. One woman coming right up to them and asking, *What did you do with his body? Did someone stay with him?* And Cal turned to Lauren, the same lost-child-face, and she had said, *Yes,* because that woman at the mortuary had said there was always someone on duty, though she guessed that this was not what this woman meant, this small woman, immaculately dressed though her face was collapsing with age. And this woman looked her up and down, and then shuffled away tutting. Others staring at them too, one man, in his fifties perhaps—handsome, dishevelled and worse for wear—coming right up to Cal: *I don't believe it,* he'd said, *I can't believe he left it all to   you. I've never even heard of you. He would have wanted me there. If he was really that sick, he would have wanted me to know.* And someone else had pulled him away. Through all of this, Cal had been a kind of sleepwalker. God knew what he did in the daytime hours, but she'd care for him through the evenings, set out meals and paperwork for him to sign, and line up happy films for them to watch together, and offer affection of various kinds to try to mitigate against his lostness. Still standing, still pushing through, keeping them going. Trying to making the house theirs, to create a space for them to live. Trying to give them a future.

But through the long night-times, things are so bad. Cal talks in his sleep. Sometimes he calls out. Sometimes he wakes and startles and says, *I'm coming, József, hang on, hang on.* And then she has to tell him again, sometimes kindly, sometimes less so, that József is gone, that József is dead. And Cal has to re-learn it, only half-awake, has to go through it all again, and then sometimes he cries and berates himself and says, *I was drunk, I was so fucking drunk, he must have called out and I didn't hear him. I should have gone with him, I should have gone with him to the mortuary, how could I have left him on his own?*

And once she's soothed Cal in the night, she's left awake. And her phone flashes at her through the small hours, her mother calling again and again, leaving drunk messages in the voice of a sedated child that she will delete in the morning after listening to just the first slurred word: Laaaaaw-ren—

And when she does sleep, these unanswered calls from her mother interfere even then. Dreams of the estate and of her sister. Dreams of that bus trip across to Leeds on a Saturday night, her and Amy with their overnight bags on their laps, the tower blocks zoning into sight. The field that they walk across first, the solitary Shire horse tethered with a heavy chain. The betting shop, the motorway junction, the Jewish cemetery. The tower blocks shutting out the light. The lift that smells of urine and skunk, ammonia paint-stripperling the back of their throats. Disembarking on their father's floor. Amy in front of the TV, their Dad playing cards with his mates in the kitchen, Lauren spiking her coke with their vodka and watching the sun set over the M1 out of the big living room window. The sky the brightest auburn-pink, a colour like gold melting in fire. Those friends, those friends of her dad's. Red-gold sky. The colour of blood in your urine. Yeah, alright, give it a rest, I'll go with him, yeah yeah, I'll go. Amy's staying at home with you, right? Just keep Amy at home, yeah?

And these dreams are nightmares: the men take her to basements or derelict mills or train tunnels, and their hands smell of cigarettes and hot fat, and they fill her mouth with stones and leave her for dead. And where is her sister, where is Amy, and what is happening to her?

When she wakes in the night in József's dead black spare room, heart beating heart pounding phone flashing, she has no idea where she is. On the estate? That rippling sea of carpet moths seething underneath her now, underneath her childhood bed? In the dark derelict mill? Is she even alive? Trapped in that dark space between life and death: next to József's bed, hand on his throat in the dark, him swallowing down, swallowing down again.

It is her, then, who reaches out for Callum, who shudders against him.

But it is almost spring. A whisper of warmth in the blue morning air. Soon the nights will not be so black, nor so long. They need to move on: it is time to move on. Six months and counting. The house is theirs now. It's softly, softly with Cal. That's the only way to get anything done with him: stealth and softly, softly. József's room and his old studio are off limits. So are the pictures. But the rest of the house: she's putting things together little by little, and it's almost there, almost ready. Little by little, she has already begun making changes. Every spare moment, scouring Pinterest and Insta, compiling her interior moodboards: rejuvenating colour schemes; healing palettes; millennial rose-pinks; neo-classical greys and mushrooms, with fresh white accents for the bones of the room; glazed ginger woodwork; plum-and-black opulence.

So far, she's had the living room walls repainted (green is the colour of relaxation and healing: oil green, sage, brindle, dark olive). She's had a new suite with energising coral upholstery delivered, and she gave the men fifty quid to take the old dull leather stuff away. In their bedroom, she's replaced the furniture piece by piece. Carbonised wood. Ochre accent wall. Rich blue bedspread. There are new bronze accessories in the bathroom. In the kitchen, new lighting and pops of jewel-colours: glassware in amethyst, emerald, sapphire. Nearly ready, the house, nearly finished, just in time for spring.

The other rooms, the forbidden rooms: not yet. Cal won't even let her clean them. Says they still smell of József. He looks wild when she says she should just run the hoover around at least. She looks in on them sometimes from the threshold, these rooms where Cal goes to commune with the scent of József, with whatever lingers of his hair and his sloughed-off skin. The studio, which smells not of József's body, but of the astringent processes of his old work: paint thinners, oil rags, turpentine. The bedroom, which smells vaguely medicated— of fungal powder preparations and mothballs—as well as of something sweet and rotten—blown flowers, bruised fruit, mulch in the earth. She kept one of her nan's jumpers, salvaged it from her house before it was cleared. For months, she could still summon her that way—mohair fibres, Chanel No.5, factory-line baking. Until one day she put her face to it and all she could smell was dust and her own perfume. József, József's scent: this too will thin away to nothing soon.

And then, softly, softly, the whole house will be theirs. She is going to set a date. The snowdrops at the edge of the canal, little white clusters fighting their way through under the plane trees: they're already finished. They will have Mina over when spring has properly broken this winter. They will eat and drink and move around the house freely, like real people, like people who have a future, the past cleared away, as though the house is theirs, as it is by right, as it is now by legal deed.

Mayfair. A large iron gate set in a red brick perimeter wall.
Key the code into the security pad. From the street, the
wall obliterates everything except the top two floors of the
apartment block. But behind the wall: a new development
of apartments and townhouses; a large private square, four
quarters of lawn, fountain at the centre. Cal nods at the
concierge, Roy, who salutes him. Shoes scrunch against the
gravel path; there's no other sound here. It's just after six and
only one light on in the row of houses at the other side of
the lawn. Cal's been here three times before and he's never
seen an inhabitant. *I call it the ghost ship*, Roy, showing him
the ropes on his first visit. *None of them are lived in. It's all
Russians and Chinese. This is what gets to people, isn't it? This is
why we're going the way we are.*

The apartment block is in total darkness. No one else here.
Somewhere far off a blackbird calls. No other signs of life. But
nowhere is really empty, not in central London. Inside he'll
do the kickboards under the kitchen counters, checking the
trays of bright blue poison left for rats. Saw one, once, in the
kitchen sink here. Desperate for water? Poison already eaten?
Bright little eyes. Clean-looking fur. Didn't report it. Willed it
to escape and live. Was it here, on the back step, that he found
the shape of a bird once? All meat and almost all the feathers
gone, but the intricate bones of the wing and the tiny ribcage
intact. Even here, cats and foxes and rats finding a way to live.

Cal lets himself into the property. A large, square house, with four equal-sized bedrooms. It doesn't take long to do the checks, even with the poison traps. The house is minimalist, no real valuables other than a couple of expensive Afghan rugs. The owner's never seen the interior. Bought off-plan, dressed by an interior designer. Check, check, check. Everything's in order for the handover tomorrow. He gets out quickly, locks the front door.

There's something he's meant to do on his way home. What is it again?

Blackbird still at it. Bright evening sky overhead. Spring, isn't it? The swallows are back, at József's—*Don't call it that. It's ours now, Cal, it's our house*—fussing round their nest in the guttering. She hasn't noticed them yet. Christ, they'd better fucking keep themselves secret; she'll eradicate them. The back garden is immaculate now. They have a man, Terry, who comes to brutalise it every month. Terry has excised most of József's old plants: the wizened, haphazard roses, which he said had some kind of disease; the rosemary bushes, which he said had *gone rampant*. The garden has been reordered in the *French style*: symmetrical and neat. But the crocuses: József's crocuses still came back through, all brightly haphazard. Even more than before, erupting all over the place. *Ah, they're here! They've naturalised!* József saying one morning last spring. József making him tea and looking out across the garden, where the first of the bright gold buds are pushing through the black earth. *That's what they call it, you know, my dear?*

These crocuses. You plant them and if they thrive, they're said to have naturalised—*which means that they come back each year, more and more of them, even more beautiful! These are special bulbs, from a very special cultivator. Would you like to hear the story? Do you have time, Cal?* He did. He always did. *Well, these bulbs come from a nursery garden in Latvia. A remarkable man called Jānis Rukšāns has devoted his life to cultivating and cataloguing these tiny flowers. He studied at the best horticultural school in the Soviet Union—this was in the 1960s—and then he travelled everywhere he could—not to the West, but through Central Asia, Ukraine, Caucasus, Siberia, looking for all of the bulbs that he could find. The crocus is native to Asia and Southern Europe, not to England, of course: it probably came to Northern Europe via Constantinople, but that is another story, my dear! This man, Rukšāns, has written beautiful books—I have one upstairs. And he's catalogued and cultivated hundreds of new species, maybe thousands. Once Latvia gained her independence, in the 1990s, he came to London and shared his great knowledge. He was the first man, I believe, to say on public television that Latvia should be free! A horticulturalist! A man who had devoted his life to tiny, beautiful, fragile things, daring to say this! This type, you see? This little saffron flower? It's the korolkowii, which he found in many places across the Soviet Union. The others are still to come: the white, the Carpathian Wonder, which he found in the mountains; and the purple Yalta, which he gathered from the Crimean peninsula. Isn't life strange and beautiful, dear boy? The world springing up like this in my back garden? Naturalised! Ha!*

He had fought to save József's things; he had. And he'd succeeded with some of them. József's giant thistle, for instance, had been wrested from Terry's grip. It's starting to come again now too, its strange, desiccated grey-green body, its self-shredding leaves and its enormous, spiked mouth of a flower gasping open at the very top: a suffocating fish at the surface of water.

No flowers here: wet green lawns, pebbled pathways. He's meant to get something before he goes back. But what? Things forgotten. All of the time. Crowded out. Lauren says he's depressed, that's why he can't remember properly. When he talks about József, she changes the conversation. A growing list of things he's supposed to eat: oily fish and sunflower seeds and certain berries. Why would eating mackerel make him not want to talk about József? Why would walnuts stop him thinking about that night, about József, just across the hall? Alone. That was the worst bit: that he was alone, while Cal slept, fucking drunk and out of it. And he must have called out, must have, and got nothing, no response. Not there, not there when he needed him. And then afterwards: he didn't even travel with him. With his body. Did nothing at all. Lauren sorting everything. Useless. Pathetic. Absolutely fucking useless. *This isn't helpful thinking*, Lauren says. *Guilt is backward focussed. We've got to look to the future.* They'll get married next spring. They'll have a family, she says. She's come off the pill, to prepare her body. All of this will help him to *move on*.

Her boss is coming over—that's the thing that's happening tonight. He is supposed to do something. What is it? The bench at the edge of the darkening lawn. Sitting on it; killing time. Tonight will be the first time they've had people over to József's house for dinner—*don't call it that don't call it that; it's ours*. Shouldn't they have invited his parents first? Not seen them in weeks. Maybe months? Lauren and him had visited them together to collect some of Cal's things just after the funeral. The funeral. Christ. All of those people, all of those strangers. Eyeing him suspiciously. Coming up to him: *Are* you *Callum?* What were they expecting? Something more impressive. Someone who looked fit to be József's executor. Days, weeks, whole chunks of time he can't really remember. Long dark months when the sun barely seemed to come up. Everything a blur. Lauren moving in and taking care of him. How had that even happened? He'd never seen her flat; doesn't remember a conversation about her moving. But she'd stayed with him, every night, and then, one evening, her boxes had appeared in the hallway. Then that was it: they were officially living together. Introducing her to his family. Ma and Da coming out into the hallway to meet them when they went across, formal like when Aunty Lib, his mum's posh sister, came to stay. They hadn't believed it, at first, when he told them that he'd inherited a house and that he was living in it with a woman, with his—what was she, exactly? Girlfriend? Partner? Fiancée? None of these feel   right. His da, perplexed: asking him the same things over and over about death duties, as though there was some kind of loophole that he was bound to fall foul of. Ma suspicious too—nervous, accusatory even. *What did you do?* she'd said on the phone when he called to tell her, *Why would he give you his house? Are you in trouble, Callum, love? None of this seems right.* But József's solicitor had gone through everything with him and Lauren. Lauren took notes. Asked lots of questions. It was all kosher, Lauren said. József had set it all up properly: he'd even set aside a painting to be sold at auction to cover the inheritance tax.

His ma had fussed over Lauren that first visit, cooing at how lovely her hair was, asking about her job in the city. Dead warm—relieved that she was a real person. His da had looked bewildered. Staring from Lauren to Cal and back again. How had he pulled this off, eh? Lauren had answered his mother's questions politely enough, but she'd asked none in return. Barely touched her shepherd's pie. When they went into his room, she'd looked pained; she stood by the window and stared out of it while Cal collected some essentials. Before they left, he wanted to tell her something about this room, something of the twenty-three years he'd spent in it. He tried to think of something significant that had happened here. Surely there was something in his whole fucking life of significance or interest? And then he remembered seeing something, out of this window, something that he'd thought about often: *Once,* he said to her, *I was smoking out of my window when some fireworks started. Right over the other side of the estate, beyond the woods. I could see them detonating above the trees. It was still a bit light. It was the middle of summer, so there was still light in the sky even though it was late. And as the fireworks started, all of these birds started to rise up from the woods. So many. Filling the sky. You wouldn't believe how many. Panic struck. Flying so close I thought they were going to hit us. I had to close the window. And they kept coming for ages, even after the fireworks had stopped. And I realised, that must happen every single time. All of these birds, woken from their sleep, flying like maniacs through the sky, totally terrified every single time there are fireworks. Only we can't see them, because it's usually dark.* And he wanted to say more, but didn't: like, that's what it's like, isn't it? Life? All this suffering that we can't usually see, except in these moments, these bright, rare moments, when it's illuminated.

Lauren had looked at him with something like pity. *That's really depressing thinking, Cal. Let's get home,* she said.

Home. Where the fuck was that now?

Come again soon, his mother said on the threshold, kissing him. *You are alright, love, aren't you?* whispered into the place behind his ear. Cal nodding. *Finally out from under your feet.*

Da: *Don't be soft, lad.*

When he asks Lauren about meeting her family, he gets stonewalled. At least he used to, when he still tried to ask. Before Christmas, he definitely asked then. Should they go up to Yorkshire, or maybe invite them down to London? She did used to talk about her sister, every so often. But she says she's making a definite break now. Says she used to send them money, to try to help them, and it made them dependent. That her mother kept asking for more and more and neither of them were doing anything to help themselves. She can't trust her mother, she says. They need to stand on their own two feet. Tough love, she says. But sometimes, late at night, her phone rings over and over again and she says, *It's them, it's them again, why won't they leave me alone?* and she puts the phone on silent. And he wakes to find her checking it, the flashing face of the phone in the middle of the night. And sometimes she wakes and wants to be held and she's breathing hard and her face is wet.

Wine. He is meant to get wine for dinner. He's still at the edge of the square. The sky is burning out in a blaze of pink. The houses all in darkness now. Nothing moves on the surface. Closing his eyes and listening for József's voice in the dark there; Bartók; *I'm still alive.*

Elgin Mews. Carrier bag cutting into his palm. Feels for the key in his pocket. When he opens the door, Lauren will be there, waiting for him in József's kitchen. She'll be getting ready for her guests to arrive. Her skin will shimmer under the new lights. She's done something to it, her face. She won't say what, but the skin is newly taut across her forehead and under her eyes, and there's something strange about her upper lip too. The new lights she's had installed in the kitchen make her skin reflect in the way that slick, photographic, non-human surfaces do. It makes him feel extra lonely, the brilliance of her skin.

And when they're together, in bed, in József's spare room, he can't look at her. It's not that she's any less affectionate. That's not it. But it's sometimes as though she's not really there. She arrays herself before him. She glazes over and she arches and moans. But something about it is   vacant. He'd never realised that regular sex in a steady relationship could be so   desolating.

These people, these people who are coming over tonight: they have never met József. The people that Lauren invites over for coffee—women she's met at hot yoga classes or HR courses, someone she introduced to him as a 'wealth manager'—they're like replicas of modern London people, with their talk of Brexit and house prices and the job market. Walking news articles; decoys. And whenever he tries to tell them about József, about the house and the paintings, Lauren shuts him down. She wants to empty everything out. She wants to get rid of all of history. *It's ours*, she says, *It's ours now. He wanted you to have it. You have to move on.*

Sometimes he finds himself on the upstairs hallway with his cheek against the wall. That's where   the box is. That's where it'll remain, and she can't do anything about it. It's safe because Lauren doesn't know it's there. A couple of weeks after the funeral, taking the Márton picture off the wall. Keying the code into the pad. Ceremonial, like. His fingers saying a vow. When he opened the dark space of the safe box: a battered metal box and an ivory envelope. A letter, addressed to him, telling him what he already knew: that the box held in there, unprepossessing as it is, contains the ashes of the great artist Tamás Márton; that József wished to be kept alongside Tamás; that Callum was to be the custodian of their ashes. And then, a line in quotation marks:

I keep you like the earth keeps all of its fallen matter.

An unfamiliar line. He had wracked his memory for it, but couldn't find a conversation, couldn't recall József speaking it. Was it written for Tamás? But it was in English: written for him, then, perhaps? He had put the new box inside the safe. And they are there together now. *I'll keep you like the earth keeps all of its fallen matter.* He loves to linger close to them in the hallway. He hears József's voice, still. His rich, warm voice. He can conjure the smell of his skin before bath time: talcum and fresh sweat and brandy.

He's still on the street. Outside. Foot moving against some loose cement at the edge of the step. Tiny violet flowers growing there. Lauren must not have seen them. *Plant violets for love*, József saying, and now he's kneeling in the soil in the back garden on a sunny afternoon, pulling up some tiny purple flowers. And he's describing Millais's Ophelia for Cal as though it is right there in front of them, painting the picture large for him because Cal has never seen it: *You haven't! Oh, my dear boy? Imagine! Well, it's huge. And the greens dominate: it's a deep green scene, with the dark river at its centre. The weeping willow is overhead, over the river, for forsaken love. And just behind the rushes there's poor Ophelia, lying back, letting go of her flowers, sinking into the water. There are floating daisies next to her, and they're for innocence. And the pansies spreading now above her dress, they're for thoughts and for lost love. The poppy, so red in that green water, that's for sleep. And then—you could almost miss them, they're so fine— the violets around her throat, which show her faithfulness in love and her too-soon death. I would give you some, but they withered all when my father died!* József says, clutching Cal's hand melodramatically. *You don't know the great play, either? What do they teach you at school these days? I will take you, I will take you to the theatre, and we'll see it together, dear boy!*

They say he made a good end. Cal stands on the doorstep listening to József's voice; he does not turn the key.

She asked him to get the flowers and wine from the good Italian delicatessen on his way home. But he's late. Again. Every chance that he'll have forgotten or that he's gone AWOL. Again. Should have done it herself. He's erratic, still, at best: she sent him out for goat's cheese and vodka a few days ago and he came back two hours later with a block of cheddar and some cider and no explanation of where he'd lost the time.

Crystalware lined up on the counter. Shining up the wine glasses with a damp tea towel. So many lights in the kitchen now, studded into the ceiling, that the brightness catches everywhere. When she told Mina about the changes she was making, she'd arched her mouth sceptically: *Don't over-light. Uplighters are very 2000s.* But the house had needed more light. The sheen on the parquet, the glinting chrome-work, all the glassware set out in the Welsh dresser. The light glancing off her too. She is properly prepped for tonight. Full body salt exfoliation and a light spray-tan. Toenails magenta. La Perla, demi-balconette bra with matching French knickers in pink silk. The dress, an investment piece by Burberry: embellished green lace, deep square-cut neck. Her shoes are maroon suede, a stiletto heel. Skin on her face primed the night before with glycolic acid—top layer sheered away, the new skin pink and plump. In the dark kitchen window, her cheekbones glisten along with the glasses and the sparkling cutlery on the table and the knives in the block.

She had wanted to make things brighter; she had needed to. This is the backdrop; she is the foreground. The house is theirs; the house belongs to them. And she is foreground, it is background.　　　　But still. Sometimes　　　　sometimes in the evenings, it's hard to tell one surface from another. It can be hard to determine what it is that is scattering the brightness: her own hard, lacquered nails, glittering cold light across the kitchen wall—or the chrome kettle that moves in her hands? All these glinting, vibrant surfaces.

The wellington is in the oven, browning slowly. The hors d'oeuvres are prepped, synchronised on a silver platter in the new fridge. Dessert is crystallising in the deep freeze— dark chocolate and beetroot ice-cream, a spectacular puce confection. As long as Cal is back soon with the flowers and the wine... Sherry. She'll serve sherry first. Very dry. Mina is always going on about a Spanish bar near Kings Cross: the centre of the London sherry revival. There'll be sherry glasses somewhere. This is the sort of thing József has. Had. A chill through the extremities of her body: a cold pulse in her fingertips and her nipples. Nausea back again: nausea for weeks now. A thick knot in her stomach.

Her phone is flashing on the worktop. Cal? Or Mina checking on directions? No. Of course not. It's her mother. Another incoherent, drunken, abusive voice message on its way.

The things you try to get rid of. The things that won't ever truly disappear. The ghost apple. The massive landfill on the valley side. As a child, thinking about it obsessively. Namely, where did it all go? All the stuff that people didn't want, all the plastic and the poisons and the tampons? *To the tip,* her mother saying, *or out to sea. You don't need to worry about it, Lauren love. We just flush it away.* But at school, they were told about global warming and environmental toxicity. They had to do a project about landfill: that warm, teeming, degrading mass just across the estate, leaching out volatile metals and chemicals and methane, a giant liquefaction of dangerous, lively matter. You can smell it still when the wind turns, and the sound of the gulls circling above it carries right into your childhood bedroom. And you were meant to just forget about it. To know it and not know it. Now they're protesting, all of the kids. Because those things didn't just go away. Nothing stays inert. Christ, that fucking condom from outside Roxy's. Where is it? What happened to it? Is it there now, degrading into her cervix? Toxic shock. Endometrial spill. Those men, those men who would pick her up from her father's flat on a Saturday night, who would pick her up and get her gatted and then put her down in the back seat of the car in a layby on the dual carriageway next to the White Rose Centre, burger van up ahead all shut up for the night, that man shrugging down his jeans, spitting on his fingers, *Your dad wouldn't like it if you pissed me off. You look dead, love. Put a smile on it.* But she wasn't dead; far from it. She was concentrating, she was taking all of that energy and she was compacting it into something hard and bright and fierce.

Incandescent. She was more alive than any of them. So who really knew? Who knew what was alive and what wasn't?

Something at the edge of the kitchen. Light glancing across the wall like a razorblade as she turns. The empty door of the kitchen: the dark stairs that rise beyond to József's empty bedroom. Weird refractions. Fuck's sake. She's getting worked up again. She'll have to reapply her base if she doesn't calm down. Anxious thoughts. Wild anxious thoughts. They are passing clouds. Breathe in, breath out. Would Mina let herself be unnerved by her own kitchenware? She would not.

There's a sound. At the door. Muffled voices. They're here. It must be them on the doorstep. God knows where Callum is with the wine. I am foreground. The house is background. I am foreground. Gathering herself up, gathering herself into the full power of her person. She knows where she is. She knows who she is. The idea of herself pulsing into her fingers and her nipples and her toes. She is an immense erotic charge through the air. She opens the door.

Three figures on the doorstep. Suspended animation. A weird urban tableau. Mina at the front, right foot forward in a nude stiletto. An eel-skin trench coat—dark, gleaming, slippery green. Maliciously delighted; her round, blonde brimming face. Tim behind her: massive head of hair, pale pink shirt skimming his stomach, making him look, at first glance, naked. Off to the side, leaning against the wall of the house,

Callum. His key is pointing forwards in his right hand, a blue carrier bag cutting into the flesh of his left.

We found him, Mina says, just hunched over in front of the door, Lauren! Delivered as though this is the most extraordinary and wonderful thing. I said to Tim, I think someone's trying to break into Lauren's house! There's someone crouching at the door! Perhaps it's a drunk who's going to be sick right there! Or, what do you call them here? Someone looking in through keyholes? Tim, how do you translate *tirkistelijä*? A voyeur?

Peeping Tom, Tim says.

Yes! A peeping Tom! But we were terrifically brave and we came right up to the door to apprehend him, and it was Callum!

Yes! says Tim.

Oh. Thanks. He's just on his way in with the wine. Aren't you, Cal?

Mina moving into the doorway. Leaning in to kiss her. Do you think he's had one of those mini-strokes, darling? Trilling with laughter. Pushing past Lauren into the hallway. Tim following her. This is not at all how it should be. Right now, Lauren should be taking their coats, she should be ahead of them so that they see her in the living room doorway. And instead, they're already in there, nosing through the cinnamon-laced air like sharks scenting the blood of domestic crisis.

Callum still huddled against the wall. Cal. Has something happened? Are you alright?

He doesn't speak. He slowly pushes the fingers of his right hand under the blue plastic handles of the bag, and holds it out towards Lauren.

You got wine, then. Taking the bag from him. That's something. Please, Cal, don't be like this tonight. A little nudge, barely a push, so that he stumbles towards the door.

Attempt to restore the proper order of things. Take their coats and pass them to Cal; give the tour of the house, even though Mina has already marched through the living room and kitchen. Talk about József's pictures, tell Mina about the artists. Highlight the new things, the little jobs that have been done. Uhu, Mina says at each turn.

It's charming, Mina says when they're sitting back in the living room. Just the right size for the two of you. I suppose we'll eat through there in the kitchen-diner? Very kitchen supper. She raises her glass.

Callum, you wouldn't believe Mina and Tim's place. They've restored all the original features. What is it, Mina, six bedrooms?

Well, eight if you count the attic rooms. Waving her glass of wine. She talks about the work they've had done, the designers and architects and craftsmen they've employed. We're thinking about investing in a place out of town now, aren't we, Tim, now your bonus has come through?

Well, if that's what you still want. Tim, topping his wine glass right up. I thought that, according to you, this country is going to be fucked when we leave. Didn't you want to invest back in Estonia or Finland? Honestly, I can't keep up with her.

Mina rolls her eyes. It's not going to happen. I've told you that. I know that British people like to blame everything on the EU. But they're not suicidal, hey? We've had a search and acquisition agent working for us. I don't know how people can bear to look at all these tiny pictures online and then go around all these different properties when they're out of town. I mean, who has the time? Anyway, she's found us a couple of places to look at, one in Norfolk, one in the Cotswolds. And there's also an architect she's bringing in to meet us, in case we decide to build our own place. You can't tell the difference between some of these new designs and the real thing. Except, of course, ours would be better than the older properties—more efficiently designed.

An alarm beeping in the kitchen.

Oh. I think things are probably ready now. Shall we go through? Passing Callum, slumped in his chair, and scuffing the edge of his foot with hers.

Serve the meal with the ceremony of a magician. Pulls an asparagus mousse from a spotless kitchen. Mina disappears the bright green goo in seconds.

Wonderful, darling. I could eat five of them!

There's venison wellington coming up, so you'll need space.

Moves the plates away and lifts a glossy parcel of pastry from the oven. Hot steam, good smell, cutting well.

This is quite a special meal. Looking over to Cal. This was the first meal Callum and I ate here. Callum brought a private chef in, a French chef, one of his colleagues, to cater for us. Last summer. It's almost a year ago now.

Oh, well done. Lauren, Callum. Mina raising her glass. Then she begins on her food. Perfect, darling! Tearing at the meat with her knife. Important to mark these things you know. Holding out her left hand and twisting it from side to side. Milestone jewellery. You're going to need to think about this for a first anniversary. This is my engagement ring. White gold with rose cut diamonds. And then you see, the wedding ring slots on top. All the rings interlock. Bespoke combinations. And then on top of that, the eternity ring, rose gold. It doesn't have to be rings, of course. Pushing platinum hair behind her ears. Earrings. Cartier, gold and diamond. These were for our first anniversary, weren't they, Timmy? Now it sounds like a lot of money, when you just say it, but we all live until we're a hundred these days, so if I wear these, say, five times a year until I'm a hundred, then they're an absolute bargain.

Callum is cutting his food into squares. He cuts until everything on his plate is cubed and then he starts to put one forkful after another into his mouth.

So, Mina says, placing her cutlery on the side of her plate. A mid-meal pause, a new focus for the group's attention. Looks at Lauren and then at Callum. What will you do now you're all settled in? However will you fill your spare time now you're not house hunting, Lauren?

We haven't thought too far ahead. Cal is still getting used to József   not being here.

I can recommend an excellent woman in Putney. When my mother died I was back at work after two days. And I'm sure your father—

My father? Cal says, through his meat mouth. My father?

She prepared him in advance for this. Of course she didn't correct the story with Mina: it's too humiliating. But she told him about this and he said it was fine; at least, he didn't object. Did he even hear her last night when she ran through it? Has he forgotten this too or did it never register in the first place? Staring, staring at him hard, willing him to remember.

Right, says Cal. My *father*.

Oh, says Lauren, this is a bit of a   melancholy topic for dinner!

Callum throwing down his cutlery, masticating his way through his final mouth-load of meat. Melancholy. That's me.

Mina raising one eyebrow: deeply gratified arch. Well. So what will you fill your time with now you're not hunting for houses, Lauren darling?

Oh. We don't know what will happen in the future. But perhaps, if we *do* have a family, I might develop some   side interests. I have a few ideas for   projects.

Oh you do? *Do tell*.

Nothing definite. Just, I don't know, you hear of some very successful start-ups. HR consultancy. Events management. Property management. That sort of thing.

Property management? Mina laughing: peals of laughter. Darling, what *are* you talking about? The thing about this girl. Turning to look at Callum. The astonishing thing about this girl, Cal, is how good she is at getting rid of people. She's got a real talent. No one has managed as many exits for us as Lauren. Most people don't have the stomach for it. They need a sabbatical after just a year or they request a transfer or they resign! The New York office tried to poach her, but I wouldn't let her go! Darling, be serious, if you're going to do anything freelance, it's got to be simplification and severance services.

Back in the lounge. Mina telling stories about their last trip and Tim, otherwise slumped over his drink, roaring into life only when he is summoned by name. Offer top-ups and lavender biscuits and tablet fudge. Every so often Mina looks at Callum while she is speaking and then she turns to Lauren, widening her eyes in the way she does in meetings when she wants to indicate to Lauren that someone is behaving in an alarming manner. This kind of look is usually followed, after the meeting, by a direction to carry out an occupational health assessment. When people lose it: that's the worst kind of exit to manage.

Mina's glossy orange lips. What is she saying now? He has *the* most wonderful work ethic. He trained as a surgeon with the US Marines and I've got his direct line, so he's on call to me any time if I need advice. They're molecular products. He extracts proteins from your *own blood* and then infuses them into the serum, so that your own proteins are regenerating your skin. Who are you seeing, darling? Who's your dermatologist these days? You're looking a little bit strained, if you don't mind me saying, a little bit stiff, across here, you know. Mina taps under her eyes and up to her temples. Here, let me give you Dr Sterum's card.

Mina hands it over, then yawns ostentatiously. Making eyes at Tim, who is slow on the uptake. Lauren offers to get their coats. On the threshold, Mina leans in close, squeezing Lauren's upper arm. We need to talk. He's not well, darling. You should have told me. You need to do something. We'll talk on Monday. I may be able to reach out to him. Kisses her loudly, sucking the air through her lips twice, leaving sheer mandarin gloss on the apples of both of her cheeks.

They're walking back down the Mews towards the tube, disappearing into the darkness. Mina's laugh still ringing when they're out of sight. Cal hasn't even come to the door to say goodbye. Moving back inside, back into the kitchen: plates and cutlery all over, lingering food congealing on the porcelain. Something unpleasant moving in the pit of her stomach. The rich food there, the meat and the scallops and the sugary fudge pieces. Her stomach distended when she touches it: hard objects, refusing to break down. Wave of nausea. Was the venison high? Perhaps right now, tiny organisms sparking into life in the darkness of her gut, multiplying in there to make her sick.

Are you feeling ok? shouting through to Callum. No answer.

When she enters the living room, Cal is sitting in the same position as before, slumped in the armchair, staring at the Tamás Márton picture.

I am not. Feeling. Ok, he says.

Is it your stomach? I feel   sort of queasy. Maybe the food was—

It's not the food. Cal interrupting her. Has he ever? Has he ever interrupted her before? Something wrong. Something different.

What's wrong with you tonight? Mina thinks you're that you need some support. I've told you, we've got to do something about your mood. Mina knows someone you could go to see.

Callum speaks slowly and quietly. Did you hear him?

Blood running cold. Clenching, something clenching in the pit of her stomach.

Did you hear him? József? Did you hear him call out for me? He's staring at the painting still, not at her.

What are you talking about? A deep pain in her belly. Sharpening to anger. She does so much: she works so hard all of the time to make sure that things get done, to do the things that he won't do, to keep them moving forward, and then there's this: this cold tone of accusation from someone sitting still, from someone totally stuck, from someone staring into a picture like it's a sacred portal to the past. Like the past is such a wonderful thing anyway. She knows the past, and it's no beautiful vista: József's shitting helpless body, curled around Callum's. Amy's little-girl eyes, her flinching helplessness. Her mum, wasted and totally fucking clueless. She's done what she needs to do, so they can all move on. Nothing to regret. Nothing to feel sorry for.

Shouting now. Wildness in his voice. Did he call out for me? Did you hear him? Did you hear him when he was dying?

She—jolt of panic—stands up and goes through to the kitchen. Begins to clear the surfaces. Picks up side plates, quickly, stacks them by the sink; rinses them, stacks them in the dishwasher. Then the dinner plates. Rain outside. A dull anxious sound. The air alive. Moving fast now, wanting the whole mess cleared away. Remnants of blood and cream and fat rinsed off. Her stomach is hard as a fist. Another lurch of nausea. The more she clears away, the more she sees the disarray of the kitchen: glasses all over the place, champagne flutes with puckered lipstick on their rims, tumblers with thumb prints grubbed all over the glass.

Shouting again, shouting through to her. Did he call for me? Did you hear him calling for help? I'm here too, you know. I live in this house too. Answer me at least.

Knocks a glass over with her right hand. Bright shards on the floor. Things moving. Energy in all the corners of the room. Pick up another glass and smash it on parquet. Then a bowl. Pick up a filthy plate and fling it hard against the kitchen wall.

When they are in bed—after he has led Lauren upstairs, helped her to the bathroom to throw up, cleared up the worst of the mess in the kitchen, crawled into the warmth of the bed next to her, turned off the lights—he still has to ask. Because now it's there: unavoidable. The sense of something coming to light that he already half knows. Is he going mad? Maybe, maybe. But something pressing him to keep on. Because how has she always been so calm about it? How? How did she take it in her stride that morning, barely missing a beat; calm, low voice. *Cal, Cal, wake up. You don't need to worry. There's nothing to worry about anymore. It's József. He's   gone.* And how did she even know? How did she know, that morning, unless József had called out in the night and he had been too drunk to hear?

Did he call for me? Did he call out? I need you to answer me.

Lauren is quiet, but she's super present—her body hard, tense, awake.

Why? Why do you keep asking this? Why can't you just move on? It's what he wanted. We've had this conversation so many times. Over and over. József wanted you to have this house. He wanted   things to end when they did.

Yeah but. I still think about it. All the time. He was so close to us, just across the hall. But alone. I can't fucking bear it. And I was so out of it. What if he called for me? What if I never heard him, and he needed me?

Quiet between them. Then:

So, are you saying if you knew he didn't call for you, you could stop thinking about it?

I don't know. Maybe.

Another long, dark, silence.

He didn't call out for you. Lauren's voice, but extra flat. I know, because I was awake.

Yeah, but you weren't awake all night.

I   went in there. I was with him.

You   went in there? His own voice strange to him; a voice from elsewhere, materialising from the dark of the house. But why would you? If he didn't call out?

Something made me get up. I knew that   he needed something. I got up and I   helped him.

You   helped him?

A crackling sound in the space around them.

I   helped him. Yes. I helped him. It's what he wanted.

Lie still in the dark. Can't speak now. Can't cry out. Can't say anything. Totally unintelligible. All of this: totally unintelligible.

Are you ok? Her asking. Fear in her voice, newly tentative. I did what he wanted, so that you didn't have to. So that you didn't have to go through with doing it. I was with him so that you wouldn't have to be. So now we can move forward, right? He didn't call for you. He didn't call out at all. He was peaceful. It was what he wanted. You can stop thinking about it, Cal. I did it for you.

He waits until she has stopped crying, until her breathing has slowed, deep and long, her exhalations almost ecstatic. Extricates his body from hers. Exits the bed. Thick carpet under the soles of his feet, toes clawing into it as he moves around the room, silently gathering up his things: phone, wallet, keys. Puts his trousers on in the hallway and then he opens the door to József's room. One quick look around. One deep deep surge: everything good and everything bad in this one place.

He closes the front door behind him, gently. Those violet flowers, colourless in the dark, latticed at the edge of the step. Violets are for love. *I would give you some, but they withered all when my father died. They say he made a good end.* Stooping to pick one, pushing it inside his jeans pocket. Crushing it there, hard between finger and thumb; fingers stained with cool ink. József in the sunshine in the back garden. József describing Ophelia. József telling him about crocuses. How cold and delicious and full the Mews are in the darkness as he walks with the thought of József blooming vividly inside him.

Walking. Walking. Walking unconscious of destination. Tracking along the side of the canal. This is the route towards Paddington. On the way to the theatre again with József. The dark, derelict buildings the backdrop to József's excitement for Chekhov. Empty backstreets. Look down, keep looking down, that's the way to stay out of trouble. Then walking along the edge of Hyde Park. Gates locked up for the night. Men in sleeping bags shifting every so often in the rhododendrons. *You're very good at taking care of people, my dear boy*, József saying. Cal has taken away his half-eaten dinner and tucked a blanket around him. *You have a rare skill. Caring frightens most people, you know.* Turning onto Park Lane. The traffic here is busy still, taxis and sleek cars dropping people in front of hotels. Cutting through Knightsbridge, towards Sloane Square. Streets that he knows well, streets where people in the daytime strut, trailing behind them their expensive appendages—suitcases, dogs, staff, young children. He has taken care of so many properties here— these creamy facades, these blocks of monochrome wealth. József loves colour. Always waxing lyrical about the vividness of Tamás's work. His colour saturation. *It's there even in those final pictures, when Tamás's sight was failing. Blue! Such a rich and wonderful colour. Do you know about its history, Callum? Renaissance Italian painters used ultramarine made from crushed lapis lazuli. You'll have heard of it, I'm sure, this precious blue rock? It's shot through with gold, my dear! It was incredibly rare and expensive, mined from Afghanistan and saved only for painting the holiest things. The virgin's mantle, for instance. On the Bayeux tapestry, it's only the blues that hold a trace of their pigment. The colour life is centuries long. Blue was the last thing Tamás saw, my dear, when his sight was failing. There's a blue frost, he said to me, across everything. If it weren't so inconvenient, it would really be quite beautiful. Ha!* All of this, József gave him all of this from a single blue brushstroke on a painting in his living room. Cal will repeat and repeat and repeat all that József told him, every conversation and kind moment, until he can be sure that he will never forgot it. This is what Lauren can't understand—that he doesn't want to *move on*; that the world is richer and bigger and more beautiful with József.

What did she do? What did she do? Fuck. Fuck. How could he have let   all of this happen?

GuestHouse home up ahead. It's not one of his but he looked after it once, covered a swap-over for Fadi. It's massive, stacked up over four floors, and they've dug down to make a two-storey basement—a home cinema and a swimming pool at the very bottom. This is what people do now, the super-wealthy. They dig down, try to make iceberg houses. *Thing is,* Fadi had told him when he'd walked him through the place, *they done this excavation, right? And then they're stuck with this massive digger right at the bottom of the house. What do you do, man? How do you get the digger back out? I'll tell you what they do. They just get the digger to dig a bit further down, and then they bury it. Fam, it's dark: the digger digs its own grave. Bishop's Avenue, it's full of JCBs, buried under houses. Millions of pounds worth of kit. Someone needs to get onto it. Find a way to dig down and get this stuff back out. Rob the robbers, man.* Cal had told József about the house and its digger tomb: he thought something would appeal to him about the idea of these enormous machines interred under pristine mansions. *Oh, yes,* József says, *I've heard about this building downwards. The neighbours get cracks in their walls; trees in their gardens begin to tilt. You can bury things as deep as you like, but they'll find a way up to the surface,* he says, biting into a plum and letting the clear juice run down his chin. *Having said that, my dear, the lowest thing sometimes lasts. Whole buildings in Buda were felled—five, six-storey apartment buildings. Sometimes the facade remained and there was absolutely nothing left behind it. But the basements stayed intact. When I was growing up, there were people living in basements with no buildings above them. Ha! Perhaps these rich know exactly what they're doing.*

Keeps on walking and crosses the river. Everything thins out towards Battersea. When another person turns onto the street—awareness of one another, instinctive, heightened. Friend or foe? Head down, head down. Humming Bartók, making little clicks in his throat. Yes, I am good at looking after people. *My mother*, József once said, *was the fiercest, brightest, most terrifying person I ever knew.* He had shown Cal a photograph of a tiny, beautiful woman with wild eyes. Cal thinks of his own mother, of her agitation recently on the phone. He hasn't seen her in time and she's evasive when he calls. It is not just that she asks about his 'job' as though it is a code they are both using; it's not just that she mentions 'Lauren' as though she is a distant, untouchable entity; she's evasive about herself too. *Your mother's not well*, Da said the last time he rang. *Why don't you speak to her?* And then he does, and she says, *I'm fine, I'll be fine. Stop fussing. Has your da put you up to this?* He's in the middle of Clapham

Common. A couple sitting on a bench repeatedly fall into one another; the woman shrieks and then falls silent. There are empty plastic bottles and carrier bags and cardboard takeaway boxes all over the grass; there is no breeze and the debris sits entirely still, giving the common the air of recent desertion. It has been the first mild day of the year: a few hours ago, people would have been sitting here, drinking and eating and thinking of summer. József's name day, two years ago, they had celebrated together in the sunshine of late spring on Hampstead Heath. József introducing Cal to the Hungarian tradition, telling him that it was necessary that he buy him a present. *Perhaps a good brandy*, he says, and winks at him. Cal had bought a French Armagnac that he knew József liked—*French brandies are the very best; I first tried this in Montparnasse, in a bar where the great artists used to drink, those monstrous geniuses who made great art before the wars.* And they drank shots of it—*ponies*, József calls them—and tiny cups of demitasse. And József tells him about name day celebrations when he was a child back in Buda. *They are more important than birthdays, because you share them with everyone else who has your name. My mother would always somehow find sweets. We would go out to the edge of the city, where the hot water bubbles up from the ground; or we would go to the Rudas steam baths, with the shattered glass roof, and swim there in the hot water. My mother, on our name days, would sometimes grow nostalgic and tell me about Upper Hungary and Transylvania, the areas that her family came from. She would tell me about the cities and forests of the north, the Tátra Mountain Chain and the Carpathians. These areas were lost to Hungary, scissored up and given away in the settlement after the first war. They would never last long, my mother's reminiscences: There is no point in nostalgia, she always said, the world has changed and was far from perfect in the past. Perhaps that is why I have never been back to Hungary. We exiles, you know dear boy, we are adventurers! We are the ones who insist that the world change and accommodate us! This is what Tamás said to me, when he was young and still hopeful: My body is in exile, but my spirit is at home in my art. Isn't this beautiful? So much great art has been made in exile, you know: Josef Albers escaping the Bahaus for America, and Pissaro here in Norwood, and Mu Xin and An-My Lê working in New York. All of the people I see who have come to this city, working so hard, trying to make their living here. Driving cars and cleaning hospital wards and kitchens and caring for the sick. These people who are finding a way to survive, a way to live, even in the most   hostile situations. This   great collective energy: this is beautiful to me!*

Keep walking, keep walking. His body is an onward rhythm. After Tooting Bec, it is one long road all the way. People staggering off the night bus onto the pavement right in front of him. He has been walking for hours when the birds begin to wake. Now: people in uniforms, early shift workers, emerging from side streets in the pre-dawn light. He climbs the steep hill at the side of Coombe Wood, up towards the estate. The violet has frayed to almost nothing between his fingertips, but he holds its soft remnants still, hopes that the ink is all over his hands.

Waking in the night. Where am I, where am I, what am I?
Her stomach twists. She curls around it. And then she feels
it: feels, deep inside, that there is something there, something
quickening. Search for Callum in the bed. We're not alone,
she wants to say. A tender surge, a tender surge of feeling
towards the empty room across the hall, towards József and
that awful, close moment in the dark. His dark throat. She
helped him. She helped him, didn't she? Reaching out for
Callum, but fingers grasp right through him to the creased
sheets where he was lying and the warmth of his body—gone,
cooled to just a trace.

Two days of messaging him. His wallet and keys gone from the side. She had checked the house first. Every room. It was before five in the morning, still dark. Perhaps he was somewhere talking to József? Smell of turpentine as she opens the dark studio. Camphor, a ghost of camphor, as she peers into the dark bedroom. Nothing. No one.

Messages him then, casual at first. All like,

Just checking where you're at? Xxx

You ok? Ring me when you get this. Xxx

Hurtling on the train back and forth to work, checking for a reply. Whole journeys watching the screen. Glancing up, then straight back down   no new messages   *Are you coming back to the house tonight? Maybe you're working? Let me know! xxx*   the backs of houses   no new messages
   scaffolding   no new messages   satellite dishes
no new messages   red brick walls, long graffiti tags

Then: *Cal, I'm worried about you. Please let me know you're ok xxx*
   no new messages   glass and fretwork and cranes, a whole cluster of them   no new messages   another train speeding past—BAAAAAAM—like a narrowly-avoided collision

   no new messages   wet washing on balconies
no new messages   *Are you coming home? Xxxx*   an open window like a scream in the middle of fire damage, high, high up in a block of flats   no new messages

rail track workers in bright orange   no new messages
    Cal??? xxx   the black coal smell of the underground
tunnel, the moan of the train approaching   and   then,
finally, this:

Please stop messaging. I'm fine but I need some space.

The nausea has not left since the dinner with Mina and Tim. And now there are cramps too. A week since Callum left in the night and nothing from him but that one cold message.

She cannot sleep in the house. Not really. She is waiting. She is waiting for a message to say when—or if—he will come back. In the evenings, she drinks wine and eats breadsticks. She turns on all the lights. She moves between the rooms she has curated so beautifully—the oil green walls and ochre accents and jewel glassware—but she cannot settle. She scans through her emails and her news feeds and she edits work documents on her phone and she sometimes falls asleep on the sofa—a moment, an hour?—waking with a cold shiver. Dry mouth, disorientation. Woozy, woozy feeling. So tired. She has never been so tired. And yet sleep will only come in these fragments that leave her even more exhausted.

When she tries to sleep in the bed, *our bed, our house,* when she tries to turn out the light, it is too much: dark, dark, hands on his throat, hands on her throat, stones in her mouth. She gets back up, drinks what she can find in the kitchen, stares again at her phone.

Tonight the cramps are worse. The tenderness that marks the start of her period? That coming on now too?

No. No, this is different. A tightness in the hips, behind the kidneys, like that time before. That thing that happened before. Toxic shock. Endometrial spill. No. Nope. No way. Don't think so. Not that again, not that happening again.

Into the kitchen. Open a new bottle. Breathe, breathe. Your thoughts are passing clouds. Fuck, fuck this pain coming back on, tugging inside her. It can't be the same. Can it? Lightning never strikes twice, etc. If you don't think about it, then it can't be happening. Can't be happening again. Drink, drink the red wine right back. Sting of the throat. Then into the living room. Coral sofa. Coral for energy, bringing good energy. But can't sit down: up on her feet again. This feeling, Christ, she knows this feeling. This feeling   this feeling is summer two years ago. This feeling is the very specific wording used by the doctor—an older man, firm but gentle—at a clinic paid for by another man. This feeling is the doctor taking his time to talk to her, trying to make things less painful. It wasn't the problem she had been anticipating. Take care of yourself, you've got to take care of yourself. She should have taken better care of herself. She was expecting that she might have   fallen pregnant because she hadn't

          taken care of herself. A lapse. A stupid lapse. But the doctor was telling her about a different problem that she needed to consider. You *have* been pregnant, the doctor says to her—such a strange fastidiousness to his tenses. You *have* been pregnant. But the scan revealed an *early pregnancy failure*. These last words. Spoken. Very. Slowly. And then more words, a slew of them, clinical words, ringing darkly in this weird new conversation: Remaining tissue. *There are a number of ways for us to deal with it.* Material. *We have ways of expelling the expectant material. Some people prefer to manage things at home, so that they can collect the tissue for burial or cremation.* Spontaneous miscarriage. *May not happen. There are risks if the expectant material remains inside.*

She had chosen to bleed it out. She had taken the pills and bled it out over days, the *tissue dispersed by the medication* drenching pads and her tights and guttering into the toilets at work and, one evening, all over a toilet cubicle floor at Victoria station. Fumbling for 50p, turnstile rush: nothing to see here, nothing out of the ordinary, just the usual one-in-three spluttering of livid chromosomes, warm strings of endometrial matter, great black clots of nothing, nothing worth collecting, nothing to bury or to offer up to the great fire of the CleanSolutions clinical waste incinerator. Mina's voice from outside the toilet cubicle at work, *You alright in there, Lauren? Do you need something? The meeting starts in five. Nothing, no I don't need anything, I'll see you in there.*

But this is not the same. Can't be. Off the pill six months, but using protection, Cal always using protection. That fucking condom. That condom lost somewhere inside her since 2008. Is this it? Finally rotted into her cervix. Toxic shock syndrome. Septicaemia. Breathe. Breathe. Your thoughts are passing clouds.

Pain now so bad that she cannot stay still. Pacing in front of that painting. Pacing in front of that massive fucking painting of József's that hangs still in the front room, a painting of fire in the sky. Blood in your urine. Infection. Septic shock. Haemorrhage.

She takes the stairs quickly. Collects towels from the bathroom. Hot, it's so hot up here. Instinct, all instinct now: she strips to her underwear. She paces along the upper hallway, back and forth. Behind that door ahead of her: József's room. She enters. Why? Why in here? Why back in this room of all places? Because there is a bed and an adjacent bathroom. Practical to the end. The carpet in here, thick and soft between her toes. The hairs on her arms rise. Her body knows; her body knows that it is happening again.

And then it kicks in proper. She doubles, dropping the towels and holding on to the edge of the bed. The pain is so fierce—hot and sudden and tearing. It is everywhere. It is everything. It bleeds into the orange air and across the pink-cast plaster. And at the same time: it is so specific; shrinking, now; she is shrinking into her own dense black inner-material.

It passes as suddenly as it came. Slowly able to stand upright. Breathe deeply. The pain, now lifted, has the quality of a temporary delusion. She picks up the towels from the floor, spreads them across the bed. Thinking clearly and practically: here for the long haul? Should she fetch her phone? And then it kicks in again. Laughing, laughing out loud, laughing at its sudden ferocity. Fucking hilarious. Fuck you. Then bending double. Stripping off her briefs. And then it stops. And then it begins again. How many times, she loses track. It starts and then it stops again. It might be over. Is it over? Coming up for breath, gasping, into the still room. Nothing moves. Sitting up, slowly, on the bed. Motes in the air, tiny dazzling stars picked out in the dying light. A cold tingle down her spine. Something brushing against her. And turning, there, she sees it there, behind her on the bed: a long clot of dense purple, connected to her inner thigh by a thick string of clear viscous material. Crying out now, crying to see it, so vivid and so   dead. And then the pain kicks back in, blotting out everything.

Afterwards, there is this wine-dark sea of matter. In the midst of it, one lucent, bright form. József's bed, the receptacle of this sad fisherman's haul. This time, there is enough. Enough to collect up. But what for? What for? And what to use?

Down to the kitchen, searching for something. Not a carrier bag, for Christ's sake, Lauren. Not tinfoil. An empty ice-cream tub on the side. Beetroot and chocolate. Rinsed out for recycling.

She works quickly. The smell is rich and grassy. Scooping with bare hands. All of the dark, wet, tender material. Still warm, but cooling quickly. When she has   it   all gathered, sealing the lid on the container. Walking down the stairs and back into the kitchen. Opening the chest freezer. Puff, puff tiny cloud of frost. Moving aside the other frozen objects. Thickly furred with ice-crystal. Depositing the carton at the very bottom. Oh little thing. O little warm clot of stopped life.

What time is it? Is it still night? So very tired. Death is a warm bed. Death is a long, dark sleep. But it is almost morning. Look, look at the arc of light outside, at the pale violet rising above the rooftops. She will not do it. She will not sleep. She will not   death. It is almost dawn. She vomits and then she showers. She showers ferociously. Muscles in her body ticking in strange places: her perineum, the folds of her hips. Skin is clean and fingertips ridged like prunes. Stepping out from under the hot water. Pat pat dry with a thick, clean towel. Pushing her face into the soft cotton, feeling only textures: the pleasing coolness of the tiles against soles of feet, the pulse in her vulva. Everything falls away. Vertiginous rush of physical sensation. For a moment, there is no organisation; sensations are the whole; the house is her body; there is no past. There is only future.

She gets dressed and she goes to work.

Part Three

SAFE BOX

Summer 2019

These are the things that he does now:

One: He cooks. RN, for instance, he's chopping an onion, a fat red bulb that keeps slipping under his knife. He finds the biting point: cubes it. Fingertips purple. Wipes them on his jeans, tips the onion into a pan, where it spits for a moment. He likes surprising his parents with a tagine or goulash. New-found skills, isn't it?

Evening sky out the window: dense with heat. This summer is officially a scorcher, but not of the blue skies variety. All humid and clotted thick cloud. How long has he been home now? Still spring when he first came back, when he first came back from József's, cold dawn light, his da in the kitchen filling a flask for work; he'd had no idea what to say. Why was he back? What would he do now? Must have looked a right state: walking through the night, white-knuckled. *Take your time, boy,* Da saying. Making him a coffee. *No need to say anything. You take your time. Your ma'll be pleased you're home any road.* Clap on the back. He'd slept that first day, back in his own bed, heard his parents in the hallway outside, fussing. *Should I check on him? What if he's ill? How did he look?* But they were distant voices, faraway like the rest of the world is when you have a fever. He slept and checked his phone every so often when it buzzed. Messages from Lauren. Breezy messages as though nothing significant had happened. He turned the phone over and let it run out of power.

That night, his mum had knocked on his door. *Tea's ready, love. Come and eat something, if you can. Or I'll do you a tray?* Bleary-eyed at the table. Shovelling the food in, chewing, chewing, swallowing. Her, his ma, seeming tired. Drawn. Her mouth pulled down, as though trying not to cry. Him, making things worse. Bringing her down. Worrying her.

Ma, he says, when Da is clearing away. *Please don't worry, Ma*, he says. *I'm ok. I just   need a break from things for a bit. I won't stay for long.* Her, squeezing his hand. Not meeting his eye. *You'll stay as long as you want to, my boy.*

And then, that night, Da hissing at him in the dark hallway. Cal on his way to the bathroom, toothbrush in hand. His father making the reverse journey. Da pulling the cord to turn off the bathroom light and bumping into Cal. *Cancer*, he hissed, *that's what they're saying. That it's cancer. Your ma doesn't want you to know. Don't say anything to her. Bloody hell. Sorry, sorry. I shouldn't be—* one sudden sob, a surprisingly high sound, like a gasp. Cal trying to embrace him—an awkward, half hug of his shoulder—and then his father darting away.

He wasn't scared. That was a surprise. He lay back in his bed that night, and he thought about everything sleeping in the darkness around him: all of the birds roosting in the blackness of the trees of Coombe Wood, all of the rats nesting in the drains under their block, all of the hidden creatures in tree roots and bins and stumps: all of them just trying to survive through each dark night. And he didn't feel lonely, or paralysed by fear or uselessness. Resolute. That's it. He would find a way to help her. His ma. He wouldn't turn away, not for a moment, not this time. He'd be there day and night. He charged his phone: a blinking stream of messages. Two from GuestHouse, the rest from Lauren. Multiple kisses. Lauren: trying to pretend that there was nothing wrong in the world, that the future was easy and assured, the past already swept away. He would wait to speak to her until who knew. Until things were different. Tomorrow he would send her a message. He would tell her that he needed space. And then, he would try to work out how he could help Ma.

Two: he takes care of her. Of Ma. Not that she told him anything at first. He was left with just that one conversation with Da, which sometimes felt as though it had been a dream. But he found evidence of new night-time anxieties. He'd hear her early in the mornings moving around the flat; he found new lists. The first one was headed EMERGENCY:

Dressing gown
2 x nightdress
Underwear
Soap bag
Jewellery pouch

Pound coins
PHONE CHARGER
Book and notepad, biros
Address book
Stamps

The other had no heading:

Lace linen—Pat's daughter
Mam's crockery set—Lewis and Cheryl
Silver baby cutlery set—Lewis and Cheryl
Mam's photo album—Lib
Dad's photos and medals (black shoebox)—Lewis
Jewellery—Cheryl and Lib
Mam's coats (bin liner in wardrobe)—Lib
Family letters (green shoebox)—Cal
Diaries (blue shoebox)—Cal
Paperwork (large box file under spare bed)—Trev and Cal
Baby clothes (bin liners in Trev's wardrobe)—Lewis and Cheryl

In his first few weeks home, he had had to work surreptitiously, finding ways to help that wouldn't be too obvious. Doing the washing when she was out, organising the shopping before she could, insisting that he wanted to try out a new recipe for dinner. Useful. He had started to feel useful again. He is good at thinking about what might help her. He can tell when she needs something without her saying: offering tea when she looks tired; making her sit down with a magazine while he cleans the kitchen. He learns that she likes soft, mild, sweet things when she is feeling worst. Nauseated, maybe, though she never says what she's feeling. He buys camomile teas and marshmallow and pistachio nougat from the big supermarket; he brings her cones of freshly baked cinnamon doughnuts from Boxpark, the fancy new food stalls that have opened behind East Croydon station; and when he's in town, if he's been to the GuestHome office, he walks up and down Wardour Street looking for something that might tempt her: Jamaican Grillhouse, Starbucks Open as Usual, Wasabi, Strip Intimate Waxing, high-vis jackets, white vans, Deliveroo, Delicious Edit, and then the run of shops that he is looking for: Hummingbird and L'Eto Caffe. Browsing the windows for her. Will a black forest meringue be too sharp, too acidic? He hunts for those mild flavours she likes best: coconut and mango, pistachio and almond dulce, cherry and vanilla ice-cream cake, honey cake, date and caramel, lemon, elderflower and blueberry, tahini cream-pie, that bright green cake made from spinach and ricotta. Sometimes she can only manage a mouthful, but her face always lifts at the sight of the small box tied with ribbon. *Callum Thomas! You shouldn't, you know. I dread to think what these cost.* But her fingers already catching at the ribbon.

One morning, standing at the kitchen counter with her back to him, she says it: says that Da is having trouble getting time off work. That she needs to get to an *appointment*. Still not saying anything explicit, not the words *cancer*, or *hospital*, or *treatment*. But initiating him into her code of illness. *I'll come with you, Ma*, he says, *I've got nothing on today*. Trying to sound casual. *Ok*. And she moves off to dry some mugs.

The ward is shabby and noisy and full of people. He sits next to her on a chair with a torn plastic covering: no bed, no river view, no faded Monet. A world away from József's private room. There are pictures on the wall by a local artist. Made of felt. Green landscapes of the chalk downs, of the Addington Hills that rise from the edge of the city, just beyond Coombe Wood. Small scenes woven in bright threads. He imagines them through József's eyes. Likes the colours, in spite of the clumsy lines. You are party to small devastations in this ward. Some areas are partitioned with fabric dividers for privacy, but you can still hear every word. *How's your digestion, my love? Is the diarrhoea any better? And the mouth sores, my darling? We've got a list of wig-makers, my love, some really excellent ones up in town. Are you eating, Mr Eze? Yes, I know it's hard to, but you must keep your strength up. Have you tried massage? Some people find it really helps with the pain and the sickness, and with sleep.* The intravenous line is fastened to a port in his ma's chest, close to her armpit. He watches the nurse carefully. He is not squeamish about it. Not at all. In fact he is fascinated by the painful intricacies of this care, and by the small kindnesses: the way the nurse places a hand on his mother's shoulder, squeezes once to let her know that the line is secure. Some folk sit silently once they're hooked up, staring off into space. Others swipe their phones repeatedly. Some lean back, eyes closed, groaning as though they are being drained of blood, rather than filled with something. That first time, after a few minutes sitting together in silence, Cal's mum asks him to tell her one of his stories about József. *It's so cold,* she says, though this summer is hotter than the last already, and Cal's back is damp with sweat, *I want distracting.* And so he tells her about the Siege of Budapest and Klara and Tamás taking refuge in the hidden village on the Danube and the Soviets in Hungary and the 1956 Revolution and József's escape to London. Another afternoon, a few days later, he talks her through József's art collection, walking her through his front room, telling her about the artists and their lives. *Barbara Hepworth survived cancer of the tongue, you know*, he says. His mother has still not said the word *cancer* to him, and he doesn't know what kind it is, or where it is growing in her body. *So, Hepworth survived cancer of the tongue and then she set herself on fire in bed with a cigarette ten years later. Very committed smoker.* His mother locks eyes with him then. Starts to laugh.

Sauce spluttering on the stove. Whenever he cooks one of József's old recipes for them, it's an opportunity to tell them more about József. Not that his da had wanted to hear at first. He tolerates it now though. *Here we go again*, he says, *off to Budapest.* Ma and Da bickering in the living room. The news is on, so probably they're on about Brexit. His ma has started a stockpile: a cupboard filled with toilet rolls and pasta and canned fish. His da wants to leave: *I don't blame these workers coming in,* he says, *it's the bosses that force wages down, and this bloody government who've done nothing to stop them. I know that. But it's simple maths. We've not got the resources for everyone who wants to come. Think about your mother. Think about that ward. We need money for the NHS here, not going on someone from* Moldova. *We can't take care of everyone. This country's at breaking point.* When Cal says, *I don't think Moldova's part of the EU, Da*, Da gets defensive. He's being taken for a fool. *This* is what the EU does: it bamboozles you in your own home. Wrong-foots you. PC gone madness. *Well, whatever, wherever they're from. The point's the same. It's just naïve to think we can take care of everyone.* There's no talking to him then, and Ma says: *Leave him to it, love. He'll see, he'll see who's naïve, who's been lied to, if it goes ahead.*

Tonight they'll eat together, then he'll tuck Ma up on the sofa with a cup of tea and something sweet, and he'll retreat to his room. He's started reading history books again. First person is what he's most into: so that he can feel as though he is having a conversation with someone from the past, someone who lived through József's lifetime. He looks for anything about the Second World War and the Soviets. Anything about Hungary, especially Budapest. He reads the diaries of Victor Klemperer. And a memoir by Sándor Márai, whose name he recognises: József had books by him, all of his novels. He wants to know everything he can about the last century, about those great forces of fascism and communism and capitalism that József talked about so fluently. So intimately. And as he reads, he'll try not to think of her. He'll try not to think of Lauren alone in József's house. But sometimes he does. Sometimes he pictures her in that place. That house is a place they once visited. A place he was briefly allowed to take care of: a place that was never his to own.

Warm grey morning. For weeks now, it's been tropical: humid days, breaking at night in electric storms. She turns to check that she's locked the door: a jealous habit. The façade of the house is immaculate. She's had all the dense little weeds removed from the cracks in the front steps and brickwork. Out back, she's had the monstrous thistle cut right back. She's had the windows repainted and an old nest removed from the guttering. The decorator brought it into the house to show her, a fascinated look on his dirty, keen face. Holding it out to her in one hand: a brittle little circle of twigs. In the centre of the nest a solitary speckled egg, unhatched, and beside that egg a tiny, naked chick. Dead. *Why would you bring that inside the house? Why?* The man had taken the nest towards his heart and then he'd left with it.

The sky is curdled grey. Should she take an umbrella? Perhaps she should? But she looks towards the dark apertures of the house; once she's left it, closed the door, she hasn't the nerve to return. Not sober. The windows are black. Behind them: cold, something so cold.

There's a new girl at work, a temp who talks constantly. Her desk is opposite Lauren's and she narrates everything she's doing. Right now, she's talking about sealing up a job offer and sending it off. She's describing the process of locating the correct postage code. She's calling out the name of each folder as she searches for the coding document: S drive, yep? HR department, yep? Costing codes, yep? Jamila, the assistant sitting next to her, catches Lauren's eye with a look of some desperation. Lauren's trying to prepare for a difficult exit tomorrow: a breach of contract. She needs to go back over the processes to make sure she's got everything straight, to make sure it's clean. But the temp's still going and she can't focus. Air con blasting down right over her. Static noise. Cold shiver.

And what is happening   back in the house?   What is happening   to that once dense   once warm   matter?

Tiny needles of ice   slicing into incipient liver
dendrites pushing,   cold and white,
into   juvenile kidneys;
minute shards splintering
into   purple clot of the heart

Shake it off. Shake it the fuck off. Lauren shouting across at Molly. For Christ's sake, Molly, we don't need to know what you're thinking every moment of the day. We don't need to know that you like the taste of envelope glue, or the exact temperature of your hands, or how asparagus colours your urine. No one cares where you're going on your *holibobs*, or how you like your steak cooked, or how your date went. You're a temp, do you understand that? It means that you're temporary. Thank God we don't have to hear all of this on a permanent basis.

Molly now looking across at Lauren; her habitually keen expression; her mouth open, ready to laugh, ready to take this as a joke. Where is the joke? Glancing across at Jamila.

But Jamila is removing herself from the danger zone: staring at her screen, head bowed.

Molly swallowing hard. Closing her mouth. Dashes up from her desk, leaving her chair to spin half a turn.

Well, says a voice from behind Lauren. That was quite a performance. Mina standing in the doorway. My office. Now.

Do you know how I can tell when you're really angry, darling? When you're not in control of yourself, when you're not able to be professional anymore? It's your voice. Your voice changes. You start to sound more   regional, is it? All of the charm flattened out of your beautiful voice. Now then, we need to have a little talk about how you're going to get back on top of things.

Mina's polished desk is almost entirely empty. Behind her, a large window; a small helicopter suspended next to her right ear. Her lipstick today is magenta, her skin bronzed. New freckles on the tops of her cheekbones from her recent trip to Sardinia.

I am on top of things. That was just   a   momentary slip. The temp, she's driving everyone to distraction. But I shouldn't have said that to her. I'll apologise.

Mina pouting. Lauren, darling, I hardly need say how much you mean to us. To me. How much we've invested in you. But I'm becoming   concerned about your reliability. You're not consistent, not like you used to be. Do we need to be thinking about some additional support for you? You took up the counselling I suggested? After   everything at home?

Knows what to say. Says: Yes, thank you. The sessions were really useful. I'm continuing to work through things. Making good progress.

She did go to see the counsellor Mina had recommended. This was after she told Mina that Callum had gone back to his parents. For a while. Time period unspecified. *This is why I urge people to marry quickly. It would all be so much more straightforward for you with the house,* Mina says. Gives her the details of a woman who smells of cigarettes and wears terrible sandals. In the counselling session, the ridged, yellow nails of both her big toes visible. Lauren secretly diagnosing a fungal infection. How could you take advice from a nicotine addict with openly terrible feet? And the woman wanting her to go over everything in excruciating detail. Asking her to describe what had happened, and every feeling it occasioned, giving each feeling an intensity rating on a scale of one to ten. As though re-hashing everything would do any good, when what she needed was to get back on it, to push on through. After that first meeting, she'd not gone back.

I wish I could believe that you were making progress, darling. Mina talking again. But you still don't look yourself. Puffy around the eyes. If I didn't know better, I'd think you were drinking too much. Terrible for elasticity. *Wine face.* Haha! Mina leaning back in her chair, making a gurning expression. You know. A very demanding job, like ours, requires athleticism. You have to train yourself. Keep yourself mentally and physically fit. You have to channel your reactions into producing positive results, keep focussed on your goals, never let what might be going on in the background interfere with things. Of course, you're right about the temp. Emotionally incontinent. Absolutely no good to us in the long term. But what worries me is your outburst. Why are you letting your feelings run away with you like that? Tomorrow, now that's an important exit. You're going to need to have everything under control. If you're letting yourself get thrown by some   inane temp, you can see why I'm worried about your ability to manage a big player.

I'll be absolutely fine tomorrow. It was just a momentary lapse, like I said. I was going back over the details before the procedure and Molly kept   Anyway, it doesn't matter what she did, I was wrong to let it get to me. I'll regroup, I'll be back on form. I'm totally committed to the seeing this through.

That's my girl. That's what I wanted to hear. Mina leaning forward. No one else here knows about Callum. No one else needs to know. In a few more months, perhaps, at worst, it might take a couple of years, you won't believe how   rarely you think of it. Holding her gaze. I've been there too, my darling. I spent a decade, in fact losing things. My mother, as you know. Then the whole   IVF thing. But it didn't drag me down. I carried on and I certainly didn't let it interfere with my work. Now I   rarely think of that time at all.

Carry on. Rarely think of it at all. A cold echo; a pulse in her lips.

Have an early night, darling. Go home if you need to. Get some rest. Come back to me fresh.

But she cannot bring herself to go home. Not before a drop of Dutch courage, which she can't allow herself before it goes dark. And it's not that she *needs* it: it just helps to dull the static through her body, the shiver she feels at the threshold of No.12 Elgin Mews. She works late. She works until the cleaners arrive and scuttle about in the corridor. Until Kasia comes in and starts on the bins. Kasia is in her forties and wears headphones and listens to rave music and sometimes sings along in short bursts, loudly and tunelessly. When Lauren first started at Lane&Hobart, working late one evening, Kasia had asked her how she was settling in. *Fine thanks.* Surprised to be asked; surprised to hear Kasia's voice: sweet, high-pitched. *Some of us*, Kasia said, *go to the Half Moon on Fridays for karaoke. The other side of Isle of Dogs. Near Limehouse, you know it? Cheaper drinks than here.* And Lauren had been horrified. Some of us. Us. Us was the cleaners and the porters and the security staff. Us was the third-party contracted staff. Us was not the HR executives and vice presidents. Why had Kasia asked her? She'd thought about that over and over. She was sure Kasia had never asked Mina nor any of the others on the graduate scheme. Was it her voice? Her accent still? She was wearing LK Bennett; she'd paid London prices for her lowlights. How could she possibly look as though she'd be interested in cut-price drinks and karaoke on the other side of the Isle of fucking Dogs? She'd been too stunned to reply. *Well we're always there, every Friday.* Kasia putting her headphones back on, head nod to the beat, walking away. She'd been frosty, Lauren had been frosty ever since. No eye contact. No encouragement. But she looks up now, watching her for a while. Kasia's movements to the music, Kasia's evident energy despite her shitty wage and her shitty hours. Joy wrested from the other side of the Isle of Dogs and the beat of the music and having an *us*. Lauren tries to catch her eye. Is she even here? Can Kasia even see her? Nothing. No acknowledgement. Kasia tipping out the bins and nodding along to the music that Lauren can't hear.

She is focussing on the future. That's what she's doing. She is re-establishing her energy. Not looking back, it's always a mistake to look back. That's where all her problems lie. Keep on. Keep on. Push right through to the future. Walking down Elgin Mews. Crescent moon sharp in the petrol-warm sky above. An early night. Come back fresh. But it is the worst at night. Coming back to the house when it is all shut up. What is happening? What is happening right now   deep inside? Shiver. Cold in her mouth. Cold in her fingertips. Crystals. Little white hexagons. Symmetrical. Spreading. A new capillary system of ice. Losing her nerve. Walks past, walks straight past the house and down to the end, turning right and then right again into the Brazilian place on the main road. As she does often now. High stool at the bar. Double gin and tonic, please. One down. Two. Then three. Then: My darling, it's time to go. The kind Brazilian woman who runs this bar, whom she watches with her customers as she drinks. Warm. This woman is unfailingly warm; she has the gift of turning any encounter, no matter how hostile, into something convivial. People ask about her accent over and over, and she never seems to lose patience. *And how do you come to be here?* One supercilious shithead, the night before. *My darling, I took a very long flight*, she says, touching his arm, *Now, what do you think of my cooking? Your steak was delicious, yes?* Time to go, my beauty, she's saying to Lauren. And Lauren wills her to touch her, to touch her lightly just on the arm, like she does with other customers. Warm. Solicitous. But the woman turns away and goes back to the kitchen.

Alone on the street. Glinting stars, impossible distances. The smallest sounds ringing out coldly in the dark. Check behind for someone, anyone: just her own shoes on the pavement, just the rush of her own breath in her ears. Push on through. Onto Elgin Mews. Key in the front door, key in the code, run through to turn on the lamps. Stumble, a stumble on the rug in the living room (*his rug his rug József's rug, she should have gotten rid of it*), falling, catching her cheek on the corner of the table. Some warmth at least, finding something warm now with her fingertips in the darkness, the warmth of blood. Not much. Not much. If she just lies here, will the cut mend? Too afraid to move. Curl up small.

Frost spreading

       capillaries hardening

a new internal system of ice.

Nothing fancy tonight. Just spag bol. Dicing the onion, throwing it in the pan. He's back late from St Leonard's so there's no time for anything more elaborate. This will do though; Da will enjoy it at least. Train back from Orpington was rammed: tropical weather, everyone's skin blurred with sweat, desperate scrabble for seats and then, at the last minute, just before the doors were due to close, a pigeon fluttering into the carriage. *Bruv, what are you* thinking? this very tall dude, full Kappa, shouts at the pigeon, in a not unfriendly manner. And Cal laughs, and the two of them pincer-chase the bird back out of the doors, and there is a little round of applause for them both and the train sets off on time. A good fucking outcome. A feeling like, despite everything, still some way to work together in this world. Still these moments of: yes! Good fucking outcome. And a good session at St Leonard's too. He volunteers there twice a week now. His mum set it up. Befriending, it's called. He did a short course and now he goes in to play cards with an old chief called Oswald who has lymphoma. His days are varied now: when GuestHouse need him, he travels into London, to the new empty houses on his list in Putney and Westminster and Soho. Enters the anonymous, gleaming spaces of the super-rich. Checks over the beige machinery of good taste. Ticks his list. Gets out as quick as he can and locks up these secret bastions of wealth. Works his way back through commuters and after-work drinkers and tourists and low down, low down, those men and women and dogs in doorways—the cardboard signs and cups for coins sometimes just feet away from the doorstep of one of his houses. In the daytimes, if he's not meeting GuestHouse clients, he takes care of Ma. And Tuesdays and Fridays he travels across to Orpington, to see Oswald. All sorts of people come to St Leonard's. Palliative teams of medical staff: standard; but also priests and counsellors and music therapists and rabbis and aromatherapists and writers and yoga teachers. The place is bright and always too warm and it smells of cabbage and patchouli oil. Oswald is usually in the lounge. Oswald eats boiled sweets from a tin; he wears shorts and socks pulled up to his knees, even in this heat; he's sharp and incredulous and good humoured. If he's frightened, he doesn't show it. *I don't want you feeling sorry for me, young man,* he said to Callum on his first visit. And the way he leans in and enunciates very clearly and properly, and speaks as though there is a great audience even though it is just the two of them: it gives him that old good feeling again. *I'm the lucky one, even with this sickness, young man. There are grandmothers, you know, grandmas who've been taken away to detention centres! Denied their medications! Grandmas who've been here fifty, sixty years—since they were girls—and some bit of paper has gone astray. This country! Only wanting to get rid of people now, anyone they can, for any tiny reason. Just numbers, we're all just numbers to them. And folks still trying to get here, like they haven't got the memo. In these boats, just dinghy boats. And in these lorries. You read about that? Poor souls. Those poor souls, I'm praying for those poor souls.*

Oswald came to London in the 1960s from Trinidad. Oswald doesn't seem lonely. Not at all. His room is filled with photos of his family: his three children and their partners, and their children too. But Cal gets the impression there's been some kind of argument about Oswald coming to the hospice. *I watched my Lucile die,* Oswald says one afternoon, apropos of nothing. *I nursed her at home. I don't want it for them. Nah. Not with them working so hard.* He sucks a sweet clean away. *That's not for them. But now they're all getting at me about it.*

Maybe they want to help, Cal had said. This was within the parameters of appropriate conversation. As a befriender, he was not to counsel. He was not to offer advice. But he could give information on services, he could make suggestions of how to access help, and he could offer *alternatives* to certain ways of thinking. This was an alternative, right? *Maybe they want to be the ones caring for you?*

Oswald had thought for a while. *Lucile, my Lucile was in a bed downstairs,* he says. *Afterwards, I couldn't sit in that room. In my own living room. Do you understand? I don't want to make their homes   like that.*

Right. Ok. I get that, Cal says.

Because, what does he really know of   actual death? He only saw József's body   briefly. Briefly enough that he could forget it, that it seemed like a double, a swap-in, a weird

251

waxy replica, and quickly, so quickly, that body vanished and he was able to remember only József alive: quick and forceful and animated, his voice still ringing through the house. It had been Lauren who'd dealt with the actual   death bit.

And had that left some sort of   mark? On her?

Nah, hadn't seemed to. She'd just pushed on through, trying to eliminate József everywhere she could: new paint smell, gaudy vases, József's old furniture shipped off in a van while he was at work. But   maybe: is that what you have to do? Do you have to change things if you've seen death inside your house, the house that you eat in and sleep in? And is that what Lauren's   domestic brutalities are about? The gardener and the bleaching of the grout and the desire to clear the past away? Is that why she always tries to erase everything so   murderously?

She had done something terrible. Really fucking terrible. But her doing it—it meant that he hadn't had to, didn't it? It meant that he'd stayed clean. And then he'd left her there. He'd left her there, alone in that house—

I see what you're getting at, young man, Oswald saying. *But what you've got to understand is that you always want to   protect your children. That's the last thing you have, you know? The last thing you can try to give them. You want to protect them from seeing you   dying.*

That's the only time he sees Oswald weep.

Rich juice bubbling around the mince, marbled with little gold droplets of fat. Dinner's ready. Shouting through to his parents. Serves up and then they all take their plates into the living room. His da wants them to go away next summer. *Maybe hire a car and drive down through France? Or get that Eurostar through to Paris? Or the ferry up to Scandinavia?* They haven't travelled since the 1980s. Ma has always wanted to. The treatment's going well; the doctors are hopeful that the chemo will be curative. Ma seems   different. Is it just the tiredness? She sleeps more. And she seems less anxious. *I'm not afraid anymore, Cal,* she said one day at the ward. *I'm not afraid of it.* He hadn't asked her what *it* was.

Da wants to make plans. But his ma is saying she'll not go abroad: she's embarrassed, she's too embarrassed to be in France or anywhere else. After Johnson and all this idiotic posturing.

I can't bear it. And who knows what'll have happened by then?

Right. Suit yourself. Llandudno it is then. Not a problem for me. It's you who's always saying we should go abroad. And what about you, lad? his da saying. What will you be doing next summer? Not still hanging round here with your old ma and da? Or with those old fellers at the hospice? Cutting his plate of food across in one direction, and then across at the perpendicular: a lattice of diamonds of spaghetti to fork into his mouth.

Hush will you, Ma saying. He's got plans, haven't you, my love?

Plans for what? Go on, surprise me. He's secretly training to be a plumber? A butcher? A special forces agent?

Shut up, Trevor, Ma says. Honestly, sometimes I wonder how I ever stayed married to you.

You stayed married to him because he has the sky in his eyes, Cal says. This is the story they've always been told. Since being children. That Da had worked on the rooftops from being a lad, a big handsome beast of a boy who could sing like an angel and fight like a bear, and that when Ma met him she could see it: the light of the sky in his eyes, the light that would keep them both going through the worst of times.

Righto, Cal, that must be it, she says. Tell your da, then. There are some courses you're looking into, aren't there?

Yeah, he says. It's not exactly a trade, Da, but it is something useful. Something that's always needed.

Cal's phone flashing: GuestHouse swapping his shifts around again?

Knock, knock? Anyone home? You telling me about these courses, then?

Nursing degrees, Da. Maybe. I could get on, with my A-level points, from before. I could specialise. In palliative care.

What's that then? Palliative? Is that, what, terminal illness?

Yeah. End-of-life care, Da.

End-of-life care. Right. Gulp of beer. Bloody hell. Queer thing to want to do while you're still so young. Haven't you had enough of   all of that by now?

Glances back down at his phone.

One new message: Lauren.

Nothing, nothing from her for weeks. For months now. Nothing since he told her he needed space.

I think it's true bravery. Ma now. Not many can face it. Caring for folk at the end. Nearly broke us, didn't it Trev, nursing your dad and then your mam so soon after? We'd have been lost without help. You remember that nurse, Trev? Teneta, wasn't it? She used to sing with your mother, didn't she? All those songs that we couldn't remember? She went out singing, singing with her, she said.

Da exhales. A long blow. She did. That's what she said. Right enough. But can we not   not at dinner   I can't

And then Da is up from the table. He staggers, holding onto the doorframe, then folds right over, hands on his knees in the hallway.

Later, when he's cleared away, settled Ma in with a blanket and a plate of macarons, he takes his phone to his room. Moves it from hand to hand, as though weighing its contents. Lauren. Lauren. Lauren. Finally swipes to read the message.

Did she sleep? She must have slept. Came to on the floor, stiff and cold: phone saying 05.07. Shower, body oil, a slight tremor in her right eyelid as she applies her base coat. Quick as she can, heavy foundation, three layers for the cut on her cheek. If you rush, if you move very quickly, then you barely feel the shivers. Out the door, street stall at the station, man just setting up in the dark: sugary coffee. Train judders. Can smell her own breath, sweet and cadaverous. Front pocket of bag, fishing in there, shake out the mints. Cold, cold, mouth tingle. Big day, big day, focus in. It's just adrenaline. Like athletes. They know how to use this shudder of energy. She'll use it too, just like Mina says. It's just energy, that's all it is. Even if her mouth tastes like her body is dying.

She's in by 7am, making headway. Gets the call at her desk before anyone else in HR has arrived.

Ms Haigh, there's someone at reception to see you.

Oh. There are no appointments before ten in my—

No, she says she doesn't have an appointment. But she says that you might see her anyway. Amy, Amy Haigh. Would you like me to tell her to contact you for an—

No, no, I'll see her. I'll come down.

Lump in her throat. Pulse rate quickening in her neck. Eyelid really ticking now. Amy, Amy here? Amy sitting on the grey velvet chairs in the reception area, doing what? Expecting what? It's been a year—more than—since she saw her last, since she stripped Amy's room bare and cut off contact. What can she be thinking coming here? Is she here to make a scene? Has something happened? Something with Mum? How did she even manage it, the journey to London, the cost of the ticket, finding her office?

Fuck's sake. Fuck's sake. She's here, really here, her hair wild and her bright red lips, and an outfit she can't parse: dungarees and black tights in this heat and high tops. Strong instinct to rush at her, to fall on her, to push face into hair and neck. Equally strong instinct to march her off the premises. There are people watching—both receptionists, other people coming through the doors, suited and booted, side-eye their way.

Amy stands up when she gets near. Looks to the side of Lauren and doesn't step closer.

So this is where you work? It's even fancier than I imagined. And then she does look up at Lauren: looks at her eyes and then at her bruised cheek, and her bottom lip is palpitating, chin dimpling up, super-fast eyelid flinch-flutter. Amy's going to cry, she's going to cry right here if she doesn't move her on quickly.

Let's go get a coffee, taking her by the arm, manoeuvring her out of the foyer.

Glass-fronted coffee shop, full of people, thrum of activity to cover, to try to cover whatever   this   is. She orders a rooibos tea for Amy, a double macchiato for herself. She pays contactless on her phone, though she has the change in her purse: important always to limit physical contact with different surfaces in central London, in order to mitigate against the risk of infection. Do not look at Amy. Do not look at Amy, so small and bright in the corner of the café. She uses her small bottle of anti-bac. A translucent pearl of gel: works it over palms, and into the backs of her hands, knuckles, nailbeds, between each finger. This makes the skin feel taut. Takes a small tube of retinol-A hand cream, and works this back over the same places, until the skin is gleaming clean and the barista calls her name.

She feels sick as she approaches the table. The desire to touch her sister so, so strong.

Didn't know rooibos had reached Dewsbury, she says and sits down opposite Amy. Lame, it's a fucking lame gambit.

How would you know about what's happening in Dewsbury? Amy says. She stirs her tea, concentrates on her cup.

So hard. To speak. To know what kind of conversation this is. To know what is happening between them. Amy silent. Introvert still. She'll have to do all of the work. As usual. Keep it moving, keep it neutral.

So how did you get down here?

Got the Megabus.

No bags though. Amy's travelling with just a satchel. Maybe she's only here to see her and then go straight back?

Did you travel overnight?

No, I came down on Monday.

Oh. Right.

Blood out of a fucking stone. Amy still not looking at her, messing about with the teabag string. How can Amy have been in London for two days? The thought is unnerving. She wants to take her home, wants to tell her to go back to Dewsbury right now, to stay put up there so she knows where she is.

So where have you been staying?

I've been staying in Finsbury Park. With my girlfriend. She looks up now, looks up to check the expression on Lauren's face.

Processing fast. This is her special skill. But wtaf? Finsbury Park? *Girlfriend*?

Amy smiling—a tiny little smile. That's surprised you, hasn't it?

Right. What's it like? This place you're staying in Finsbury Park?

That's what you want to know about? Right. It's really scummy, Lauren, it's practically a squat, and there are dogs and drugs everywhere, and we're all off our heads on ket and spice all the time, and you'd absolutely hate it.

That's not funny.

Your face is funny. Blowing her tea, then sipping it. It's an ok place. It's a bedsit. Sorry, *studio*. But nice. Lucy's made it nice. And it's only for a year. She'll be back in Leeds after her course has finished.

All of these alien words from Amy. She's speaking a new language. Finsbury Park. Girlfriend. Studio. Lucy. She's different. More sure of herself. More animated. Good. Good on you. But the distance is so   cold. Her sister part London-stranger now.

Right. So you're staying in *Finsbury Park* with your *girlfriend, Lucy,* in her nice *studio.* Got it. And Mum? Is she ok with you being away?

Amy looks back down. Then saying: Like you care at all about Mum.

I… What does she?

Yeah, don't even try. There's nothing for you to say. A year without hearing from you. She was heartbroken. I can't even   But I took care of her and she's   better now. So if you were thinking you'd come back at some point? You can't. We can't   I won't let you do that to her.

Cold, cold, stone cold. Flooding with cold.

Aimes. There's a lot that you don't know—

Yeah, right. Whatever. I'm not going to feel sorry for you. I won't.

Aimes, listen, I've always just tried   to look after the both of us. I spent   years   protecting you. You have no idea…

Amy's face. Cheeks flushed, eyelids going. Like when she was sick, like when she was a feverish five-year-old. Reaching out for her hand, for her hot little hand.

Amy pulls back. Don't touch me. Don't you dare fucking touch me. Protecting *me*? Protecting *me*? By going out every Saturday night to get smashed and leaving me on my own with Dad? You still have no fucking idea, do you? *I* protected *you*. I took it. I took it for *you*.

She's crying now, hot tears, flaming red face. But she's not stopping, she's not falling apart, she's keeping on going. She's getting louder.

I mean it, Lauren. Don't try to get back in touch. You've done it now. You've properly done it. Leave us alone. No, I mean it. Fuck off. Don't touch me.

Walking the corridor. Breathing, breathing, deep breath. But this wild feeling: this feeling like sliding across ice, sheering, sheering away from the objects around her—the corridor floor, the bad art, the closed doors, her sheering away from all of it.

Shake it off, shake it off. Just adrenaline, use the adrenaline. An important job to be done. Picking up the manager from his office: Riz Hanfi, rising star. Young, good-looking, cocksure but not reckless. He's not one she should need to worry about; he raised the alarm on the employee and he's handled a dismissal before.

Walking down the corridor together. This might get messy, she says. Is there a tremor there? A slight tremor in her voice? Talk louder, talk louder to cover it. And if it does, we don't need to worry too much about smoothing things out. Gross misconduct is rarely amicable. But we need to make sure we don't compromise our own dismissal procedure. He knows it's coming, so he might have built up quite a head of steam. If we need to, we'll leave the room and have security deal with it. Just follow my lead.

I'll be surprised if he's got any steam left. Surely that's what he releases all day long. Riz strutting. Enjoying the build-up to the confrontation or trying to psyche himself up? Either way, this sort of showmanship rarely makes for a clean exit.

There's nothing we need to get worked up about. This is a very straightforward case of misconduct. We just need to get rid of him, we don't need to settle any scores. I'll have him out of your team today.

Arriving at the boardroom. Two men inside already. Sitting close together on one side of the large table. Peter Gerard, the employee to be terminated: staying seated. He's wearing his cheap-looking shiny blue suit, staring at the table. An unusually large face, which is almost concave, the shape of a donut peach, features bunched in the middle.

The other man, a stranger, is up on his feet, smiling broadly, extending his right hand. Mr Hanfi? he says. I've heard a lot about you.

Riz not responding to the man; turning to Lauren. Unexpected, this additional party at the meeting. She should have prepared for this possibility. Of course, of course he would bring someone. Why didn't she think to prepare Riz for it? Breathing in to steady herself. Focusing on the purpose: termination. A procedurally clean exit. Nothing else matters in this room, none of the usual rules of sympathy or social courtesy apply. This man, this stranger, is trying to play a trick on them, trying to change this into the sort of social encounter where it would be unbelievably rude to terminate someone's employment.

She needs to take back control. Extending her hand to him. Good morning, Mr Gerard. And good morning to you, I don't believe we've met? I'm Lauren Haigh. I'm Mr Gerard's HR representative and I'm here to—

To make sure due process is followed. I've heard about you too, Ms Haigh. The man sitting down now, and spreading some papers out on the table in front of him. Then glancing up at them. Do please have a seat, both of you. Make yourselves comfortable. I'm Fergus, by the way. I'm here to support Pete in what we sincerely hope isn't intended to be an unlawful termination meeting.

This guy, this Fergus, with his overconfident stubble and his chin cleft and his perfect poise, is set on derailing them. Is he a lawyer? Sounds and acts like a lawyer. Focus, like Mina said, focus like an athlete would: drive things forward, keep them going in the right direction. The future the future the future. All that matters is the outcome. Sitting down, motioning for Riz to sit too. They mustn't be on the back foot. They need to attack, rather than defend.

Good to meet you, Fergus. You are of course very welcome to accompany Mr Gerard. But can I clarify your relationship at this point? You're aware, of course, that legal representation isn't permitted in this kind of meeting?

Of course. Of course. I'm Peter's brother. And I can confirm that I'm not acting as his legal counsel   at this time. I'm here simply in a supportive capacity.

Ok. Is that ok? Grey area. He's a lawyer but not acting as a lawyer RN. In this moment. Try to think, try to think. Nothing there. No memory of the protocol for this. White out. Keep on, got to keep on. Push on with the script.

Ok, thank you, Fergus. I've invited Mr Gerard—Peter— to meet with us today to discuss some concerns relating to the recent performance of his role.

Peter Gerard remaining impassive, hands clasped in his lap, large, radial face angled downwards.

That's interesting, Ms Haigh, because Peter also has a number of concerns related to the *management* of his performance recently. Fergus smiling at Riz. Yeah, this Fergus is a pro: knows exactly how to provoke through ostentatious courtesy.

There's been very little from your   brother that you could call   'performance'. Riz coming back, already riled. There's been nothing to bloody manage, that's the problem.

Peter still not looking up.

Now, Pete, don't let this man intimidate you. Performative hand on the shoulder. I'm beginning to get a sense already of the kind of environment of fear in which you've been made to work, and how that level of stress might push you towards certain *kinds of behaviours*. Fergus looking to Lauren here, to see if she's picking up on the direction of travel.

Keep on. She's got to keep this on track. Let's focus on the issues at hand. Mr Gerard, are you aware how much time in the working day you spend looking at internet sites? Well, I can tell you. Over the last month, it's averaged five hours a day. On certain days, you've spent in excess of seven hours active on particular sites. And let's not be coy. These are highly inappropriate sites, which are entirely unrelated to the performance of your role. These are hardcore pornographic sites. I have here a breakdown of your visits to these kinds of sites over the last four weeks. Pushing her papers over to Peter Gerard. Fergus scooping them up before they make contact.

Carry on, carry on with the script. Now, as you will be aware, clause 52 of your employment contract sets out what constitutes gross misconduct; conduct that will be grounds for instant dismissal, without the usual preliminary procedures. Misuse of email and internet, including the retrieval of indecent images during working hours, constitutes gross misconduct, and it is for that reason that we are regretfully forced to terminate your contract of employment today.

Riz doesn't say a word. He bounces back in his chair, hands balled into victory fists.

Fergus, leafing through the records in front of him, making a show of concern. My, my. What an involved record of my brother's internet use. Is it usual, Ms Haigh, for you to keep surveillance records on your employees' internet use over such a length of time? These go back over a month.

Consider. Consider words carefully. There's every chance they're being recorded. As you might know, Fergus, all employees' use of the internet during company hours is subject to monitoring, in order to ensure compliance with our contract of employment.

Yes, but, aside from a potential GDPR issue here, it looks to me like you've been aware of Peter's *problematic* use of the internet for over a month, as I think you've just admitted. Pete himself has overheard his manager, this young man sitting across from me, referring to him as—Fergus making a great show of referring to his notes—a *dirty little pervert*. Now, the thing is, Ms Haigh, these records demonstrate that you've been aware of Peter's *problem* for over a month. And I'm speaking here of a very serious and pervasive problem, a problem that particularly afflicts those who work in high-stress environments. That problem is *pornography addiction*.

Riz, slamming his fists down on the table. High stress? Pornography addiction? You've having a laugh! This guy hasn't brought in any money in over six months. He's not stressed, he's a blank bloody sociopath. Doesn't talk to anyone, just hunkers down behind his screen. He's a chancer. Got a bit of mathematical nouse, lands himself in a cushy role, plays by the rules for six months till he's through probation, bringing in just enough to keep us happy. And then, bang, he goes AWOL, off to the land of the wank bank all day long.

Placing her hand gently on Riz's arm, trying to calm things down, but he shrugs her off.

Fergus leaning back in his chair. Extremely pleased with

himself. Now then, Ms Haigh, this is exactly what I'm talking about. My brother has had to put up with this macho, bullying environment for the last year. This sort of derogatory, pejorative language is used as matter of course by your managers here and I'm afraid this all adds up to a detrimentally stressful environment. People do funny things when they're under a lot of stress: they get sick, they turn to substances for relief, they develop addictions. And you, as an employer, have a duty of care for those suffering from work-related stress. My brother has had to develop certain   habits for relief from the day-to-day pressure he's placed under. It's become a compulsion, an addiction for him. Now, a compassionate employer, noticing through internet records that their employee was exhibiting *unusual* behaviour, might have stepped in to offer support. I notice that you have a clear company policy on addiction: you offer counselling and a staggered return to work after treatment. It's laudable that you're so aware about the possible problems caused by your high-stress environment. But this hasn't been offered to my brother. You're persecuting him just because he's buckled under the pressure *you've* placed him under. You can't just get rid of the unpalatable results of your business practices, Ms Haigh. Pete's not just going to disappear.

You fucking dirty little nonce. Riz, rising up out of his chair. Have you seen what he looks at?

Oh dear, oh dear, oh dear. Fergus smiling. I'm afraid that

a termination in this environment of personal animosity is almost certainly going to appear to a tribunal as *unfair dismissal.*

Getting up on her feet too. Collecting things back together, trying, trying to take back control. I'm sure you have a proposal for us, Fergus. Why don't you and Peter pass it across and my colleague and I will take a moment to consider it.

Fergus smiles tightly. Passes across a document.

Out in the corridor, Riz exploding. This is bloody unbelievable. So I'm meant to be a bad manager now? I did exactly what you told me to do, I followed everything you said. I've been polite to that shit for the last two months, knowing what he's doing, sitting in that corner. You said it was a straightforward case. This isn't going to come back on me, you know.

Let's try to stay calm. Controlling her voice, though she feels a slackening in her stomach. Let's see what his proposal is, and if we can work anything out.

Work anything out? There's nothing to work out. I've got daughters you know. And he's bringing my whole team down. We're missing our targets because of him. There's no working this out. He needs to leave. Immediately. This is your problem. What is back-of-office for if you can't even sort this out? Look at the state of you. Shaking when this is meant to be your job. Sort it out.

Fuck. Fuck. Fuck. Alone in the corridor. Riz off down the other end. Windowless. Blankness. Blankness. Total adrenaline whiteout. Cold thoughts.

Cold. So cold. Fuck off. Leave me alone. Amy exiting without a backwards look.

The ice that forms on the surface
A hoar of frost   creeping over lipless mouth   over eyeless lids
over thin-skinned cheeks

Shake it off, shaking her hands until the cold jitter goes. Breathe. Breathe. Your thoughts are passing clouds. Clouds full of snow. Dense, cold matter. Can't shake it, can't shake it off, but both of them still there, waiting in the meeting room, waiting for her.

Back in the office, explaining the outcome, trying to explain it at least. She'd tried to salvage what she could, she really had. She'd gone back in, future-focussed, determined to give him nothing more than a month's salary to leave. Fergus had proposed two options: one, that Peter be admitted to a luxury addiction treatment complex, paid for by the company, followed by a staggered return to work; two, that he be relieved of his duties on the grounds of ill health, with a year's salary as a gesture of goodwill. And then there she was, somehow agreeing to the year's payment. Spooked by all of Fergus's talk about how things would look in front of a tribunal, what bad publicity it would be for the company, how the public hated financial institutions, how scrutiny of their working conditions and their bullying managers would make for terrible PR. Anything to make this go away, anything to make this whole thing disappear.

Mina going fucking apeshit when she reports all this. When Mina goes apeshit, she does it very quietly. She begins to whisper: Lauren, breathing into her ear, deadly soft. We need to talk about this. Right now. In private.

In Mina's office, and her pitch still so quiet that Lauren has to lean in to hear her. This would never have happened a year ago. You would never have let this happen. You didn't leverage anything. You had so much to counter-threaten, and you just let him intimidate you. You didn't focus on the outcome, you let yourself get unnerved by his lawyer's ludicrous threats. A man who views borderline illegal pornography all day long at work? What tribunal is going to be sympathetic to that? Her voice dropping even lower. I can't trust you, Lauren, your judgment's gone. I knew it yesterday and I should have intervened. Go home. I can't bear to look at you. Your face Lauren, what's happened to you?

The journey back to the house through the centre of London: the towers half built, the cranes lit up in the dark, the sparkle of planes circling overhead, the dark office blocks with lone workers making bright orbs of light in the sky as the daylight thickens to evening. So much in process, so much half built: everything half done or half undone.

She used to feel the momentum of the city, the way that everything was surging, the shared velocity of all of the people who had left things behind, who had hurtled here. But now she feels the ways in which it is   dying too.

And Amy in Finsbury Park   close-by, but further away than ever.

And what does she really know of this city? Living at the edge of Deptford for two years and not speaking once to anyone born there. Until that woman in the office—was her name Sylvia?—an older woman who had grown up in New Cross who insisted on telling her something about it. It was at a drinks reception for new starters, they'd been talking about where they lived and that's when Sylvia said: *Oh, that's my neck of the woods. I grew up near there. I guess they're marketing it differently now. I've heard that even Lewisham is gentrifying these days.* Grim laugh. And then she told her about a fire. Years ago. *The New Cross Massacre*, she called it. *Thirteen black kids killed there, you know.* And she hadn't wanted to know. She hadn't wanted to know the history of that place. Hadn't wanted to hear the words *massacre* and *black kids* and *killed* at a drinks reception she'd helped to organise. All she'd wanted to know was the best route to walk to the station to avoid the indigenous poor, and the best place for a strong sweet macchiato. Why couldn't people keep things   clean?

Because nothing is. Clean.

Superimposed. She had tried to superimpose herself on Deptford. And then on Little Venice. And what does she really know of anything in this city? Triangulation through coffee shops and tube stations and new bars on well-lit streets. No history. What does she know of these streets? Of the people all around her? Of Elgin Mews and the house she lives in? Of   József? What did she really know of him? His dark throat, seeming to move under her fingertips. But had he wanted her help? Oh God oh God   what have I done?

No use, no use looking back. But it's all still there. Inside.

Rotting condom. Toxic shock. Endometrial spill. Dulled to purple now, to blue to grey to white.

Finally, frost covers all. White cocoon. Powder snow.

In the Brazilian bar on the high street again. Second double gin and tonic, bitter, fizzing. Can't shake today's disasters. Mina's right: totally off her game. That feeling that she's sheering away from everything. Can't decelerate now. And she can't even go back to the house. At the threshold, she feels it. When she opens the door, the static collects in her clothes and her hair; it makes her skin prickle. The twinge inside her; the weird, cold pangs, shivering through her. *Expectant material.* Had to keep walking down Elgin Mews, right to the end and then into the bar. Trying to blunt the cold, trying to take the edge of the shakes. But it's not working. The shakes only getting worse. Jitter, jitter, cold jitter.

Checks her phone over and over. For what? As though Amy might have messaged. *I mean it. Fuck off. Don't touch me.* No one for her to call. No one to message. The woman in here, the warm Brazilian woman with her undercut and her easy manner, looks straight past her to the couples and the families. Fuck. Is she even here? Where is she? Can't go back there. Can't go back in there alone. Is there anyone now who isn't a stranger?

She needs to see him. To see him, to touch him: warm blood.

She types: Please Cal come if you can. Come back to the house.

He walks along the canal path, the cool air at his cheeks, the damp air in his throat. Cuts back up onto the road when the canal goes underground. The keys are in his pocket. He's not wearing his work suit. He breathes in. Breathes deep, breathes the dark, green, damp air. All of the low-rise flats, the pollarded plane trees, the chemist's where he used to come to collect József's prescriptions and to pick up menthol sweets and talcum. And then, here he is again: Elgin Mews. Walking past these low, safe, colourful houses. He stands outside No.12. The house is in darkness. He could put his key in the door. That old good feeling: metal in metal, bite of the lock. Nice one. Safe as houses.

But this isn't József's house any more. Lauren's at the bar round the corner. He should go there first. It's her home, she lives here. For now.

She looks different. Not her skin. Nothing surgical, at least. It's her eyes. Her eyes are full, but tearless. And her cheek: a mark on it, a bruise is it? Yeah, a grey something across her cheek, like a mark on a peach that has been handled too roughly.

It's good to see you, she says. False bright voice.

Yeah, he says. Is it? He doesn't know. Still doesn't know what to say to her.

He gets a drink. Sits down on the stool next to her, both of them facing the bar, staring forward in parallel.

What are we going to do? she says.

I don't know, he says.

Do you want me to   leave? she says. The house?

I   I don't know. Do you want to? Leave? Do you have anywhere to go?

I…

Cold, cold shiver. At the heart of the house. The dead and the unborn, waiting for her there.

I don't know, she says. That's the problem. I don't know what to   do. I can't just leave   it.

Leave it? Leave what?

This is what he's agreed to. He will go back first. He will return to the house without her. He's asked for a few minutes there, alone. And then she'll come and she'll tell him what *it* is, what it is that she has left in the house that she cannot leave. *I can't,* she'd said in the bar, after another long silence. *I can't talk about it. Not here.* He'll try to help her, if he can, but there's something he wants to do first.

It's properly dark on the Mews now. The front of József's house is still and black. Feeling for his key in his pocket. The key in his hand, the key in the lock, the bite as it turns. His body tessellating with shadows and the night sky. Stepping inside, pressing the code into the alarm—1 9 4 6. József's house is fresh coffee and polished wood and verbena from the fat yellow candle that József lights to keep away mosquitoes and evil spirits in the evenings. But the smell is all wrong now. Violently clean. Bleach.

If he were doing his checks he would search through the kitchen cupboards now, cleaning off his own pawprints afterwards. He would survey the paintings. But he knows what he will find if he looks around: new things, dotted here and there. New things that József would hate. Garish, bright, crudely optimistic.

He climbs the staircase up to the Tamás Márton painting. Leans so his cheek is against the cool plaster; nuzzles the wall. Behind the plasterwork, inside the safe: József and Tamás.

József's voice, over breakfast one day, talking about people returning. People released from the camps, walking back into Buda, disoriented by life, by life still going on. Circumstances that Cal could hardly imagine, the most extraordinary suffering, and József talking about it with the same pragmatism as their arrangements for lunch. *When you are persecuted*, József is saying, *you know what you must do. You struggle and struggle to escape it, to survive it, the bit of suffering between your teeth. But what then if you do escape? What do you do then? After such hardship? People are sometimes crushed by it, dear boy. You are still struggling, you are still fighting, but now it is against those around you who are still living: against yourself even. You must work, then, to find out how to live, how it will still be possible to live. There is always something you can do.*

What does Cal know of suffering? Nothing. Hardly anything. But there must be something *he* can do. Something that he can do with the immense cluster of good fortune that is his; with the immense cluster of good fortune that is sealed into this house. He removes the Tamás Márton picture with a sense of deep ceremony; he keys in the safe's code. Tender, so tender, as though his fingers are saying a vow. Inside the dark space are the two metal boxes containing the ashes of József and Tamás, and the ivory envelope, which bears his name in József's lavish hand. *I keep you like the earth keeps all of its fallen matter*. Fallen matter. Fallen matter. What can he do?

He rushes back down the hall, down the steps, out into the back garden. *Violets for love. Violets for a too-soon death.* But there are none to gather. His fingers scrape against the edges of the paving stones, against hard lichens. The garden is immaculate. *I would give you some*, Cal saying under the stars, into the cool night air, but they withered all when my father died. Cal's heart is full; he feels his life, he feels all his good fucking fortune blooming inside him, blooming all around him; he searches for other flowers; he pulls at roses and the agapanthuses and lilac, hands full of crushed petals; he runs with them back inside and litters them into the safe.

Fallen matter. Fallen matter. How does the earth keep its fallen matter? Warm. The petals of József's old roses that would collect on the summer soil, marked and worn. Pinkness giving way, leafing into soil and ground. Softened, dispersed. Until   indistinguishable: earth, world, fallen matter.

The house must go. Everything in it must be dispersed. The money must go back into the world. All of this is fallen matter.

She sits and drinks until the woman behind the bar tells her, kindly, as she did yesterday, that it's time to go. She's given him time enough now. An hour, or more. She walks slowly. The traffic is starting to thin; soon the dark streets will belong to foxes and the night shift and street cleaners and all of the other desperate wanderers of the dark. She turns onto Elgin Mews. Most of the houses have their curtains closed now. Their sleeping faces. The house with the recently glossed cerise door exhaling the wisteria that rises above it. Walking slowly, closer and closer to the red house. Some scuttling: a tiny, secret catastrophe in a tree across the way. In No.6: the lights on downstairs. A woman in the kitchen in a long silk dressing gown; palest oyster. Depressing bread into a toaster. Then moving suddenly over to the front window. Has she been seen? Has she been seen staring in? No. The woman stoops. Scoops up a baby—a crib just below the window. A white muslin cloth now thrown over her shoulder, and the infant, the tiny bundle of the child, held against it. The woman's mouth moving in a soundless song. Her face: not beatific. No, not at all. Hollow; a face harrowed by tiredness.

Keep on. Keep on walking. No.12 and the lights are all on. Callum is in the living room. Moving around, looking at things. Checking, checking like he used to, that everything's still there? Moving from one picture to the next. Coming to rest in front of the fireplace. In front of the enormous Márton picture, that patchwork canvas of a sky on fire.

He's thinking of József, not her, of course he is. But then he looks towards the window. She flutters her fingers towards him. He doesn't respond. Can he see her out here in the dark? Will he even let her in? She's on the outside, she's on the outside again. After everything, after everything she's done, here she is still. Always on the outside.

But she will not leave. Where would she even go? There's something of her in there. Something something something. Shiver. The pangs, the pulse in her lips and her fingertips. Her own cold material calling to her.

Little brittle thing.

Oh little cold.

Oh little brittle.

Oh little, little mine brittle cold thing.

Let me in let me in let me in.

The door opens. A slice of light on the pavement. And then she is inside, inside the house again, in the living room, and shivering, shivering, shivering, him looking for something, a blanket, but the words shivering out of her now with his back still turned—

I had to   collect it up. I couldn't   I couldn't just get rid of   it. The   material

What? he's saying. What material? Lauren, are you ok?

Shaking, she's shaking: though the evening must still be warm—summer air, thick and amniotic. But her: so cold.

I had to. This time. I had to try to. Gather   it. Just, just it was just clotting. Mostly   clotting. But I had to try to   gather it

Upstairs, in that dark room. That clot of dense purple connected to her inner thigh. That wine-dark sea of matter, the grassy smell, the warmth of those strange tissues. And in the midst of it, that one livid, small, bright, beautiful form.

Sorry, is all she can say then. Sorry. Sorry.

And his arms are around her. Warm. Steady pulse. He is a stranger, will always be a stranger, but a warm one at least. Both of them: alive, still alive.

This is what they'll do: next year, when springtime and the dangers to come are still just a hint of gold in the sky. It is dusk. They will meet on the street. They will stand together outside No.12 Elgin Mews and look up at the house. Windows dark. Interior oblique.

Are you ready? Cal asking.

She, nodding.

He'll draw the key from his pocket for one the last time. Biting point in the lock. That feeling, that old good feeling on the threshold: gone. Stepping into the house, her following. A new smell of dust and damp plaster in the hallway. Cold and empty, the house has been, all through this winter. Dark patches bleeding out through the paint on the chimney breast. Grey felt of dirt along the skirtings. In the corners: scrags of cobweb. And everything of József's cleared out now: the furniture gone to auction, the pictures gifted to a public collection. Empty space above the fireplace where that enormous patchwork of a sky in squares of blue, and below it, squares of orange, red and black, hung for three decades or more. Sunset. Scorched earth. Nothing. Contracts on the house exchanged, completion due for tomorrow.

They are here to retrieve the things that they have left behind.

Him: walking the staircase alone. No looking around now, not in the bedroom, not even in the old studio. No searching for the smell of József's skin in these damp, empty rooms. He keys the code into the safe. Collects the two boxes, and the letter addressed to him. Sweeps with his fingertips around the interior: flowerheads he left behind, crisped and brown, which he scrunches into his pockets. Fallen matter.

Meanwhile, she: alone in the kitchen. Puff, puff, little puffs of ice from the deep freeze. That tub, furred with frost. Inside: frozen chrysalis. Oh little brittle. Prickly cold to the touch. Grasp it, draw it in to chest. The thawing is immediate: her fingerprints appearing on the surface. Her shirt cold and wet with it.

They file out to the back garden. The last of the light fading fast. The world around them is a silhouette: black roofs, bare branches, the song of a blackbird, small body in eclipse; dark buds not yet green; all of the life around them, bound into the world in blackness.

Callum will walk the garden. Opening the first box—which one? it doesn't matter!—and hurling the ash across the wet ground, across the stumps of József's old plants, across the earth where, beneath the surface, the bulbs that József planted must be secretly moving—the tips of the crocuses, even now, their tender shoots just beginning to break apart the darkness. József's Latvian flowers: *Naturalised! Ha!* The little saffron and the white Carpathian Wonder and the purple Yalta gathered from the Crimean peninsula. *Isn't life*

*strange and beautiful, dear boy? The world springing up like this
in my back garden?*

And then the other, the other box is open, ash scattering
into the cold air, across the cold ground, fingers thick and
gritty with it, ash catching, catching on his lips and in his
hair. People shouting somewhere down the street. Get a move
on, get a move on, dickhead. Traffic noise in the distance.
That old good feeling: not there at the threshold of No.12
Elgin Mews anymore. Because it is here. Because József is
carrying on the air and drifting down to the soil. Falling
matter, to be held by the earth. The secret energy of life still
moving somewhere in this darkness: the energy of the world,
that wild and various energy, still here, surely still here,
proliferating under the cold dark ground.

She has been watching him. The frost that encased the tub
is soft now: her hands ringing with cold, a wet patch over
her heart.

Where? she says. Where should I   bury it?

Callum looking around: that patch of earth around the
giant thistle, the giant thistle that still bursts through each
summer, gasping for life—the patch of earth around its
stump is clear.

What about there?

They have nothing to dig with.

Fuck. Fucking hell. He'll use his hands. But he can't dig
deep: the earth is too cold and catches his knuckles.

When he stands back, she prises the lid open.

Something. Something and nothing. Something and nothing. This little frozen curled   thing.

She'll tip   it   out into the earth. Something and nothing, here, here, buried here.

They cover it. She uses her hands then too. Gritty soil. Dirt under the nails. Toxoplasmosis. Toxic shock.

And when it's covered she says: Is it too close? To the surface I mean? Is it   safe?

I don't know, he'll say.

And she will have to leave   it   there. To warm. To soften. To degrade.

Cold, cold rush in her body. Static all over. Skin prickling.

She will start again. She will have to start all over again. Carrying all of this with her. Ghost of an ancient condom degrading against her cervix. Amy. Amy as a child: bright with trust, bright gelatinous eyes. That black night   standing between life and death, her hand on József's throat. What did she do? What have I done? She's done   harm. She's done grave, grave harm. All of this, carrying all of this. A clutch of hard, bright undigestible objects inside a poisoned body. Crime scene. *You look dead, love. You look dead.* Spit on the fingers. These things that won't disappear, all of them inside her now. But also   this: this shiver of   life? She's teeming with it, isn't she? This deep pulse, this blood-gush in her veins beneath the cold surface: here, in her cheeks, in her fingertips, in the vivid clot of her own breath materialising in the cold air in front of her.

And what would he say, what would József say? You're alive. You're alive, aren't you? So there is hope.

Acknowledgements

'I keep you like the earth keeps all of its fallen matter' is adapted from a line in 'Óda [Ode]' by Atilla József (1905–1937). I am greatly indebted to the work of Sándor Márai, in particular *Föld, föld!...*, published in English as *Memoir of Hungary, 1944-1948* in a translation by Albert Tezla ([1972] 1996). Márai's work taught me much about Hungary's recent history and his lived experience of it, but the individual experiences that I narrate in this novel are fictional. I am also indebted to the following books, which found me at key moments in writing: Jay Bernard's beautiful and devastating poems in *Surge*; Steve Ely's poems in *I beheld Satan as lightning fall from heaven*—'Death is a warm dark seed bed' is one of the lines that haunts this novel; Laura E. Joyce's work on literary crime scenes in *Luminol Theory*, which opened my eyes to the colour blue, as well as to the saturation of violence through written history; Elissa Marder's *The Mother in the Age of Mechanical Reproduction: Psychoanalysis, Photography, Deconstruction,* which introduced me to the phenomenon of freezer babies, and much more besides.

I am immensely grateful to the following people: Nathan Connolly, Amelia Collingwood, and Jordan Taylor-Jones at Dead Ink, who have supported this book with unfailing energy and ingenuity through the most challenging of publication circumstances. Sabhbh Curran, Emma Bailey and Lucia

Walker at Curtis Brown, who provided invaluable support and advice at the different stages of writing (and re-writing) this novel. Camilla Bostock, Abi Curtis, Kieran Devaney, Dulcie Few, Laura Joyce, Helen Jukes, Tom Houlton, and Toby Smart, for being brilliant readers and friends. Kechi Ajuonuma, Chris Hands and Adrian Steele for specialist knowledge of various kinds—all errors are mine, mind. Thank you also to everyone who supported my previous books, and thereby made writing this one possible, especially Gary Budden, Kimberly Campanello, Tom Chivers, Nasser Hussain, Kate Murray-Browne, Sophie Nicholls, Nicholas Royle, Davi Lancett and all at Titan, the wonderful folk at New Writing North, and my colleagues and students at York St John University and at Durham University.

To my parents: thank you for your encouragement, generosity and all kinds of practical support. To Michael and Betty: thank you for sticking with me when I disappeared into this book, and for still being there when I re-emerged.

About the Author

Naomi Booth is the author of two previous works of fiction: *The Lost Art of Sinking* and *Sealed*. Her short story, *Cluster*, was longlisted for the Sunday Times EFG Short Story Award. Her work has also appeared on BBC Radio 3, The New York Times, and The Guardian. She completed a PhD on literary swooning at the University of Sussex and teaches at Durham University. She was born in Bradford, grew up in Dewsbury, and now lives in York.

About Dead Ink

Supported by Arts Council England, we're focussed on developing the careers of new and emerging authors.

Our readers form an integral part of our team. You don't simply buy a Dead Ink book, you invest in the authors and the books you love.

You can keep up to date with the latest Dead Ink events, workshops, releases and calls for submissions by signing up to our mailing list.